E.O.N.

E.O.N.

EVOLUTION OF A NIGGER

SEAN AVERY

This book is a work of fiction. Names, characters, places and incidents are products of the author's imagination or are used fictitiously. Any resemblance to actual events or locales or persons, living or dead, is entirely coincidental.

All rights reserved, including the right to reproduce this book or portions thereof in any form whatsoever.

Book design by Crash Wilson

Copyright © 2010 by Sean Avery

Forward written by Sean Avery

ISBN 9-780984-541102

FOREWORD

Niggers are everywhere! According to the dictionary, a **Nigger** is defined as:
- A noun
- "Slang":
- Extremely disparaging and offensive
- A person of any race or origin regarded as contemptible, inferior, ignorant, etc.
- A victim of prejudice similar to that suffered by blacks.
- A person who is economically, politically or socially disenfranchised
- **A Black Person**

So in theory, they are everywhere, in our stores, on the bus, in our schools, in prisons and churches, in every city all around the world. The word is said to have originated in 1640: however, when used today, it is directly linked to its heavy use in the 1700s and 1800s to describe slaves. What's more intriguing is not the origin of the word, but the creation of the **Nigger** himself and the **Nigger** mentality.

Black people were taken from Africa. They were force fed a new God and culture. The men were emasculated and the women raped. They were treated like livestock, being brought and sold like cattle. Denied any form of education and their sacred dance was transposed into a form of entertainment. They were forced into the belief that fear and obedience was the only means of survival.

The offspring of yesterday's black people are now a generation of feeble boys struggling to be respected in the eyes of their women. The women have been forced to become the men. The children have been taught not to value education. Their family tree has been cut down, and the family structure is almost obsolete. These people have evolved to adopt the term themselves as a tool of survival, changing its spelling yet keeping its traditions. The seed of deception set in place has blossomed into a flower of genocide leaving death, destruction, and a warped mentality in its path.

This novel, **E.O.N. *Evolution Of a Nigger***, is a small cry for **"Niggers"** to awake from their inherited ignorant slumber and acknowledge the kings and queens from whom they are descendants!

Sean Avery

ACKNOWLEDGMENTS

My mother, the mother of my Earth, has given me, as a black man, my mind, body and soul. I am impossible without you! Thank you, Mother God. You are my light! To my children, I thank you for blessing me with your presence...please follow your dreams and stay awake to everything! S.M.L.A. & J.W.R.A. I love you both, eternally.

Gran/G-Squizy, you are the book that I read each day. To my family, you are my backbone, and I cannot stand strong without your constant support and love. To my father, who has helped me see that I am a king, your advice is priceless, and your love is what I pour into my children. K.B., you are always in my heart...thank you for the blessing! To A.R.S., thank you for helping me to see and understand the best man/friend/father/lover I have inside of me. Fa Garcia, the more I realize the significance of our connection, the more I know that God doesn't make mistakes. You are the essence of love. The definition begins with you! Tae, you helped raise me into the man I am today. Thank you and I Love You! Tc May, you prove to me that good people don't finish last. Thank you for being the biggest little sister I could ever ask for! Cali, you are the strength of the family and because of that we are an unstoppable force!

Dread, Markie and the entire Zeiss family, thank you for showing me how to stay sane in an insane world. It took me ten plus years but I learned Rasta, I learned! To J. Forbes thank you for always being you! Royale French, you made growing up fun and I will always be grateful, you've also made me wish we could stay forever young! OFO...thank u! 2411...thank you! Morningside...thank you! R.Thompson you are and always will be my best friend! To my dear friend PE, you have been an intricate part of my life, and I thank God for you. To AZU, thank you for allowing me to eat from your mind (W.S.) Much Love, brother. Let's continue down the road of success. JJ, you are a tremendous talent and, even more, a tremendous person. Love You & Thank You! My brother from another W.T. Hough, you are a great friend and my brother, thank you for being there from day one; love u man. To my ZU family, thank you for the lessons in business and life. Anthony Walker, you proved to me that it could be done. Thank you! I miss you! Mama, I wish you were here to share this moment with me. Your daughter misses you so much, and so do I! Love you forever. Nana & Papa you are in my heart, mind, and soul...forever! Charlie R., Thank you for the head start.

  This book is inspired by every author... past, present, and future! Thank you for the influence!

  To all who feel slighted or disrespected if you did not read your name...please fill in the blank,_____.As you all have filled in mine!

CHAPTER 1

The flashing lights from the camera's bulb flickered with blinding speed. The photographer called out to his assistant to bring another camera and quickly made the exchange while continuing to bark orders at his muse. His voice seemed to rise with each flash. The frustrated artist looked into the camera with a glare of anger as he followed the voice of authority, turning and changing his profile as he was told.

"Okay, now turn to the left." The photographer shouted. "Now to the right!" He barked at Eon. "Okay, is it possible for you to stop moving and just turn your body? Let's go, let's go, let's go," he said snapping his fingers.

Eon Montgomery, aka E the Great MC, aka $E = MC^2$, is shooting a cover for a prominent magazine. Eon's assistant, manager, Cassie, could see the aggravation building inside of him. She quickly ran over to the iPod station and pushed "play." Instantly Eon's energy changed with the loud sound of his voice blaring from the speakers. As he started to recite his verses, the entourage of continual "yes" men and bandwagon "friends," standing behind the photographer and off to the side, sang along word for word. The enticing rhythm seemed to infect the rest of his body as Eon started to move back and forth aggressively. As the contagious sounds grabbed a hold of his entourage, they all started to dance in their typical b-boy style.

Suddenly the photographer seemed to be the one who was irritated. His commands were being drowned out by Eon's world-renowned hit single "Nigger, Nigger, Nigger, Nigger, Nigger, Nigger, Please." While Eon and company continued to zone out into his music, the photographer tried to regain control of his photo shoot as it slowly began to resemble a scene at a club. The numerous scantily clothed women shook and gyrated as if they were on a video set.

The frustrated photographer gave his assistant a look, and within seconds he was off to speak with Eon's manager, the instigator who set the party in motion with one touch of a button. As the young white guy circled through the countless people, he seemed to get lost in the motion of one of the ladies derrieres as it shook, rattled, and rolled all over the place. He wobbled his head free from the trance like state and returned to his mission. As he fearfully sidestepped through the crowd, he finally arrived at Cassie. He tried to speak, but his voice was no match for the loud bass and background singers all around him. He could only place his hands together in a sign of prayer, asking Cassie to calm the savages. Cassie's head bounced up and down, confirming that she understood his wordless request. She returned to the music station and quickly stopped the song, sending the joyful children into a quick and abrupt halt. The crowd all stood in shock at the sudden stop of their dancehall moment.

"Thank you, bloody Jesus, Mary, and Joseph!" the English photographer screamed. "Now, can we get back to the freaking, bloody shoot, please?" he said with frustrated aggression. Eon stared directly at Cassie as he uncomfortably returned to his place in front of the camera. The photographer also returned to his commando style of demanding that Eon turn from left to right. His voice was clearly annoying Eon again. This time, Cassie could not and would not save the day with music.

"Okay, wait a mother fucking minute. Who is the fucking star here? I'm on the cover, not you! You're going to stop talking to me any type of way!"

Eon pushed his hands forward as if he were shoving an invisible object out of his way and strutted into his dressing room. The photographer stood in silent fear as Cassie quickly followed Eon. She walked into the room as Eon was in the midst of lighting a joint.

"C'mon now, I thought you were going to quit," Cassie said with a tone of disappointment.

"I can't quit when these mother fuckers keep

driving me to want to kill they ass! Cass, I don't know how much longer I can take this shit," Eon quickly shot back as he took his first drag. His words were drenched in honesty.

"Can take what?" she asked.

"The bullshit! The fake shit! The real shit that's really the fake shit...it's just a lot." Cassie listened intently. "The fact that a mother fucker like that could think that he has a right to talk to me in that type of manner!" Eon said as he pointed toward the closed door. "I mean, where I'm from, that type a shit just wouldn't happen, you know." Eon was looking for her approval.

"Well, I don't know if you remember, but you're from Mississippi, and to be honest, that fruit cake would have told you that and a whole lot more, to be totally honest with you, E," Cassie said in her sternest voice. She always had a way of bringing Eon back down to earth whenever he would make silly statements, which was why she was his right-hand woman. "Plus, these people are paying us one million dollars to do this week long interview, and you've already spent a good chunk of that, so unless you want the legal pricks on your...our backs, then I suggest we get it together and get out there and just shoot this shit." Eon looked Cassie directly in her eyes as she stared back at him.

"You know you my nigger, right?" Eon said while extending his hand to the only person he truly trusted.

"I know, I know, and you're mine," she complied.

"I'm just really tired of *all* of it, you know?" Eon said as his face showed his frustration.

"Well, E, we've been in this game for five years, and we've made a shit load of money, so I think if you are really serious about this, then we can do this interview and the rest of our shows for this month, and after that we can revisit this conversation then...cool?" Cassie said with sincerity.

"That's why you..."

"Your nigger, I know, E, That's why I'm your nigger," Cassie interrupted, and Eon could only smile. Cassie always seemed to know what he was thinking, in some cases before the thought even came to Eon.

"So when is this cat coming through?" Eon asked while relighting his spliff.

"Well, they were supposed to be here today, but I haven't heard anything, and with the crowd you run with, it's..."

"C'mon, Cass, now stop it. You know the hottest MC in the land has to roll with his troops," Eon said as if he was making a point.

"E, you don't know half of their names, and the ones you know are nothing more than leeches," Cassie said in hopes that her words would change Eon's choice to have such a large entourage.

"Anyway…when is our next show?" Eon asked, ignoring Cassie's request.

"This Saturday is the boat ride, and after that, we are off to Atlanta for Monday's show," Cassie shot back.

"We have to do this boat ride?" Eon asked.

"Well, again, they've given us half of the money already, and we get the other half after the performance," Cassie said as she realized her attitude was going unnoticed. "So let's go finish this shoot before this silly chump comes in here with his panties in a bunch." Cassie's choice of words made Eon smile.

Just as Eon was finishing his joint, there was a knock at the door. Both Eon and Cassie ignored the person on the other side.

"And you said you were going to stop smoking!" Cassie said as she slowly walked toward the door.

She quickly jerked the door open, scaring the already-shaken photographer on the other side.

"Good day, Ms. Shelia. I just wanted to talk to the mate, if possible." The photographer spoke with honesty in his voice. Cassie looked back at Eon to see how he felt about the possibility of a truce.

"Listen, Russell Crowe. Shelia is named Cassie, so let's call her by her name, okay mate?"

"No worries, mate, no worries," the photographer stated, hoping he didn't upset Eon any more than he already had. "Can we make magic, *Miss* Cassie, please?" he asked. Before Cassie could answer, Eon shouted as he stood from his seat.

"Let's make magic, Crocodile Hunter! Let's make magic!" Cassie smiled at Eon's sarcastic way of dealing with the photographer.

As they returned to the shoot, Eon noticed everyone looking at him. This was nothing new to Eon. He honestly liked the attention. Eon stood back in front of the tripod. The photographer picked up his camera and gave a small smile to Eon. Eon returned a grin as he looked past the photographer at his entourage.

As he scanned the small crowd, his eyes locked onto an old man with salt-and-pepper dreads. He seemed to be staring directly at Eon. His piercing glare made Eon feel as if he were looking through his shaded eyes and directly into his soul. As Eon looked over to Cassie, the photographer called for Eon's makeup artist to touch up his face. Rudi was a short dreadlocked Nubian sister. Rudi's body looked as if the gods sculpted it. She walked over and ran a brush over Eon's face.

"What up, Ms. Rudi?" Eon asked.

"I'm doing great, E. How about you? How're you feeling?" she asked.

"So, who's that dude, your new boo? He seems a little old for you, though, Eon stated, trying to find out who this new face was.

"What new dude, E?" Rudi shot back. "You know I'm a married woman. I have no time for no one but my family…well, and traveling all over the place with you," Rudi said as she took her brush and tapped Eon's nose.

"So then, who is that cat over there mad-doggin' me like I said something against Haile Selassie?" Eon said as he pointed in the direction of where he last saw the old man.

"Where?" Rudi asked as she turned to see the usual crew of people.

"Right over...."

Eon's finger was now pointing at one of the girls who wished she would be chosen by the rapper as his toy of the night. The ecstatic vixen began to strut towards Eon. She walked past the photographer, who stopped changing his lens and concentrated on her robust behind protruding from her super-miniskirt.

"I'm here, baby," the woman said in her best Marilyn Monroe tone. Eon looked at her strangely as if he didn't understand her language. Although her face was familiar, Eon knew her kind all too well.

"I'm sorry, sweat heart...I mean sweetheart, but not right now maybe a little later," Eon said as he looked past her and ran his eyes throughout the crowd trying to find the mystery man. Cassie noticed the weird look on Eon's face and walked over to find out what was bugging him.

"Everything okay?" Cassie asked.

"Yeah, I'm cool," Eon said with doubt in his voice. "Hey, did you see this dude with, like, salt-and-pepper dreads and a full goatee and beard?" Eon asked, hoping that he wasn't the only person who noticed the man.

"Uh…no," Cassie said with an inquisitive look on her face. "I haven't seen anyone who looks even similar to that description, E. Are you sure you saw someone?"

"I'm positive!" Eon emphatically stated as Cassie and Rudi looked at each other. "Whatever…listen, let's get this done so a nigger can get out of here!"

After the shoot, Eon and Cassie returned to his Harlem brownstone, leaving the entourage to return to their own lives. Eon had purchased the property with his first official big check from his successful freshman album, *Me and My Niggers*. The four-level home was once a place of refuge for Eon. He would often go there to get away from the creatures that were once his parents.

Eon's parents were born and raised in Mississippi. They grew up living very close to one another on the red clay roads in Canton. They were high school sweethearts, and both their families were descendants of slaves. Eon's great-grandmother labored on a plantation. She worked inside the Big House for the majority of her life. Her relationship with Master Montgomery and his family was so great that he willed the entire property to her at his death.

Eon was born in Mississippi and lived there until he was ten. His parents moved him to New York in hopes of getting away from the racial tension in the Deep South and setting up a better life for themselves and their son. Instead of creating a home of hope and possibilities for Eon, his parents produced a dungeon-like lair filled with drugs and addiction. They lived in a housing project infested with roaches, rodents, and his parent's habit. Eon watched his parents slowly deteriorate as the hard times continued, the sight of both his parents slumped together in a dope-fiend nod began to make Eon sick. He would run to his grandmother's home, which was the brownstone, with tears in his eyes. She would sit young Eon down and try to calm his hurt soul. She'd talk with him about his life and his options to not end up in the same situation as his parents. His grandmother would also discuss her mother's life and the things she went through living on the plantation.

Although Eon knew his great-grandmother's home in Mississippi inside and out, from his younger years of running around the large property, he never knew its origins. The stories intrigued Eon and kept him full of curiosity, curious about whom he was and his family's past. He adored his grandmother and was eternally grateful for her love and admiration. Nana Montgomery knew her grandson was special. Her heart and front door were always open to Eon. Big Mama Montgomery knew that her grandson and granddaughter-in-law were heading down a path of self-destruction. Because of this, she sent her daughter, Nana, to New York and told her to find a place for Eon to go whenever things got out of hand with his parents. As fate should have it, there were sales on unclaimed brownstones. They were selling for as low as one dollar. Big Mama had Nana send the paperwork so that her lawyers could research everything and make sure it all was legit. Once they gave the stamp of approval Big Mama sent Nana enough money to buy the property and pay for whatever decorum changes she wanted. Big Mama took pride in knowing that Eon was safe whenever he was with her Nana. Mama's stories stayed with Eon throughout his youth and into his adulthood.

Very soon after Eon's success, his grandmother passed away. Eon had never truly confronted the pain and hurt that came with losing his grandmother. Nana Montgomery left Eon the brownstone and the large amount of back taxes still owed on the property. Even though it took the majority of his first check, Eon was more than happy to acquire the property. This was Eon's most significant purchase in more ways than one. He put a state-of-the-art studio in the basement, along with a top floor that resembled a comfortable lounge with a full bar and a patio overlooking Harlem. He wanted to keep the essence of his grandmother within the house, so he left the main living room the same. Cassie had her own bedroom, along with a personal full bathroom. She had helped Eon pick out much of the furniture and was very comfortable around the house.

"You know, you really need to change this living room up a bit, E," Cassie said as they walked into the living room and set their bags down. She'd been telling Eon to change the inside of the brownstone since the day he purchased the place. "I understand your Nana was important to you, but honestly, I don't think she'd mind a new couch or footstool or something," Cassie stated.

"Mind your business, Cass, please," Eon said in hopes she would drop the subject.

"Well, I consider us family, and as family I feel the need to discuss how much better this room would look with a little facelift. I mean…"

"You mean what?" Eon interrupted. "You are not my family, Cass. You are my employee. I pay you a salary, no fucking more, no fucking less. Yes, you have been here since day one, and yes, I'm extremely lucky to have you, but at the end of the day, you are an employee, and I can get another employee if necessary!"

"So what you saying, E?" Cassie asked.

"That was one of my favorite EPMD joints." He jokingly mentioned the hip-hop group in hopes of breaking the tension that was forming between him and Cassie. Cassie looked at Eon through squinted eyes.

"Cass, I just want to leave this one space as it is. Okay? Maybe we can look into a change-up after we get out the game," Eon said with sincerity.

"Damn, you back on that again, huh? You really serious about leaving hip hop?" Cassie asked. She was slowly coming to grips with the realization that Eon was truly considering leaving E the MC behind.

"Well, again, let's see how things feel after these next few shows, and we'll discuss it then," Eon reiterated.

"Okay, cool. Well I'm going to my room, and I'm going to bed," Cassie said as she walked past Eon.

"Good night, Cass."

"Good night, E the MC," Cassie replied with a smile. "Get some good rest 'cause we have the boat ride tomorrow," Cassie said as she sashayed away.

"Will do, Boss Lady, will do," Eon complied.

The next morning, Cassie was awakened from her sleep by the sounds of activity coming from the kitchen. As she shook out the cobwebs of the night before, she placed her feet into her Ugg slippers. She walked into the giant kitchen and saw Eon at the stove, cooking. He was dressed in a robe and house shoes, preparing his famous cheese eggs. As Cassie pulled back her chair, she sat down at the island in the center of the kitchen. Eon nonchalantly placed a plateful of eggs, turkey bacon, grits, and fresh buttermilk biscuits in front of Cassie.

"Good morning, Cass," Eon said in a proper tone as if he were a world-renowned chef.

"Thank you very much," Cassie said, her voice still groggy and unclear. "I haven't even had a chance to brush my teeth," she said with little to no embarrassment. As Eon prepared a second plate, Cassie walked over to the refrigerator and took out the orange juice. She picked two glasses out from the cabinet and placed them on the table. Eon placed a plate across from where Cassie was sitting as she poured the two glasses full of orange juice. "So you're going to enjoy breakfast with me. That's really nice…"

Before Cassie could finish her statement, a lady came out from what seemed like nowhere and sat in the vacant seat. Eon slowly kissed the lady's lips as she returned the favor.

"Good morning...oh, orange juice!" Ms. Unknown said as she snatched up the second glass while smiling from ear to ear.

Cassie stared at the woman with uncertainty and anger. As her eyes continued to survey the woman's features, she realized where she had seen her before. She was the girl from the photo shoot who had thought Eon was talking to her when he pointed to the mystery man.

"I think I'm going to eat in bed," Cassie said as she grabbed her plate off the table.

"Dad E, you ate *well* in bed, didn't you?" Eon smiled mischievously at his lady friend. Cassie could only suck her teeth in disgust over the one-night stand camouflaging as a relationship.

After Cassie finished her delicious breakfast, she stayed in bed for an hour, flipping channels. She then went into the bathroom and started preparing for the day. In the midst of brushing her teeth, Cassie heard Eon arguing in the hallway. She walked out of her room and was extremely surprised to see Eon grabbing a hold of his lady friend.

"You scandalous Tramp! You go and try to steal from me!" Eon said while pulling the half-dressed woman toward the front door.

"Dad E, I just wanted a picture of you, that's all. I...I just really wanted something to show..." she said tearfully.

"To show the rest of your trick bitch friends! You lying whore, I have hundreds of promo pictures! Shit, I would've autographed it and everything...but you go and try to steal from me!" Eon said while grabbing a handful of her hair.

"No, Dad E, no," she said while trying to fight the inevitable.

Just as Eon got to the front door, he opened it with his free hand. He was alarmed to see a woman standing outside his door with her hand extended to the bell. Eon's presence shocked the lady as she stepped back in amazement.

"Now, get the fuck out of my place, and don't ever come back...ever!" Eon shouted as he flung the young lady out the door by her hair. Eon looked at his hand and saw that he was still holding the lady's weave. He shook his hand free of the hairpiece as if he were trying to get a sticky substance off his hand. The young lady slipped down the stairs, running barefoot as soon as her feet hit the sidewalk. Eon turned around and headed back into the house.

"And who the fuck are you, Jehovah Witness or

something?" Eon sarcastically shouted at the young lady.

"Uh, no. I'm here for the interview," the woman at the door stated.

Eon looked up at Cassie who was behind him, standing in the doorway in shock. She was so stunned by the commotion that she had forgotten to wipe the toothpaste from her mouth.

"This is where you told them to meet me?" Eon asked Cassie. He did not want to believe that Cassie would give out his home address to anyone, let alone an interviewer. "And you come out here looking like Cujo or some wild dog foaming at the damn mouth!" Eon said. His voice still carried the anger and frustration he felt not only toward his lady friend, but also now toward Cassie.

"Uh, excuse me. No one spoke to me about you coming here. You were supposed to be at the photo shoot. And to be honest with you, there's no reason for you to be here," Cassie said quickly putting her business cap on. Cassie wiped her mouth with her bathrobe.

"Well, I was at the photo shoot yesterday, but it seemed like a bad time for you then, so I left. To be honest, now doesn't seem to be any better," the journalist said.

"Yeah, well, you should leave," Cassie shot back.

"No, it's cool," Eon said. He sensed a familiarity in her eyes. For some unexplainable reason, he felt comfortable with this woman. Cassie quickly turned to him with a look of shock and disbelief.

"Just give me…give us a second, and we'll be right with you," Eon said in his most proper voice. The lady nodded her head in agreement and continued to wait outside.

"What are you doing?" Cassie asked as she shut the front door in the lady's face.

They both began to clean up the messy trail left by Eon's unwanted guest.

"It's no problem. We have to start this at some point and time," Eon said as he slowly began to regain his composure.

"Yeah, well, what was the problem with little Ms. Breakfast…Dad E? What did she do?" Cassie asked. She was attempting to poke fun at Eon while hoping to find out what triggered him to transform from chef of love to Ike Turner.

"Don't play with me, Cassie," Eon said as his eyebrows furrowed. "That bitch tried to take this," Eon said as he picked up the broken picture frame.

It was an old photo of Eon with his grandmother.

"Where the fuck do you get these scandalous broads from?" Cassie said as more of a statement than a question.

"Yeah, well, this is one of the many reasons why I'm ready to get the fuck out of this bullshit. Friends...there are no friends, just a bunch of leeches and thieving backstabbing hoes," Eon stated, still holding on to his feeling of betrayal.

"Okay, well, what about this chick outside?" Cassie asked.

"I don't know what it is, but I dig her." Eon spoke honestly.

"Damn you just got the kleptomaniac out of your house, and now you right back in love again!" Cassie stated in hopes she was convincing Eon to push the interview back.

"That bitch was a piece of tail, nothing else. This woman's energy just feels right. I can see that she's going to conduct a professional interview. I think she really wants to know about Eon Montgomery, and not E the MC, understand?" Eon asked as Cassie looked on.

"Yeah, well, first things first. Let's clean this stuff

up. And make sure we screw everything down just in case she's really down with Ms. Breakfast." Cassie's comment brought a small smile to Eon's face.

After they finished cleaning up the house, both Eon and Cassie went into their own personal bathrooms, showered, and dressed. An hour later, the front door opened, and Cassie greeted the interviewer.

"I'm sorry for the wait, I'm Cassie, E's personal assistant and co-manager. Thank you for your patience. Please come in." Cassie extended her hand to the young lady.

"Thank you very much, my name is Violet Thompson," the reporter said, shaking Cassie's hand.

As she walked through the front door, Violet examined the interior of the brownstone. Her eyes roamed the entire first floor. It seemed as if she was looking for information about Eon through the layout of his home. Cassie walked Violet into a large sunken living room.

"Take a seat, and E will be with you very soon."

"Cool," Violet said while sitting on the plastic-covered couch. She giggled to herself as she felt the synthetic cover, and began to settle into her seat.

She could not believe how unexpectedly comfortable the couch actually was. Five minutes later, Eon calmly walked into the living room, looking as if nothing had happened.

"Hello, Ms. Violet. I am E the MC." Eon took Violet's hand into his.

"Greetings, Mr. E," Violet said. Her voice was drenched in undeniable comfort.

"So, you are supposed to be with me for the next week, huh?" he asked, already knowing the answer.

"Yep, you're mine for the next ten days," Violet replied and smiled.

"Okay, so what kind of questions should I expect from you, Ms. Violet?" His voice displayed a hint of sincerity.

"Well, honestly, I want to get behind E the MC. I want to know who's behind the rapper. Who are you?" Violet asked honestly. Eon was a very unattainable person since he'd started in the business. Many magazines and countless other Mr. Smiths within the Matrix wanted to sit with E the MC, yet he consistently kept himself clear of the quotes and reporters…until now.

"Well, in the immortal words of that great negro poet, Don King, you're a nigger till you die, if you are poor, then you're a poor nigger, if you are rich, then you're a rich nigger, and if you get to be educated, you're just an educated nigger," Eon said, quoting the flamboyant boxing promoter.

"So you'd consider yourself...?"

"A *nigger*!" Eon said with honor.

"So what possessed you to allow my magazine into your life?" Violet asked with a straight face.

"Well...off the record?" he asked.

"Damn, this is a tough way to start an interview off, but okay...off the record." Violet concurred.

"Your people paid me a shit load of money for this, and I could not deny it," Eon said with all honesty.

"Well, now that we've gotten past the small talk, may I begin?" Violet asked.

"Well, let *me* ask *you* a few questions," Eon shot back. "So this is not like *The Osborne's* or *The Real World*, right?"

"What do you mean, fake reality?" Violet's reply brought a smile to Eon's face.

"Good answer...but no, I mean you're not going to be following me around with a camera crew and all that shit, right?" he questioned sincerely.

"Nope, what you see is what you get," Violet stated

while running her hand across herself as if she was on display.

"Yes, I will be with you for the next seven to ten days, but no, I will not have a camera crew. I will have my personal camera with me." Violet patted the small camera bag that sat next to her.

"Yes, I will ask you questions, but no, you don't have to answer anything you don't want to. Oh, and I must show you my final draft, pictures and all, before it goes to print." Violet looked at Eon as he seemed to have a question, but did not know how or if he should ask. "And yes, you still get your million, no matter what," she said, reading Eon's mind. Eon looked baffled.

"Well, your manager was very specific in making sure every '*I*' was dotted and '*t*' was crossed," Violet said frankly.

"That's my nigger," Eon said aloud to no one in particular.

"Okay, well, now that we've gotten all of that out the way, let us begin. What, where, why, or when?" Violet joked, quoting a hip-hop classic.

"That's 'My Philosophy' you just quoted right there." Eon bounced his head up and down in agreement. "That's my shit! Where'd you hear that joint? You seem too young to remember 'My

Philosophy,'" Eon said in an attempt to get Violet to admit her age.

"Let's just say I'm on top of my game. I was born in the South, and made my way through life with my ear directly connected to the sounds and vibes of hip hop. I felt it in my soul from day one, and even though my mother didn't want me to listen, I found a way to keep her close to me." Eon looked puzzled.

"You kept who close, your mother or the music?" he questioned. Violet looked at Eon as if he should have known who, or what, she was talking about.

"The music! C'mon, I said I used to love her! Well, I used to then and still do now...love her, hip hop!" Violet said.

"I hear that, Lady Vi." Eon's nickname for Violet made her smile.

"Well, E the MC, let me ask you. Where are you from, and how did you get here?"

"I'm from the streets, simple and plain! I've been all through these Harlem streets for the majority of my life, and I've seen it all!" Eon spoke in his "keeping it real" voice.

"Uh, Okay." Violet sounded as if she didn't believe the "gangster" rapper.

"I got here from my grandmother." Violet looked at Eon as if she was expecting more information. "Well, she kept me safe and informed as to who I was. My parents were…" Eon stopped before he finished his statement. He realized he was way too relaxed with Violet, especially for having just met her.

"Your parents were?" Violet wanted Eon to continue, but he didn't. She slowly turned her attention to the numerous pictures in the room. Eon watched Violet as she surveyed the photos.

"That there is what that disgraceful, eBay-shopping bitch was just released for," Eon said as his eyebrows furrowed with anger. Violet looked at him with doubt. "She tried to steal something very special from me." He placed the cracked and poorly taped picture frame in front of her. She examined the picture as her mouth dropped. She was surprised and shocked to see a young E the MC smiling with a woman who looked like his older twin.

"So this is your sister?"

"Hell, no!" Eon shouted, causing Violet to jump back. "That's my Nana!" Violet looked on as Eon seemed to become emotional.

"Yeah, well, we are going to this boat ride later tonight, and then I'll see you in action," Violet said with a devilish grin as she consciously changed the subject. "I can't wait to see you with your people," she said while placing her hand on top of Eon's. They gazed into each other's eyes as they silently shared a moment together.

CHAPTER 2

Eon and Violet talked for four hours straight. They spoke of everything from the battle of KRS-ONE of Boogie Down Productions against MC Shan and the Juice Crew to the honest possibility that 9-11 may have been an inside job. Their discussions made them realize that they had many things in common. As they compared life notes, they both seemed to lose track of the time.

"Uh, E, we have to start getting ready." Cassie walked into the living room, interrupting the two new long-lost friends.

"Okay, cool." Eon nodded his head at Cassie, confirming that he understood. Violet and Eon stood simultaneously. The two appeared to meet face to face as both their bodies intruded on one another's personal space.

"So I will see you soon, yes?" Violet asked.

"Of course. You're coming to the boat ride, right?"

"Yes, I just thought I was going to be able to change and get freshened up, but we ended up talking, and the time flew."

"Well, I can have my stylist come through and bring something for you, if you like." Eon took pride in the fact that he could get clothes within seconds.

"No, that's quite alright, I'll just go back to my hotel and do a quick 'overhaul' and get myself ready." Violet started to exit the living room. She didn't want to take up any more of Eon's time.

"No, it's cool. Stay. I will make sure she gets you something." Eon extended his hand to stop Violet's progress. "Cassie!" Eon shouted. "Call Pat and tell her to bring something for Lady Vi."

"No!" Violet commanded as she started out the door. Cassie came out of her room with her Blackberry comfortably glued to her ear while calling Eon's personal stylist.

"Hey, Pat, can you pull…" Cassie stopped in the middle of her sentence as she stepped into the living room where Eon stood alone.

"Forget it!" Cassie quickly pushed the button to release the call as the sound of the front door closing echoed through the house. "Let's go. We don't want the boat to leave us." Cassie seemed agitated at Eon's desire to help Violet.

"Be easy! There's no way that boat is going anywhere without me!" Eon spoke with a strong tone. He wanted to make sure he was heard and obeyed. Cassie's silence confirmed her compliance.

As usual, Cassie was ready before Eon. She waited in the kitchen as Eon made his appearance.

His cream-colored linen suit fit him to a T. The pants were tailor made, as was his shirt and jacket. His shoes were created by Donatella Versace herself and were never duplicated, making them originals. Eon had established great relationships with only a few of the top designers with whom he chose to spend his time and money. He called most designers big-money drug dealers who were trying to peddle their product to everyone with the financial ability to purchase it. In staying away from the swarm of dealers, Eon made himself more and more desirable. He knew the only reason they were even considering him was his status, both financial and worldly. Because of his outlook on the clothing world, many designers did not like Eon, and he was comfortable in knowing that the feeling was mutual.

Eon stepped in front of a mirror that ran from the base of the floor to almost the top of the high ceilings. He examined himself, and a giant grin ran across his face.

"Alright, let's get a move on." Eon demanded as he checked his watch. He clapped his hands to alert Cassie that the time to leave was now. Cassie walked out from her room with her phone glued to her ear.

"Okay, we are leaving right now. We're in Harlem, so we should be there in about thirty minutes." Cassie inspected Eon from head to toe.

"Listen, we will be there!" Cassie's frustrated tone immediately caught Eon's attention.

"What the fuck is their problem? Give me the phone!" Cassie held the phone against her chest as she shook her finger at Eon.

"Stop! I got it!" she snapped at him.

"Fuck that! They better recognize who the fuck I am! That boat will sink without me!" Eon spoke loudly, hoping that the person on the other line could hear him.

Cassie continued talking as Eon strutted in front of her and out the door. He walked down the stairs to the awaiting chauffeur. The driver opened the car door, and Eon hopped into the backseat of the giant SUV. Cassie finished her phone call just as she entered the truck.

"What's their problem?" Still annoyed, he pulled the middle armrest down and grabbed the plastic bag hidden in the compartment. He removed some of the contents from the bag and began rolling a joint. Within seconds, Eon was lighting his marijuana stick and releasing the smoke from his lungs out through a small crack in his window.

"It's nothing. They just wanted to make sure you were going to show up. I took care of it!" Cassie emphasized.

"What's wrong with you?" Eon's face wrinkled with confusion.

"I thought you were going to quit," Cassie said, answering Eon's doubtful glare.

"C'mon now, Cass. With the morning I had with that slut, and then having to deal with this interview shit, a nigger needs to breathe." He strongly inhaled from his medicine stick.

"And of course this helps you 'breathe' better, huh?" Cassie said sarcastically.

"That's why you my nigger. You understand a brother like me," Eon replied, clearly ignoring Cassie's evil stare.

Before long, they were speeding down the West Side Highway. They pulled up to the pier as the restless crowd waited on and outside the giant boat. Cassie stepped out of the truck while Eon sprayed himself with cologne to camouflage the hemp stench exuding from his body. She walked halfway to the boat, and then phoned Eon to tell him that the coast was clear. Since Eon didn't walk with security, Cassie would always survey an area before him to make sure that everything was safe.

Eon's eyes bulged at the sight of the massive ship. He read the back of the boat: Eclipse. Multiple women did double and triple takes as they noticed the famous rapper. Eon was forced to put on his shades as more people became aware of the main attraction. He walked up to the large entrance of the boat where Cassie stood. She smiled to herself as she saw the innocence in her artist's face. He had never been on anything so large that did not fly in the air.

"You ready?" Cassie asked.

"Please, ready. Are they ready for me? That's the question." Eon stuck his chest out.

The two walked onto the boat as the remaining passengers rushed to the entrance, hoping that they wouldn't miss the ship. Eon slid through the crowded vessel, led by Cassie. He gave a few handshakes and kisses to some of the men and women as he made his way to his V.I.P. section. Once he was seated and comfortable in the roped-off section, Cassie went off to find the promoter. Eon poured himself a double shot of Hennessy from one of the many bottles sitting on his table. There were ten unnecessary bottles of champagne, all chilling in buckets of ice, two to each pail. He sat and watched the guys and girls mingle. His eyes zeroed in on the usual crew of bandwagon riders and wannabe friends. He was amazed at how they always knew where to find him even though he wouldn't tell them his next location. Eon watched as a crowd of onlookers began to form.

"Hey, E!" a random woman yelled from behind the velvet rope. He returned her greeting with a smile and a peace sign. Eon observed Cassie as she pushed her way through the small mob that was forming in front of his sector.

"She's good," he said to the security guard camped out at the entrance of the V.I.P. section. Cassie sat next to Eon with a smile on her face.

"Okay, so we will be pulling off in about..." The boat jerked forward. "Now-ish," Cassie joked. Eon stared at Cassie as he sipped on his drink. "So you go on in another hour, so get ready."

"I was born ready! And what's up with the check?" Eon asked curiously.

"Well, we've gotten paid. All that's left is the performance," Cassie answered.

"That's what's up!" Eon said in a happy tone. "Wow!" He grabbed a hold of the plush couch as the boat thrust forward.

"You okay?" Eon's face showed worry.

"Yeah, I'm cool. I'm just not used to this uneasy ground, that's all." Eon spoke with honesty.

"You sure you'll be okay performing?" The look in Eon's eyes made her worried.

"Hell, yeah!!" he quickly shot back. "As long as you let my guy in here." He pointed at the guy standing directly in front of the security guard and anxiously waiting for Eon to acknowledge him. Eon did not know his name, but he did know his product--marijuana. Cassie sucked her teeth as she walked over to the rope and told the guard to let the "weed man" in.

"He's okay," Cassie said to the security guard angrily.

"Thank you, Ms. Cassie. Thank you so much," the exuberant man said. Cassie rolled her eyes in disgust. She was more upset with the "stranger" knowing her name than with the fact that Eon was smoking yet again.

"You have about forty-five minutes, E!" she yelled, walking away from Eon and his new best friend.

Thirty minutes later, Cassie returned. She shook her head in hatred. The section now held the usual groupie girls and guys. Cassie walked through the clouds of marijuana smoke and grabbed Eon.

"Let's go!" she said, clearly aggravated. Eon held Cassie's hand as she followed a giant security guard though the crowd. They descended down four sets of large circular stairs. Eon joked as he walked down each flight.

"You got me going in circles," he sang while Cassie guided him toward the stage, holding his hand as if he were a little boy.

The stairs were on the side of three balconies, all filled to capacity with party people. They reached the final landing and walked behind a curtain where the stage was set and ready. Eon looked up in amazement. He turned his eyes up toward the sky and noticed that the stage was the bottom of a coliseum-like area.

"You ready?" Cassie yelled over the loud music, bringing Eon out from his comatose state.

"Uh…yeah…hell, yeah!" Eon was trying to regain his cool. "I feel like Mad Max in the Thunderdome," he said in a joking voice, yet he was very serious.

"Two man enter, one man leave!" Cassie said, trying her best to sound like Tina Turner in the classic film. She stood behind Eon, allowing him to take in the moment. He closed his eyes and took in a deep breath. He exhaled and looked up into the mass of people. Eon shook his head in confusion as he spotted the old man from the photo shoot standing dead center on one of the balconies.

"What the fuck?" he said to no one in particular. Suddenly the rocking and swaying of the boat seemed to become a new reality to Eon.

"*What?*" Cassie asked.

"Nothing. It's nothing," Eon said as he refocused his energy on the task at hand, struggling to regain control of his equilibrium. "I'm ready. Let's go," he said with confidence. Cassie passed Eon a microphone. He clutched it and took another deep breath. He panned the throng of people in search of his male stalker, but just as before, he was gone.

The deejay sat behind the curtain. He looked over to Eon and gave him the thumbs up. Eon returned the sign of approval. The curtains pulled back, exposing the deejay, and the people cheered loudly.

"Y'all ready for the hottest rapper in the game?" the deejay asked. The multitude of partygoers screamed with anticipation. "I don't think they ready, E." The deejay egged on the mob. The crowd's screams grew aggressively stronger. Eon spoke into the mic from backstage.

"Where my niggers at?" Eon's voice made the people go absolutely crazy. "Where my niggers at!" The natives went restlessly insane. Eon stepped onto the stage and froze immediately. His feet began to tingle, almost as if he were about to have an orgasm. Then suddenly, his hands began to sweat and his eyes started to flutter...

Eon looked around in horror. The screams of love and admiration now were moans and whimpers of pain. His eyes ran around the circular levels in confusion. His ears registered the new sounds, but Instead of seeing his adoring fans, Eon looked out at multiple dark faces uncomfortably intertwined. The people were on top of one another while chained at the neck and legs. Eon began to zoom in on certain people. He noticed a man chained to a pregnant woman. His face was cloaked in desperation as he gripped his stomach. The throbbing inside of his intestines could not be denied. The man released his bowels onto the woman. She immediately vomited. The woman held her large stomach and screamed in agony. The continually consistent pain of labor had come to a climax. She sprawled her legs out and began to grunt persistently. Even though the people below her and on her sides were cramped and confined to the tight space, they all supported a part of the woman. Each dark face showed a look of want and anticipation. They silently rooted her on while she turned and twitched in pain and discomfort through the excruciatingly beautiful ordeal. Eon shook his head, trying to remove himself from this bout of insanity in the twilight zone, but he couldn't turn away. His nose caught the strong stench of human feces, urine and unwashed body odor. Each level held bodies, both dead and barely living. With every face he saw, there were feet, arms, and hands sticking out in an unorthodox pretzel. The luxury liner had quickly transformed into the guts of a slave ship. Time stood still as Eon noticed the same black dread locked man mixed in with the others. He appeared dead with his eyes closed shut. Eon fixed on the man's face. Suddenly his eyes popped open, and his face came alive. Without effort, he disconnected from the hordes of dark people, never taking his eyes off of Eon. His piercing stare burned into Eon's soul as he started to walk directly towards him. He spoke with conviction as he came closer and closer. "What's your problem, Nigger? What's your problem, Nigger? What's your problem, Nigger?" Fear and panic began to take control of Eon's mind, body, and soul. He felt the same feeling in his feet returning, and before he knew IT...

"*Ahhh!*" Eon belted out in a high soprano.

The crowd of people stopped their applause and enthusiastic chatter and fell silent. Eon looked around in hopes of regaining his bearings. Within seconds, the lasting smell of the slave ship returned to Eon's nose, and he began vomiting on stage.

"Oh!" the crowd shouted in unison. Embarrassed and ashamed, Eon quickly walked off the stage. The large group of people looked on in total confusion. Eon ran directly into Cassie's arms. Although her arms were embracing him, her face showed doubt and uneasiness.

"Are you okay?" she asked in her most motherly tone.

"I need to get out of here! I need to get off this slave ship!" he said unconsciously. Cassie wondered what Eon was talking about. She began to walk Eon away from the stage and his disappointed fans. Eon stopped as if he wanted to return to his performance.

"What, you want to go back?" she asked, hoping Eon was over whatever strange sickness had taken hold of him. Eon nodded his head in agreement and slowly turned back to his place on stage. Before he could take three steps, he started to shake his head no. Without warning, he projectile vomited. At this time, someone was on stage cleaning the area Eon had previously decorated, and Eon seemed to be aiming for the exact same spot. Some of it landed at the feet of the cleaner. The crowd again blurted out in unison.

"Oh!" Cassie immediately grabbed Eon from his back and steered him through the backstage area.

Because Cassie always visited the locations where Eon performed beforehand, she knew every exit and emergency area just in case they were ever needed. Cassie carefully maneuvered Eon through the small crowd backstage. They went down a small flight of stairs, turned right down a long corridor, and walked into an empty room that was labeled "DO NOT ENTER." She sat Eon down and tried to hand him her bottled water.

"Drink!" she demanded.

"No, I ain't drinking nothing else. That Henny is what got me fucked up like this now! Plus, my head is throbbing!" He was oblivious to what was in Cassie's extended hand.

"Listen, you need water…drink!" Cassie commanded. She placed the water into Eon's hand, and stood over him like an angry principal.

He slowly turned his head to the water bottle in his hand and then up at Cassie. He unscrewed the top and took a taste of the cold water. Suddenly there was a knock at the small office door. Cassie looked confused and bothered by the unknown intruder.

"Hey, it's Violet. Is this a bad time?" She spoke softly from the other side of the door.

"Yes!" Cassie screamed like an annoyed parent.

"No, come in!" Eon said, holding the water up to his temple. Violet tried turning the handle to no avail.

"What the fuck, E?" Cassie asked aggressively, while Violet struggled on the other side of the door.

"She wants to know who I am, so I'm going to show her!" he said in a matter-of-fact tone.

"Well, this ain't *you*!" Cassie emphasized. Eon just stared at Cassie as he moved toward the door and unlocked the handle. Violet walked in with a very worried look on her face.

"Are you okay?"

"Well, I think I need to work on my stage show," Eon joked as he sat back in his seat.

"There's a short, stocky white guy running around the boat screaming and cursing," Violet said.

"Shit! That's the promoter. Listen, I will be right back, don't move!" Cassie ordered as she made her way out the door. Violet locked the door behind Cassie. She looked Eon directly in his unsteady eyes.

"What happened to you? That was crazy," Violet said.

"I didn't think you were going to make it. Where were you?" Eon sounded as if he wished Violet was on stage with him.

"Well, I wanted to come over to your VIP section, but it got real tight, real quick. When you were going on stage, I was trying to make my way through the crowd, but by the time I got close to the stage, you were…" Violet stopped, hoping that Eon wouldn't relive his worst moment as an artist.

"Throwing the fuck up!" Eon finished her sentence. "I don't know what happened to me. I just started to feel like I was outside of myself. It's like I was seeing shit." Eon spoke with pure honesty as he stared off into nowhere.

"Like what?" Her words were drenched in curiosity.

"Like niggers were just on top of one another," he said slowly.

"Like sexually?" Violet asked, oblivious to the severity of Eon's words.

"Nah, not like that at all!" Eon quickly snapped out of his trance like state. "Just forget it, man!"

"No, what was it? Tell me." Violet pried. Eon quickly realized exactly who he was talking to, a reporter.

"So what? So you can make a fool outta me? So you can write some *bullshit* about me! You bitches are all the same! Get the fuck outta here!" Eon shouted with frustration.

"No. I'm sorry, I just…" Violet pleaded.

"Get the fuck out of here!" Eon turned his face away from Violet. Violet opened the door and was met by a smiling Cassie. She'd heard Eon's tirade from the other side of the door and was more than happy with Violet's dismissal.

"Excuse me," Violet said with pain in her voice.

"No, excuse me," Cassie replied sarcastically as Violet exited in a hurtful rush.

"Anyway, so I've spoken to the promoter, and he says we can get only half of our fee, and that's only 'cause I put that in the contract. He didn't want to give us a dime. Now, unless you feel like you could go back and do the show." Cassie looked sheepishly at Eon.

"I can't! I really can't!" he said with all truthfulness. "I really just want to get off this thing, Cass. Can we get off this thing, please?" He spoke with a rare sincerity. Cassie looked at him and knew that he was serious.

"Yeah, I have them taking us to a dock close to where we are now. And we are leaving through a path where no one will see us," Cassie said.

"Great!" Eon took a giant swig of water, finishing the bottle. Before he could bring the plastic container down from his mouth, Cassie snatched it away Eon looked at her, shocked, as she quickly handed him a new bottle of water. Eon replaced his shaken look with a brief, small grin.

"My nigg…"

"Yeah, I know, I know…save it," Cassie said,

interrupting Eon's usual commentary. "And you're going to tell me what the hell you were talking about when you said that slave ship shit, too," she said with a definite look on her face. Eon could only shake his head as they waited to disembark from the boat.

CHAPTER 3

As a child, Eon was a chunky, plump kid. Having a Southern diet didn't help at all. His classmates and so-called friends always teased him. Although Eon was one of the smartest children in his school, he was always treated unfairly. The kids would ridicule him for living on the land of a former slave owner, but in reality they were all jealous because he lived in a much bigger home than anyone else in his school. They called him everything from a house nigger to a cotton picker. Eon would go home to his great-grandmother with tears in his eyes. She would sit and discuss the past and the truth behind his family's connection with the large estate. Eon would listen intently as Big Mama, told in vivid detail, the many stories and adventures that had transpired over the past 100-plus years. He heard about everything: family separation, arranged marriage, childbirth in the cotton field, and lynching. Big Mama would describe the best and the very worst of times on the Montgomery land.

Big Mama was the matriarch of the family. She would walk Eon through the entire agricultural estate, checking on the many different plants and livestock. Eon had learned everything from picking cotton to feeding pigs by the time he was six years young. As Eon grew older, he'd begun to desire the stories more and more. He felt pride in knowing that he came from a long line of strong men and women who went through a great deal of hell so that he could taste a small piece of heaven. Racism was still very much alive, yet he knew that he was extremely lucky to have just missed the old days when he could not even go to school.

From the first to fifth grade, Eon went through a metamorphosis. He learned to take the negative energy from people's teasing and harsh words and combat it with sarcasm and humor. As Eon entered the sixth grade, he was a different person. The usual suspects would say things like,

"What you looking at, cotton picker?" and he would reply.

"That dirty-ass cotton jacket your Mama brought off my land!" Or they'd say,

"You having fun over there in your slave shack?" while he'd shoot back,

"No, *you* live in the slave shack, and I'm sorry, but niggers like you still aren't welcome in my house." He'd say that their families weren't given any large amounts of land because they were small, menial niggers. Eon's quick banter made him less and less of a target as each school year went on.

After eighth grade, Eon felt an unbelievable amount of self-confidence. Big Mama watched her little timid boy turn into a bright, secure young man. He learned more about true history from within the confines of the plantation than he'd ever been shown in school. This gave Eon a feeling of true purpose whenever he was in class. He'd listen to the teachers as they spoke of history. Most of their curriculum was based around explaining how essential the white man was to the world and its continual growth. Eon would shake his head in disgust as he listened to the teachers and their trick knowledge. He'd sit in silence, referring to the mental notes and dates he had recorded in his mind from the stories of Big Mama and Nana. Eon would go through his own personal timeline and compare the information he knew to the teacher's lessons. Although Eon knew the "real" history, he still managed to keep an A average.

    Eon's parents never noticed the change in their only son. They were extremely young mentally. From the time Eon was born, their inexperience showed in their lack of support for him. One summer afternoon before Eon's freshman year of high school, his parents announced that they were moving to New York City.

"It's time for you to pack up, son. You're going to be a big man in the big city," his father stated.

"That's right. We leave in seven days!" his mother interrupted excitedly.

"What about Big Mama?" Eon asked.

"Oh, she'll be right fine, right here!" both parents agreed.

During the train ride, they were so anxious to get to the "big city" that they never noticed Eon crying. He felt like he'd just found comfort in his own skin, and now they were taking that away, and most of all his Big Mama. Eon never forgave them for their selfishness.

Eon stepped off the train into a whole new world. He felt as if someone had pushed the fast-forward button on his life. The super-fast pace of life up north was demoralizing to Eon. People pushed and shoved their way through Penn Station. Eon watched his mother and father looking around in amazement. They walked as if he weren't there, arm in arm, pointing up at the great, grand ceilings and chandeliers. The roles seemed reversed as Eon made sure that their luggage was secure and all accounted for. The two "children" walked out from the train station and into the city. They both took in a huge breath of the dirty city air and stared into one another's eyes.

"This is like the honeymoon we never got," his mother said. Eon shook his head in disgust as he hailed a cab.

"Boy, get the bags and put them in the trunk while

we talk to this here driver," his father commanded.

"And sit in the front. Me and your Daddy got some celebrating to do," his mother said, climbing into the back. He sat in the front seat with his head hung low, hoping not to catch a glimpse of the two lovebirds kissing each other with love and happiness. The driver took a peek through his rear view mirror, and then shifted his attention to the little boy sitting to his right.

"First time, huh?" he asked.

"No, that's how they made me," Eon sarcastically shot back.

"So, how long you going to be in the city?" the driver asked curiously, as he could see they were visitors.

"Till death do they part!" Eon said with a snarl.

The driver quickly turned to Eon in shock. He shook his head in amazement at the little boy with the big attitude. The driver stayed silent for the rest of the entire ride. As they pulled up to their destination, Eon looked up in awe at the giant buildings.

"Here you go, mister." The driver spoke to Eon as if he were an adult. Eon's father paid the fare while Eon and his mother removed the bags from the car. Before the driver pulled away, he looked directly at

Eon. He pushed his own chin towards the sky with his index finger. Eon bounced his head in agreement at the silent message.

Eon's parents were astonished at how massive the city felt. They could not believe the buildings and multiple storefronts. They watched the hordes of black people walk through Harlem without a care in the world. Eon gathered the majority of the bags as his parents picked up the remaining two.

They entered their new building, and the three of them stood in the lobby looking around with uncertainty as if it were a museum. Eon's parents noticed the numbered doors that read *1A*, *1B*, *1C*, and so forth and they wondered how they were going to get to their door, *6A*. They turned to the right and noticed a flight of stairs. Eon's father looked at his son with little concern. He knew that his boy would have a hard time just getting up the first flight of stairs, but he really didn't care. Eon walked over to the elevator, pulled the door open, and entered. His father tilted his head like a confused dog as he began walking toward the boy. Eon peeked through the small window on the elevator door as he allowed it to close shut, just out the reach of his father's extended hand. Eon continually pressed the number *6* as the elevator jolted into motion. He waited as the rickety box came to a halt. He pushed the door open and struggled a few feet to his new residence. Before placing his parents in the back of their love carriage, the taxi, Eon had taken the keys from his father's jacket.

He unlocked the front door and entered his new humble abode. He dropped the heavy load at his feet as he analyzed the extremely cramped conditions. Eon walked throughout the undersized dwelling, inspecting each area. His eyes squinted in shock as the reality of the one-bedroom flat sunk into his mind. He listened as his parents stood outside the door.

"Honey, the keys are in your jacket pocket."

"Bitch, I told you they ain't here. Check your purse."

"I done checked already, Billy. I told you I never touched those keys."

"Then where in the hell else can they be?"

After about five minutes, Eon's father turned the handle of the unlocked door. They both stood silent as they peeked in on Eon, who was standing in the center of the miniature living room.

The Montgomery's quickly adjusted to life in the Big Apple. They spent their summer days walking around, and taking in the sights, while their nightlife revolved around drinking and smoking at any and every lounge in Harlem. Eon stayed confined to the little apartment, preparing for the upcoming school year. He watched both of his parents spiral down into the dark side of New York. Strange associates transformed into full-time friends, and Eon's parents spent more and more time outside of the house. Becoming well versed in the world of living life attached to the system, his parents learned to use their government assistance to regularly fund their new social addictions.

    A month after the big move, Eon received a call from his Big Mama. They talked for hours, reminiscing about the past and how much they missed one another. Big Mama felt guilty for allowing her grandson to take her heart away. She wanted him to return home, but Eon explained how he was responsible for his parents and their well-being. Even though he knew that they only cared about themselves, deep down inside, Eon still desired his parents' love and admiration. Eon described to Big Mama how he was not prepared for the school year and feared that he would not be allowed into any learning institution. Big Mama believed that going to school was not an option but a mandatory assignment that was to be carried out by any means necessary. Big Mama told him she'd make sure someone called him within the hour. Eon hung up the phone and patiently waited for the call. In what felt like seconds, the phone rang. Eon picked up on the first ring.

"Hello," he answered.

"Well, hey, boy." The sound of the soft, sweet voice immediately gave Eon a feeling of home. "Wow! You sound like a grown man, boy. Last time I seen you, you were a little boy." Her comment made Eon smirk to himself. "Boy, this is your Nana." Eon's half smile turned into a full ear-to-ear grin as he placed a name to the voice.

"Nana!" Eon shouted with love. Nana was Eon's confidant before she had left for New York.

Ten-plus years ago, back in Mississippi, Eon's parents would sit and discuss their desire to relocate to New York. As they talked about their quest to the "promised land," Big Mama tended the fields, and Nana would sit and play with Baby Eon. For the first ten years of his life, whatever love he didn't receive from Big Mama, he definitely found in Nana. Big Mama and Nana seemed more like sisters and less like mother and daughter, as they both looked more than half their age.

Big Mama was the fourth generation of Montgomerys born on the plantation. Even after slavery was allegedly abolished, Big Mama's family chose to stay. They truly believed that there wasn't life for a black person outside of working as a slave. This mentality was passed down from generation to generation, making Big Mama's family legacy one of loyalty and commitment to the plantation and its pale faced leader, Master Montgomery. Throughout her time as a worker on the plantation, Big Mama gained his trust. She was his only loyal servant. She cared for him through his sickness as the cancer spread throughout his body. Big Mama tended to all of Master's business, and made sure the plantation ran smoothly. While still in control of his faculties, John Montgomery made sure he had his will drawn up and reviewed by his lawyer. He knew that his one, true, genuine friend was Big Mama, so he made her the sole beneficiary of everything he owned. John Montgomery died without any children. He did, however, have three greedy, ungrateful ex-wives who impatiently awaited his passing, hoping to grab whatever they could from his estate. John made absolutely sure that the vultures would not receive a single penny from him upon his death. Strangely enough, John benefited from his decision in more than one way. Not only was his business going to continue to grow, but also his namesake would now live on through Big Mama and her offspring.

After John's death, Big Mama moved Eon's then ten-year-old dad and Nana from the small house where all the workers lived into the large dwelling where there was more than enough room. William Montgomery had lived without truly fearing the crack of a whip or the evil stare of a slave master. Eon's dad did, however, know his position in the real world of Mississippi. As the beginning of the 70s came along, Eon's dad began to think about life outside of the red clay and dirt roads of the South. He was in love with his girlfriend, Cookie, who shared the same desire to relocate from the country life. As the two strategically planned their exile from Mississippi and Big Mama's ruling hand, Cookie found out that she was pregnant. This created a giant setback in their campaign to move. William's mother was extremely helpful to Cookie and her needs throughout her pregnancy. She would assist Cookie, who now lived in the big house with William, with whatever she needed. Nana would keep Cookie very close to her, and their bond grew extremely tight. She would speak to Cookie's massive belly and tell the fetus just how special it was. Cookie would sit and laugh at Nana. She didn't believe that Nana's words of encouragement were reaching her baby.

Upon Big Mama's demand, twenty-five-year-old William married twenty-three-year-old Cookie. The small ceremony took place on the grounds of Big Mama's property. Amazingly, as William kissed his very pregnant bride, her water broke. Cookie was quickly rushed upstairs to her room. Nana stood next to her, encouraging her to breathe and push. Big Mama sat as the catcher, waiting for Eon to blossom from his mother's womb. William stood guard outside the door and listened to his brand-new wife as she screamed and yelled her way through 18 hours of hard labor.

William's soul rose with unexpected love as he heard the crying from his new baby boy. He walked into the room, happily held his giant ten-pound son, and cried tears of joy.

"Haven't seen that much emotion from you in eons," Big Mama said with pride.

"Eon!" William said with love. Cookie looked on in heavenly bliss. She watched her two babies falling in love with each other.

As the months turned into years, it was sadly clear that the thrill of being parents was very temporary. The young couple was truly not ready for a child. Nana stayed with Eon so much that he would cry for her. He would leave everything, including his birth mother, and make a direct line to his Nana. Amazingly, the lack of attention Eon showed his parents was accepted and even seemed welcome. The family members all were in their own worlds. Eon's world revolved around his Nana and Big Mama, while William and Cookie continued on their quest to leave Mississippi. As of 1980, Eon was a strong-willed young man who seemed to be more mature than his own parents. His great grandmother and grandmother had raised him with love, discipline, and spiritual integrity.

After John Montgomery passed, Big Mama and Nana were able to go to their own church instead of having to wait outside while John attended his. The pastor of John's church was Mister Reverend. He was the owner of the farmers' market located in town. John and Mr. Reverend shared more than just their religious beliefs. They were also business partners. Mr. Reverend and John worked out a bartering system in which they both supplied each other with necessary goods. If John needed gas for his plowing machine or his automobiles, he would have Big Mama send a servant to Mr. Reverend with a few bales of cotton or a case of eggs. This pact worked for years until John's death. Once Mr. Reverend realized that Big Mama was controlling the estate, he quickly rearranged the deal, adding a tax to all items coming in and out of the Montgomery plantation. This could have been detrimental to the continued success of the plantation, but Big Mama adjusted her prices so that the altered arrangement wouldn't affect her business. Unknown to Mr. Reverend, his account with Big Mama showed a profit with every transaction. Because of her knowledge and experience, the window for taking advantage of Big Mama was always shut with no possibility of being opened. Mr. Reverend soon realized that the only way to do business with Big Mama was respectfully. She wasn't afraid to speak her mind when she felt that she was being mistreated. She wouldn't scream and shout, but she would explain herself in a leveled, mature, smart but stern manner. It was almost impossible for anyone to take advantage of Big Mama, not that people didn't try.

Eon loved going to church with Nana and Big Mama. The loud sounds of joy and praise resonated throughout his body. The choir sang with great love, and the band played relentlessly. Eon loved to feel the bass pounding in his chest. The church was the place that introduced Eon to his hidden passion for music. He started to dissect the overpowering music. He watched each musician as they played in unison, relating every noise he heard to what he saw. Eon began studying the distinctive sounds of each instrument. His Nana would sit and watch him examine the entire band. She watched Eon bounce his head up and down to the strong, powerful rhythm without missing a beat. He moved his hands through the air, mimicking each specific artist playing his or her instrument. Nana watched her baby in awe. His love of the art grew with every trip to morning service. Soon Eon began to find sounds in his everyday travels. He would sit in school, clearly in his own world, humming to himself throughout the day.

Nana enrolled Eon in, a performing arts high school in New York so he could study music. From the moment he first walked into the specialty school, Eon knew he was going to truly enjoy his time there, and he did. Throughout the school year, he learned about instruments, music technology, harmonies, and song composition. Eon learned to make real music, and he was good at it. As opposed to being teased and ridiculed as he was in

Mississippi, Eon was praised and adored by not only his classmates, but also his teachers. Eon felt so much love at his school that he'd leave and go directly to Nana's. He did not want to diminish his great feelings by returning to the dungeon of his parents' home. They never encouraged Eon and his gifts. Whenever Eon would visit, if they were conscious, they would talk down to him and tell him that he was wrong for leaving them all alone. They tried to make him feel bad about relocating to Nana's, but it didn't work. Eon knew that they were only attempting to get money for their out-of-control habit, which had now taken over their entire will to live.

By his sophomore year, Eon had completely moved all of his belongings from out of his parents' house and was now living with Nana full-time. William and Cookie were completely engulfed in the evils of the nightlife of New York. William would work little odd jobs until the supervisor realized he was stealing from them, and then he was fired. After his appearance began to diminish, William's ability to gain employment declined greatly, and he eventually gave up all hope of even looking for work. Cookie continued to support her man as much as she could. Their need for a fix reached an all-time low once William began to pimp Cookie for drugs. Eon visited his parents less and less as they quickly transformed into full-time zombies. The house was a dungeon, filled with garbage and drug paraphernalia. Nana's continual love and affection helped to keep Eon's mind, and body, free from the clutches of his parents. She knew that her one and only son was way beyond reach, so she kept a very close watch on *his* one and only son. Eon would still check on them from time to time. At the beginning of his senior year of high school, he had done so well academically, he was offered a music scholarship to the school of his choice. He ran straight to tell his parents the great news.

Eon got off the elevator and immediately smelled the funk of smoked crack and urine. As the smell invaded his nose, Eon turned his head from left to right, hoping to erase the scent's strong hold. He placed his key inside the door and noticed that none of the locks were locked. Eon walked into what looked like a devil's lair. All of the blinds and shades were pulled over the windows, allowing no light inside the apartment. As Eon stepped into his old living quarters, he carefully maneuvered through the maze of crack vials, junk, and broken glass. He wanted to believe that he was in the wrong place, but just as he was about to leave, he heard an all-too-familiar voice.

"Who the fuck is that?" William asked. Eon looked at his father sitting in the corner on the kitchen floor, draped in a dirty tank top and worn pants undone. He slurred his words. It was very clear that

William was under the influence of his "medicine." His eyes were slits as his head slowly swayed back and forth. Eon looked at the stranger in front of him with disgust and hurt. He did not want to believe that his father had allowed himself to get to such a place where he was unrecognizable, but he had.

Eon watched as William readied himself for his next dose. His father grabbed a belt that was sitting on the floor next to him and flung it around his biceps. As the buckle wrapped around his arm, the pin seemed to slide magically into the correct hole, latching immediately. William picked up his spear and slowly plunged it into his arm. After a few seconds, he pushed down on the top of the syringe and released the happiness into his system. Eon watched his father's chin drop to the middle of his chest. A string of saliva hung from the side of his mouth and dripped toward the floor, stopping just short of its inevitable destination.

"William!" Eon shouted at his father.

"Hmmm...that bitch won't steals from me again William muttered. Eon looked at him doubtfully as he wondered what William was talking about.

"William, where's Cookie?" Eon asked.

"F...fu...fuck that trick!" he said, stumbling over his words. William's eyes stayed closed as he spoke without facing his son. Eon shook his head as he tried to ignore William's comments about his mother.

"William, where is sh...?" Eon's words were interrupted as he glanced to the right of the kitchen.

He noticed a person's body crunched in the fetal position. Eon slowly walked toward the body. The sniffles and panting coming from the figure made Eon even more curious. As he got closer and closer, he started to feel a certain familiarity. Eon's heart fell into his stomach as he turned the lady over and noticed his mother's bruised and battered face.

"No, I'm sorry Daddy!" she said as she shook and twitched away from Eon's grasp.

"Cookie, it's me...Eon," Eon said. His tone was drenched in the pain and sorrow he felt for his mother.

"Hey, she said as if she knew exactly who was in front of her.

"Hey, Cookie, are you okay?" he asked.

"Aw, you worried about me, huh?" Cookie asked as she grabbed her son's face with affection.

"Yes, I am, Ma I'm really worried about you." Eon's face began to change, and his emotions began to get the best of him.

"*Aww*, baby, don't worry about me, I'm fine." Cookie said as Eon wiped his face clear of the tears forming in his eyes. He looked directly into Cookie's swollen eyes. Eon wiped at the dried blood sitting on the side of Cookie's busted lip. "But I can tell you how everything is going to be Okay," Cookie said. Eon looked at his mom with love and sincerity as he waited to hear her solution. "You can let Mommy suck that dick for a lil hit of some good shit." Eon stepped back from his mother in shock. He could not believe what she had just said to him. "C'mon, Daddy, I know you got that good shit…I won't charge you too much, just one bag…I will suck the nut outta that dick."

Eon stood up from his mother as she reached out to him. He did not want to believe his ears. He quickly turned away and exited the apartment. His tears fell uncontrollably from his face. He never went back to see his parents and in turn never revisited the hurt that stemmed from their neglect.

CHAPTER 4

As Eon slept, his mind wandered in and out of his horrifying ordeal on the boat. He continued seeing the unknown man's eyes. His gaze was familiar, "No!" Eon said aloud as he awoke in a bed of sweat and nervousness. He shook his head in hopes that his night was a weird, unexplainable dream. He arose from the bed and immediately went into his daily regimen of 100 push-ups and 100 sit-ups. After Eon finished his routine, he went into the kitchen and watched Cassie as she poured orange juice into two empty glasses. She glanced up at the television that sat mounted in a corner of the kitchen. MTV played different videos as she prepared a plate of food for Eon. He pulled his chair to the table, and Cassie placed the plate down in front of him. Eon looked directly into Cassie's face as she returned the stare.

"Good morning," Cassie said as she smiled.

"Hey," Eon replied. "So was I dreaming or what?" Just as Eon finished his question, an MTV news flash came over the television screen.

"Last night, multi platinum hip hop artist E the MC seemed to come down with a case of seasickness as he performed on a luxury boat liner." The newscaster's statement answered Eon's question.

"So I guess I wasn't dreaming, huh?" Eon said.

Cassie grabbed the remote control and pointed it at the television. "No, wait, I want to see what they're saying," Eon said as he touched Cassie's hand, stopping her from changing the channel. Cassie looked at Eon with concern as she put the remote control back onto the counter next to her.

"I mean, c'mon, E. This is nothing but bad publicity," Cassie said.

"No such thing, Cass. You know that," Eon replied. Cassie stopped as she thought of the honesty of Eon's words. She watched as MTV showed a recording of Eon's "performance." Cassie stared at Eon with concern. She hoped that Eon was not allowing himself to fall victim to what happened on the boat. "I'm okay, Cass…I'm fine!" Eon stated.

"You sure?" Cassie asked.

"Yeah, I'm cool." As Eon spoke, the television showed him vomiting on stage. They then showed his return to the stage and his attempt to perform an encore, only to vomit a second time. Eon and Cassie both looked at each other and burst out in laughter.

Seeing him smile made Cassie feel extremely good. She knew he was strong enough to get past this bump in the road, but she wanted to feel assured that he believed it himself. Eon slowly took a bite of turkey bacon, as he became very serious.

"You don't think I'm washed…"

"Don't you dare even say it, you, if anybody knows, your words have power!" Cassie quickly interjected.

"Yeah, like *'Nigger, Nigger, Nigger, Nigger, Nigger, Nigger*, Please?" Eon sarcastically shot back at Cassie, making a joke of himself and his music.

"C'mon now, don't start that shit. You the one who say if it don't make dollars…"

"It doesn't make sense." Eon finished Cassie's comment with pride. "Honestly, Cass, I'm not going to lie. The American buyer scares me to death." Cass looked at him with doubt as she tried to understand Eon's logic. "Akon will always sell The Yardman will always make his sales. You know why?" Eon asked. "Because their fan base is loyal. Africans support Africans, Jamaicans support Jamaicans, but these fucking Americans don't give a fuck about nothing and no one!" Eon said while pointing his bacon at Cassie like an angry teacher talking to one of his disobedient students. "And you know why they don't care?" Eon continued. "Because they are the most spoiled brats to ever live on the earth." Cassie nodded her head in agreement. She knew that Eon's point was extremely valid. "Just a bunch of fucking kids who get whatever the fuck they want," Eon shouted. Cassie looked at Eon as he continued spewing his honest hatred. Eon stopped short of his next comment as he caught a glimpse of Cassie's piercing stare. "What?" he asked.

"Well, Mr. Montgomery, those same spoiled fucking brats are a major part of your fan base. Whether they give a fuck or not, they buy your albums." The reality of Cassie's statement struck a chord in Eon's mind as his frown turned into a smile.

"You know that's why you're my ni…"

"Okay, yeah, I know, I know!" Cassie said as she flung a piece of bacon at Eon. "So listen. We have a show in two days in Atlanta." Eon nodded his head as he drank his orange juice. "Let's make sure we are seriously prepared for this, Okay?" Cassie questioned. Eon brought his glass down and glanced at Cassie.

"What do you mean, seriously prepared?" Eon asked. "I'm always prepared for every show!" Eon's facial expression showed his self-doubt.

"Eon, you almost never do rehearsals, and I've been telling you for the past few years that you need to practice." Cassie could feel her motherly advice sinking into Eon's mind.

"Practice what, Cassie? Just throw your hands in the

air and wave' em like you just don't care," Eon said as he mimicked himself onstage. As he bounced from left to right, Cassie tried to look away from him. Eon stood up from his chair and stood in front of Cassie while he held his fist in front of his mouth, pretending to hold a microphone. "Let me hear you say 'ho...'" Eon said before placing his imaginary microphone directly in front of Cassie's lips. Cassie looked at Eon with disgust and anger. Eon ignored Cassie's mean stare and continued. "Say ho...ho!" Cassie shook her head in disappointment as she walked from the kitchen and toward her room. Eon stood alone in the middle of the kitchen. He looked around as if he were surveying a crowd of his adoring fans. "Thank you for coming out. God bless you. Good night!" Eon said. He took his hands, placed them over his mouth, and began making a sound of people cheering.

"This is not Def Comedy Jam, and you are not Russell Simmons. Just be ready!" Cassie said as she slammed her door shut. Eon laughed at his moment of comedy as he returned to his plate of food.

After finishing his breakfast, Eon spent the afternoon in his studio. He listened to numerous tracks in hopes of finding something for his upcoming album. Eon was looking to introduce a new sound to the world with this album. An abundant number of producers had sent their music to Eon, hoping that he would choose to work with them.

The day of the artist and producer working in the same studio was a thing of the past. Today's music business was based on email and assistants. The clear disconnection had affected the music and its all-around sound. Eon wanted to bring back the authenticity of Quincy Jones and Michael Jackson, Berry Gordy, Jr. and his Motown family. He felt that hip-hop was hurting itself by using watered-down computerized sounds. Eon was a lover of pure, authentic music. His freshman album had pieces of this idea sprinkled throughout, but the majority of the twelve-song classic was Eon's older material. His demo was so aggressive and raw that the record company left most of it untouched and released it "as is." They only changed a few sounds at the mastering table.

After spending three hours in the basement listening to tracks, Eon made his way outside to get some fresh air. As he stepped out into his small vestibule, Eon tainted his fresh air by lighting a joint. As he blew the smoke out into the cool night air, Eon's "spidey senses" went into high gear. He suddenly felt he was not alone. He scanned the familiar area. His mind raced with the different possibilities of who would want to trespass on his property. Eon's first thought was of the girl he had thrown out a few days earlier.

"Come on out, you stupid bitch, and I won't call the cops on you," he said unconsciously. Eon smelled the stench of cheap marijuana in the air, and his antennas went into hyper drive. He quickly butted his own joint so as not to confuse the two smells and sniffed through the air like a trained hound dog. He felt his keen beak zeroing in on the exact location of the smell. As he shifted to the right, the unpleasant odor seemed to move closer and closer. Eon peeked under the stairs and saw the silhouette of two people. His anger swiftly shifted to fear. He grabbed a wooden broomstick from the stack of cleaning tools sitting off to the side and held it with a Barry Bonds grip. He slowly edged closer and closer to the area and its unknown inhabitants. Eon pushed two plastic chairs from out of his path. Just before he could muster the strength to call out to the intruders, two tall dark figures emerged from the darkness.

"What the fuck!" Eon jumped back. He caught himself as the thought of running sprang to mind. As his common sense began to settle in, along with the fact that this was his home, Eon glanced over to the small gate that allowed access in and out of the lower level of his brownstone. One of the uninvited guests lunged at the gate. Eon quickly smacked the broomstick down on the gate, making a loud cracking noise, stopping the young man in his tracks. The trespassers both jumped as Eon removed the stick and stood in front of the gate, further denying their egress. The confused boys looked at one another as if they both needed the other's approval for their next move.

They were both dressed in common urban attire. One wore Timberland boots, shorts, and a colorful shirt that matched his brown construction footwear. The other had on a pair of tight jeans, a white t-shirt, and a pair of white Nike Air Force Ones. Both kids wore their pants way below their waists. The younger of the two stepped forward.

"Look, my nigger. My nigger we sorry for intruding and all that, we out!" The tall lanky character moved toward the gate. Eon stared at the kid with a look of seriousness, causing him to reverse his stride. As he stepped back, both guys focused in on Eon's face. He watched as their eyes doubled in size. Eon could see that they quickly became aware of whose house they were infringing on.

"Yo, you that nigger…you… E the MC!" They said Eon's show-business name in unison. Eon bounced his head up and down, confirming their revolutionary discovery. Eon's fear was quickly replaced with pride and arrogance. The boys smacked each other's hands in disbelief and shock.

"Yo, my nigger. What you doing here, man?" the spokesperson for the two asked.

"Uh, I think that's my question for you two," Eon

stated in a matter-of-fact tone.

"Nah, my nigger. I mean, what you doing in Harlem, my nigger? That's what I'm asking you." The young boy seemed oblivious to his whereabouts as he looked at his rap hero.

"Listen, I'm here for some studio time, plus I was raised in these streets, which explains my need to be here. However, the both of you don't spit, nor do I remember seeing either of you in the industry, so that means you need to explain to me why *you* are here and not the other way around." Eon's voice was sprinkled with humor and partial truth, as he did not want to let the boys know that this was his residence. He could see that the young men were clearly star struck.

Eon always loved seeing people's reaction to him when they saw him in the street. Many people missed the chance of talking to him because they would stand in disbelief for minutes at a time. Before they could utter a word, Eon would be gone. He was going to make sure that this was not going to be one of those times. As the two stood in silence, Eon spoke up.

"So…what are you two doing under these steps? And why are y'all smoking that trash?" Eon's first question did not register at all, but his comment about their marijuana stood out loud and clear.

"What, my nigger? We smoking that Piff, Haze, stickiest bud this side of the Hudson River," the second boy said, breaking his silence.

"We only smoke the best of the best, my nigger!" The two boys smacked each other's hands as if confirming the first statement. Eon shook his head.

"You know you need to research shit before you place it on your lips." Both of the boys looked at one another for a brief second, and then burst out laughing.

"Yo, my nigger. You needs to put some cut on that shit," one of the boys said.

"Word, yo, you need to pause that, for real." Eon immediately smirked, as he was well aware of the Ebonics meaning of the term.

People in the hip-hop community would say, "pause" when they made a comment that sounded gay or had a homosexual undertone. You "paused" your comment because you did not want to give off the impression that you were a homosexual.

"Yo, my nigger you the gay rapper, yo?" the young man asked.

"Nah, baby boy, but I was going to ask you that with those spandex jeans you wearing," Eon shot back wittily. The boy in the shorts continued laughing as his partner stopped.

"I told you them shits was crazy gay, my nigger!" he said in between laughs. His friend's smiling face quickly transformed into an angry snarl as he looked at his associate with dislike.

"Anyway, you cats need to realize what's garbage smoke and the real deal," Eon said as he reached into his pocket and pulled out a small bag of "the real deal" and placed it on the small patio table.

"My nigger, all we smokes is the real…" The young man's words were cut short by the aroma that the small package immediately began to exude.

"Yo, that shit stinks really good. What the fuck is that?" Both of the boys converged on the small sample of marijuana. They each pulled up a chair and sat down in front of the tiny bag as if it were a campfire. "Yo, my nigger, what is *this*?" the boy with the tight pants asked.

"That's real, fresh, official bud from California."

"Damn, Cali bud! Where you get this from?" the boy said while reaching for the weed.

"California!" Eon said as he smacked the young man's hand, causing him to pull it back. "Listen, who are you two?" Eon asked.

"Well, I'm Justin…and this is my boy, Will, " the young man said as he blindly tapped Will's arm. Both guys kept their eyes stuck on the California package. Eon looked at them in their trance like states.

"Okay, now I know your names. Now maybe you can answer my question. Who are you two?" Will and Justin looked at each other with doubt and confusion. "I mean, *who* are the both of you? You know, where are your people from? Do you know who you are?" Eon asked.

"I'm a mother fucking G!" Justin said with confidence. "Shit is in my blood!" Eon looked at Justin, shook his head, and quickly turned his attention to Will.

"Will?" Eon's voice broke Will's concentration.

"Man, I'm a nigger just trying to make his way through all this bullshit." Eon's face shifted at Will's response.

"You seem a little young to be dealing with bullshit," Eon said.

"Nigger, the bullshit doesn't have a age requirement." Eon nodded his head in agreement.

"Well, that's true, but you both need to know your true identity. How don't you know where you're from?" Eon asked. "You dudes walk around with No I.D.!"

"Man, I got my learner's permit right here!" Justin

said. He pulled out his identification from his pocket and tossed it on the table. Will stared at Justin with a blank look.

"What?" Justin asked, oblivious to the ignorance of his comment.

"Listen, you two need to make sure you know where you've been before you can get an idea of where you're going." Eon checked both of his pupils to see if his words were being felt and understood.

"I don't know about all that, my nigger. I know I want to go smoke some of that California goodness." Justin smacked Will's hand in confirmation of their need to smoke.

"Okay, listen. How about this?" Eon asked as he grabbed the bag of drugs from the table. "How about I give you cats an assignment, and if you do what's asked of you. I will have a 50-sack of this very same green waiting for each of you upon your return." Eon stepped back and lit his joint. Both boys looked at each other and then at Eon. Eon grinned as he basked in his Monty Hall moment.

"Okay, what do we have to do?" Will asked.

"Well, it's a two-part mission." Will rolled his eyes in frustration. "You have to find out who your great-great-grandmother and father are on your father's side."

"Okay…and?" Justin impatiently asked. Eon passed the marijuana stick to Justin in hopes that it would calm his nerves. As Justin took a giant pull from the joint, he quickly began to cough from the potency of its contents.

"Wow, is that freshman lungs right there? Slow down, son. Take your time," Eon said as he patted Justin on his back. Justin passed the joint to Will, who listened to the instructions given to Justin. Will slowly took a drag from the manmade cigarette. As Will held the smoke in his chest, the power of the strong drug caused him to cough, releasing the smoke into the night air.

"What's the second part?" Will asked as he passed to Eon, completing the cipher.

"You must find five things that a black person has created or influenced the creation of," Eon stated.

"You mean like crack?" Justin asked blindly. Eon looked at Justin before taking another hit.

"Absolutely not!" Eon stated emphatically. Will could see that Justin's ignorance was becoming more and more disruptive to Eon's calm demeanor.

"We got you, my nigger. So when do you want this info, and when can we pick up our goodies?" Will asked with a straight face.

"Well, I have to travel tomorrow to Atlanta, and then I will be back in about two or three days," Eon said as he finished the last of the California plant. "And also, if you dudes speak of my whereabouts to anyone, our deal is totally off!" Eon said in a very serious tone. Both boys nodded their heads in agreement. Eon extended his hand to both Will and Justin. He watched them both as they shook his hand. He was looking for signs of weakness and was very happy that he didn't find anything.

As they exited, Eon watched both of the boys walk down the block. A small smile escaped as he thought of their youthful innocence and how it was a gift and a curse. They had no idea of who they were; yet Eon could see that they would soon find out.

Suddenly a sharp pain caused Eon to sit down at the patio table. The feeling was familiar to him. He began to roll another joint and smoke the pain away when he remembered the moment he found out who he was.

One day in eighth grade, Eon's teacher spoke about Christopher Columbus and his importance in "discovering" America. Eon listened as his teacher, Mr. Jones; spoke about Columbus as if he were a saint. He referred to him as the first man in America. Eon sat with a face full of frustration. Mr. Jones, a black man, noticed his frown and called on him. "Mr. Montgomery, do you have to go to the bathroom?" he asked with a twinge of sarcasm. Eon shook his head no.

"Yeah, with all the shit you shoveling," Eon said under his breath but loud enough for a few of the surrounding students to hear and giggle. In disbelief, Mr. Jones continued his questioning.

"Why the long face then, Mr. Montgomery?" Eon looked up from his desk.

"Because what you're saying is false," Eon said.

"False?" Mr. Jones questioned.

"Yes, False, as in not the truth!" Eon said with conviction.

"What makes it not the truth?" Mr. Jones asked, hoping he would stump young Eon.

"Well..." Eon paused as Mr. Jones looked on with a devilish grin, thinking he had won the debate. "Columbus could not have discovered America if there was already people here." The crowd of students all sighed in disbelief. "Mr. Jones, Columbus was paid to find another route to Asia, not to discover anything. He landed on the Caribbean Islands where there was already a civilization. So he didn't discover that, either. He did, however, find many different spices and items that his government and financial backers were very happy to *take* from the original people. So in the eyes of his people, he was a great man, yet he actually only got lost and found something by mistake." The students sat in total silence as the teacher stared at Eon with anger. "It's the same thing with good ol' Abe Lincoln. Everyone thinks he freed the slaves, but he was forced to…"

"Okay, so let's move on to the next subject, children. Open your math textbooks to page 67." The kids all followed the instructions and opened their books to the proper page, all except Eon. He sat at his desk and stared at his teacher. Mr. Jones did everything he could to avoid Eon's angry glare, but he knew that he couldn't shake this young man.

CHAPTER 5

"Let's go, Eon!" Cassie demanded from her room as she zipped her suitcase shut. "Our flight leaves in another hour and a half," she said with urgency. Eon walked out of his room and watched Cassie as she rushed back and forth. As usual, she was holding her cell phone to her ear, blasting out directions. "Well, if he's not here, then how are we supposed to make our flight? Listen, if you don't have our car here in another 15 minutes, you can forget our names and our business with you!" Cassie hung up the phone before the person on the other line could say anything.

"That's my nigger!" Eon said with joy and pride.

Will and Justin walked down the street en route to Eon's studio with a bounce in their step. Both boys had done their homework and were anxious to get to their present. As they walked, they noticed a large Rolls Royce Phantom pass. They watched the massive boat on wheels as it smoothly glided past them. "Damn, one day that's gonna be me, with some better rims, of course, and everybody is gonna hate on me for it," Justin said before he raised his middle finger to the sky.

The doorbell rang.

"See, you bugging out, and the driver is here already. I keep telling you to calm down." As Eon opened the door, he could see that this was not his usual driver or any driver he'd used before. Eon looked past the man at the giant car parked in front of his residence. The clean-cut, well-dressed white man who stood in front of Eon looked and smelled more like money than a chauffeur. "Cool, I think you guys bringing the Phantom might calm my manager down," Eon stated matter-of-factly. The man glanced at him with a look of true confusion.

"Yes, I am looking for Mr. Eon Montgomery," the man said with doubt in his voice.

"Yeah, this is him, here in the flesh…but I don't know about you using my government name. I go by E the MC," he said with pride. "If you're going to be my driver you must call me by my stage name."

"Uh, sir, I'm sorry, but I already have a driver, and I am not on stage at all," the white man said with an English accent. It was clear that Eon's assumption was beginning to aggravate the man, as his frustration showed in his face. Eon surveyed the man from head to toe. Strangely enough, the man's annoyance had quickly rubbed off.

"Can I help you?" Eon asked.

"Maybe you can. My name is Theodore Black, and I am here on behalf of Thompson Gamble & Lone. That's L - o - n - e." Eon looked at the man as if he had something strange on his face.

"And?" Eon shouted.

"And, we are interested in buying this property from you." Eon inspected Theodore's form fitting tailored suit and rolled his eyes. "As you're probably aware, Harlem has grown in its diversity and continues to grow."

Eon looked at his unwanted guest as his blood boiled with anger. He realized that Theodore didn't know who he was talking to, nor did he care. He was one of the many financial giants who wanted to rape Harlem of its inhabitants and, in turn, its culture. Many of Eon's neighbors had fallen victim to the get-rich-quick proposition that the banks and real estate moguls laid before them. The worst part was that in the end, many of the people were given much less than the amount offered because of back taxes and other legal loopholes that were stated in the fine print of every contract. Eon was more than aware of how the big fish would devour the small fish and leave them homeless and broke. After watching the change in his surrounding area, Eon talked with his lawyers, and they informed him of the traps that the companies were setting. They explained to him that his best fight against the "machine" was not to sell and keep his property. Big Mama had always told Eon to prepare for darkness, even in the brightest of lights, and he took heed of every word that came out of her mouth.

   Will and Justin walked toward Eon's home and saw the same exact Phantom that had passed them parked in front. They both exploded with inner excitement as their eyes focused on the expensive car. Justin walked over to the driver's side of the car and noticed the black man sitting behind the wheel.

"Yo, my nigger, this you right here?" Justin asked. The dark-skinned young man looked up from his seat. He sat up with a twinge of pride as he realized that he was on display along with "his" automobile.

"Yo, my nigger, you sitting crazy pretty, man. Can a nigger get a spin or what?" William asked, half jokingly and half serious. The gentleman got out of the car. Justin stepped back and allowed the man to walk past him.

"You going to see my nigger, E?" Justin asked.

"You some type of producer or something?" William questioned as the man walked onto the sidewalk.

"Mr. Montgomery, we are offering you seven hundred and fifty thousand dollars. That's not an amount you would want to shake a stick at." Theodore stretched his amount in hopes of making Eon want to jump at his meek bid.

Unknown to Mr. Black, Eon was very well aware of the two and a half million dollars his house was worth. His anger tripled as he heard the disrespectful amount Theodore and his company was suggesting.

"Listen, Teddy, you and your company can shake *my* stick with your offer," Eon said as he grabbed himself. Theodore's eyes grew big as he walked out of the front door.

"Well, I never!" he said as he galloped down the stairs.

The driver walked past Will. He could see that Mr. Black was very much ready to go. He opened the back door to the Rolls Royce and stood next to it. Will looked at him strangely. He was trying to understand why the man was walking around the car. He was oblivious to the dispute that was going on between Eon and Theodore.

"Yo, my nigger, you trying to pick me up or something?" Mr. Black came rushing down the stairs and bumped directly into Will.

"Get out my bloody way, would you?" Theodore said in frustration.

"Yo, what the fuck is your problem?" Will asked angrily.

"And don't *ever* come back to my house with that

bullshit. You can tell your employers that they can *suck my dick*!" Eon screamed from the top of the stairs.

    Once he finished his tirade, he looked to the bottom of the stairs and noticed the boys, who were now surrounding Theodore.

"Pause!" Eon shouted jokingly. Justin pointed up to Eon to confirm his correct usage of the word but kept his eyes directly on Theodore Black.

"You need to watch where the fuck you're walking, Mate!" Justin said in his poorest British accent.

"Uh, no worries, hey, Mate," Theodore said as he slowly stepped between the two teenagers and into his car. The driver closed the door behind Mr. Black. Justin and Will realized his position as they watched him walk around the car.

"You bitch ass nigger!" Will said to the chauffeur. Before he got into his car, the man stopped and looked at both boys.

"You do not know me. You do not know my struggle. I am an African, and you give us a bad name," he said with a heavy accent.

"Well, you're takin' us back to driving Miss Daisy, you chump," Justin said. By this time, Eon had made his way down the stairs and was watching from the street level. "And if you knew any better, you would have called Madame C. J. Walker." The chauffeur looked at Justin as if he were speaking a different language. "She invented the straightening comb. So you could get them naps out from the back of your head, you African booty scratcher!" Justin said as the man got into the car and began to drive off.

"*You Niggers!*" he screamed as he sped down the block and out of sight.

Eon stood between the two boys. He looked on both of them and extended his right hand for a nice greeting. First Will shook his hand, then Justin. Eon could see the frustration on both of their faces. He also felt the excitement of knowing that they had researched the information he had asked them to.

"Madame C. J. Walker, huh?" he said with pride.

"Yeah, and there's a whole gang of shit that we've done that they don't give us credit for," Justin said.

"They just hate niggers cause they ain't niggers, you know," Will said. Eon walked the two boys to their original meeting place. This time they all sat in comfort as the uneasiness of the night before had passed. Eon could see that Will and Justin were still under the trance of anger. He pulled out two neatly rolled marijuana joints from his pocket and passed one to each of the boys.

"Here, this should help you calm down." Will and Justin looked at each other and smiled. They were more than happy to have their afternoon fix. Will lit his joint, and then passed the lighter to Justin, who did the same. Eon stood in front of them both with his joint hanging out of his mouth.

"What, a brother can't get no love?" he joked. Justin tossed the lighter to Eon, who snatched it out of the air. He placed the flame to his marijuana cigarette and inhaled deeply, taking all the potency into his lungs.

"Pace yourself this time now, okay?" Eon warned his pupils, hoping they didn't repeat their previous coughing episode.

"Man, I got this!" Justin said as he took his time smoking. "Just like I got all this info in my mind now." Eon smiled to himself.

"So you found out about your families, too?" he asked.

"Well, my mother couldn't give me much info on Pop Dukes. She says he was a continual one-night stand who one day decided he didn't want to stand with her anymore. She said his family is from the South, but she's not too sure where," Justin said as he pulled from his medicine stick.

"Yeah, my mom said pretty much the same thing,

except she was a little more aggravated." Eon looked at Will. "Well, as soon as I asked, she went into how we don't need his faggot ass and never will. She says he could die for all she cares and asked that I find it in my heart to feel the same way."

"Damn, she really loves your pops, man!" Justin said. The three guys looked at each other and burst out laughing.

"So, that cracker was trying to buy your place?" Justin asked. Eon pulled up a seat and sat between his two new buddies.

"Yep, but the problem is they fucking with the wrong nigger!" Eon smacked five with Justin.

"So this is yours right here, huh?" Will pointed behind him to the tall structure. Eon hesitated before he answered.

"Yeah, and I only told y'all it was a studio 'cause…"

"'Cause you ain't want niggers trying to be groupies and shit. We understand, my nigger, we do," Justin said as he continued to enjoy his weed.

"But you dealing with the wrong nigger if that's what you thinking," Will added. Eon nodded his head in agreement.

"You want to see some really funny shit? Check this out." Eon said as he glanced down the street at a young, tall, and slender Caucasian woman with dreadlocks. She was walking hand in hand with a Japanese man of the same height.

"Man, I'm so tired of these crackers coming through Harlem and taking our shit!" Will said.

"Yeah, first they were just visiting, and now the mother fuckers are here to stay!" Justin added.

"Well, you see these two right here; they are about to go on a trip," Eon joked. As the happy couple came closer to Eon's home, he put his head down. He didn't want them to recognize him because he knew they would return with a camera crew and a gang of other people whom they wanted to introduce to E the MC. A giant maple tree stood right before Eon's place. The roots of the tree were protruding through the ground, causing the man-made earth to buckle. This formed a ramp like incline. Most of the people who lived in Harlem were more than aware of the multiple deformities within the city's sidewalks, but many of the newcomers were not.

As the happy couple walked by, both of their knees buckled as they tripped over the unleveled plain. They quickly turned back to see what could have caused their embarrassment while Will and Justin laughed. After a few minutes, the boys calmed down and settled back into their seats.

"Man, I'm trying to stop this shit," Eon said. He looked at his joint as if he were looking for it to answer him.

"My nigger, are you kidding me?" Will asked. "This shit is the best shit I've ever puffed, and you want to *stop*. I tell you what; whatever you don't want, you leave to us, and we will make *sure* it doesn't go to waste!" Will said. Eon giggled to himself.

Cassie opened the front door, looking for Eon. He looked up from below the stairs. Both Will and Justin looked up from their seated positions. Justin's view was directly underneath Cassie's dress, giving him a clean observation of Cassie's personals.

"Hey!" Eon shouted at Justin, breaking him out of his trance. Cassie heard Eon's voice and glanced over the railing.

"Uh, excuse me," Cassie said, looking down at the three-man sit-down. She waved her hand across her nose as she caught a whiff of the stench below.

"Cass, this is Will…and the brother trying to sneak a peek of your goodies is Justin." Cassie looked down at Justin. She quickly caught wind of what Eon was saying and stepped back away from the railing.

"No, ma'am, I wasn't," Justin said as he felt a sting of embarrassment.

"E, we have to go. The car will…" Before Cassie could finish her statement, a large stretch Phantom pulled up to the house.

"The car is here!" Cassie said as she went back into the house to get her bags.

"Shit, that ain't a car…that's a fucking space ship!" Will said as he finished off his joint.

"Alright Cass, we're coming. You cats get in, and I will be right there," Eon said.

He entered the house from the studio door Justin and Will both stood up and looked at each other in shock. Neither one wanted to make a move toward the giant vehicle. After a minute of standing in silence, Cassie came darting down the stairs. She looked over at the boys standing in silence.

"E says you guys are coming along for the ride?" Cassie walked toward the car, and the chauffeur got out to open her door. The young white man looked at both the boys as he awaited Cassie's entry. They both smiled from ear to ear as they proudly stepped through the gate and into the open car door. As they settled into the plush leather seats, Eon hopped into the limousine and sat next to Cassie.

Moments after the car pulled off, Eon tossed two medium-sized Ziploc bags packed with marijuana to his two young passengers. Cassie rolled her eyes in disgust.

"How old are you two boys?" Cassie asked.

"Sixteen," they both said in unison.

"E, you're old enough to be these boys' father. Don't you think you should set a better example for them?" Cassie said.

"Damn, my nigger, you old like that?" Will said jokingly. Eon looked at Will and smiled.

"Well, honestly, ma'am...he has been teaching us a lot," Justin said in a matter-of-fact tone. Cassie looked at Justin with complete doubt. "I have learned more about myself as a black man than I have ever learned in school," Justin said.

"First of all, you are a boy, not a man, and what are you talking about?" Cassie asked like a curious schoolteacher who didn't believe her student.

"Well, ma'am..."

"Cassie! My name is Cassie!" she interrupted.

"Well, Cassie, I have learned how important the black man's role has been in creating many different inventions that we still use." Cassie looked at Justin and then stared at Eon. She thought he was pulling a prank. Justin continued as the car slowed down to pay the toll for the Triboro Bridge. "The brakes we using to stop were made by Granville Woods...a black man." Cassie looked on in disbelief.

"Can you turn the air down some, please?" she asked the driver.

"The first air conditioning unit was invented by Frederick M. Jones...a black man!" Justin said. Cassie looked at the teacher and student who were both sitting back, smiling from ear to ear. She ran her hands through her hair, not wanting to believe what she was hearing. "Madame C.J. Walker made..."

"Yes, I know she made the straightening comb!" Cassie interrupted Justin. "I overheard you screaming at the, uh...African booty scratcher I think was his name," she said sarcastically. Justin bashfully smiled.

The car pulled into a private hangar at LaGuardia Airport. The Gulf Stream jet sat waiting for Eon and company.

"Listen, fellas. The car is gonna take you guys back to the block. I'm going out to the A.T.L. for a lil bit. I'm gonna see you dudes when I get back," Eon said like a proud father. Both of the boys nodded their heads in agreement. They were basking in the comfort of the luxury vehicle. The chauffeur came and opened the door for Cassie and Eon.

"Okay, gentlemen, let's make sure we leave this car the same way we found it, okay?" Cassie said.

"Yes, ma'am...I mean, yes, Cassie," Justin said and smiled. Cassie gave her approval with a look and a nod as she stepped out of the car and headed toward the jet. As Eon began to exit, he turned to the boys. Will looked at Eon and grabbed a cigar from his pocket. He swung the cigar from side to side in a silent request to find out if they could smoke in the car.

"Hell, yeah. Just don't leave nothing in there," Eon said.

"All right one, my nigger," Will said. Eon stopped before he left the car. He had one foot in the car and one outside. He stuck his head back inside the limousine.

"Let's say P.E.A.C.E.," Eon said with a bit of aggravation. Will and Justin looked at each other, then directly at Eon. "What good is the one without the Love?" Eon asked. "Positive Energy Activates Constant Elevation!" Eon said. Eon's breakdown of the word "peace" took a few seconds to settle into the boys' minds. Will and Justin bounced their heads as the true understanding of Eon's message resonated. They sat back, relaxed, and enjoyed the ride back to their neighborhood.

CHAPTER 6

"E MC...E MC...E MC..." The crowd screamed for an encore as Eon left the stage. He walked directly to Cassie, who was waiting with a towel and a bottle of water. Eon smiled at her. They both knew that this was an accomplishment. Eon had gone through his entire show without a single glitch. His mind hadn't wandered off, and he felt the usual comfort of his fans and the music. He had performed a close-to-perfect show. "What rehearsal?" Eon joked as he grabbed the towel and wiped his face. Cassie took the microphone from his other hand and exchanged it for the water. He took a big swig as he peeked out from behind the curtain at his adoring fans. He could feel the love from each and every one of them as they cheered. Eon always loved the feeling of people enjoying his words. Even though he knew that he could be much more creative with his vocabulary and all-around flow, he knew that he was making an impact on people. Whether good or bad, after some of his shows, if he was in the mood, Eon would have a "meet and greet." He'd allow a select group of his fans a chance to see him up close and personal. They would take pictures and get autographs from their favorite rapper.

Eon and his small entourage entered the dressing room. He turned to Cassie and gave her the thumbs up. Cassie's eyes grew wide with surprise.

She knew that the sign meant he was going to permit people to meet him, and it had been quite some time since he'd given the okay for the post-show gathering. Cassie walked out of the dressing room to speak with the promoter and gather the group. Eon dried himself off and allowed his makeup artist to touch him up. Cassie knocked on the dressing room door just as Rudi finished dabbing him with a sponge.

"Come on in." Eon commanded. Cassie walked over to Eon and whispered in his ear.

"They're ready to see you." She said.

"Okay, let them in." Eon quickly shot back. Cassie left the room and returned with a group of twenty-five people, all displaying smiles larger than life.

Eon sat in a chair and watched as the first young lady slowly inched toward him.

"Don't be scared. I'm not gonna bite." E the MC said to the first batch of uneasy fans. He kissed and hugged fan after fan. The men shook his hand and snapped pictures while the women hugged and kissed him, some to the point where they needed to be pulled away. As the group of people dwindled down, Cassie began leading the people who had already seen Eon out of the dressing room. Eon turned his attention to the last four people. There stood a couple, their teenage boy, and a woman who was alone. As the lone woman stepped toward Eon, he stared at her with a look of confusion. He knew this woman but couldn't figure out how or when they might have met. She wore a nice long dress, and her hair was pulled into a tight bun.

"*You!*" Eon shouted. Cassie was just walking back into the dressing room. She immediately ran over to Eon and embraced him. She didn't want the remaining family to see E the MC in an angry rage. She also thought about the possibilities of a lawsuit being filed by the woman, the couple, or both.

"You cannot do this right now. Just calm down and meet the last family, and we will get her out of here." Cassie said as she slowly began to calm Eon's nerves. As she released him from her clutches, she grabbed a hold of the lady. The woman shook Cassie's grip loose and was ready to make a scene, but a gigantic security guard stepped between the two ladies and separated them.

"Time to go," he said in a calm, deep, serious voice.

The lady knew that she had won the battle but not the war as she composed herself and walked out of the dressing room. Once they were outside the door. Cassie turned to the lady and looked at her with a strong glare.

"What's wrong with you, woman?" Cassie asked.

"There's not a fucking thing wrong with me...you are what's wrong with me! You and that bitch-ass nigger in there!" she said as she pointed over Cassie toward the closed door.

"Are you insane? You spent the night with him, and the next morning, you tried to steal from him," Cassie said.

"You don't know what the fuck you're talking about...and neither does he!" The lady's eyes began to fill with water. Cassie looked directly at her.

"You need help. Are you seriously that attached?" Cassie asked. The woman's tear-filled eyes were now full of anger.

"I'm more attached than you will ever be, bitch!" the lady said. Her loud voice shook the people in the hallway where the two women were talking.

"Get her out of here!" Cassie said as the security guard grabbed the lady by her arm and whisked her away.

As Cassie returned to the dressing room, the couple and their son were leaving. She gave them a phony smile and bid them goodbye, as the excited child looked at all the cool stuff he had received from his hip-hop idol. Once they were gone, Eon went into a tirade.

"How the fuck did you not see that crazy bitch

when you got the people together, Cass, huh?" Cassie looked like a child as Eon continued to chastise her. "This is why I don't do the fucking meet and greet, because of mother fucking cunt bitches like her." Eon's use of the forbidden four-letter word sent chills throughout Cassie's body. "I mean, do I need to get someone else to scan the mother fuckers before they come in the dressing room, Cass? Do I?" Eon's loud voice was making Cassie's blood boil. "Listen, you have to…"

"No, *you* listen!" Cassie interrupted Eon. "You cannot and will not blame me for not keeping a record of the stink nasty whores you sleep with that go crazy and want to follow *you*! I am not your personal condom keeper, nor do I keep these airhead bitches in some type of pussy Rolodex. So don't blame me for that crazy ho's actions," Cassie said as she pointed toward the closed door. "I don't even remember what the girl looked like, E!" Cassie said as she finished her rebuttal.

Eon looked at Cassie, as she was clearly upset.

"I do," Eon said in a matter-of-fact tone.

"I remember what she looked like, and I know I've seen her before," Eon said as he looked off to nowhere.

"Yeah, she looks like the bitch you threw out your house a few days ago," Cassie said.

"Yeah, but I mean before that, Cassie," Eon said. Cassie could see Eon trying to place the woman's face.

"Oh, so now you want to call the crazy cunt back and get reacquainted!" Cassie rolled her eyes. She was upset with herself, not only because she allowed herself to lose her cool, but also because she used the forbidden word to describe another woman. Eon looked at Cassie. A few moments passed, and they both allowed themselves to calm down.

"You know you my nigger, right?" Eon's question brought a smile to Cassie's face.

"E, you have to be more careful who you lay down with. Some women are really scandalous." Eon nodded his head in total agreement.

"What about you?" Eon's question stopped Cassie in her tracks.

"Are you fucking kidding me right now?" Cassie asked. Eon stayed silent for what felt like an eternity.

"Eon Montgomery, are you fucking kidding?"

"Yes, Cassie! I'm fucking with you!" Eon interrupted her before she could finish her statement.

"Well, don't fuck with me like that!" she said.

"Well, Cassie, pretty soon you won't have me to fuck with you at all. Cassie looked at Eon as he sighed.

"You really going to get out the game, huh?" she asked.

"I'm getting more and more sure of it by the day. But for right now, let's just get the fuck out of Atlanta." Eon's comment put a smile on Cassie's face.

"Amen!" Cassie said as they exited the dressing room, eager to make their way back to New York.

"Ah." Eon plopped down on the sofa. "I'm tired," he said.

"Damn. I remember when you were able to do two or three shows in a week," Cassie said as she looked at Eon sprawled out on the couch.

"I'm more tired of the game as opposed to being physically tired," Eon said as he yawned.

"Are you seriously ready to say goodbye to all of this?" Cassie asked as she ran her hands across the plastic-covered couch.

"I'm more than ready. I'm set to let go!" Cassie laughed at Eon's wordplay.

"Cass, we have enough money saved, right?" Eon asked.

"Yes more than enough," Cassie said as she bounced her head up and down. "Well, we can leave now if you want. We can leave this slave ship," Cassie said. She peeked down at Eon to see if he would take the bait.

"Nah, let's play the rest of this little stint and then revisit this conversa...what did you just say?" Eon asked as the tail end of Cassie's comment settled into his mind. "What did you just say?" Eon asked again, hoping he was hearing things.

"Nothing," Cassie said with a sneaky tone.

"Cassie, do not play with me," Eon said as he made himself more comfortable by readjusting his horizontal position. Cassie could hear the seriousness in Eon's voice.

"I told you, we will discuss this issue, and any other issue, after we finish this run!" Cassie held her hands up as if someone were robbing her at gunpoint. She knew when she should leave things alone with her client, and this was definitely one of those times. Cassie walked out of the living room and left Eon to fade into la-la land.

As Eon began to fall asleep, he could hear Cassie's voice. "Slave ship...slave ship...slave ship." Eon began replaying his moment on the boat. He saw the people's arms and legs uncomfortably interlocked together. He recognized the woman giving birth within the massive amount of people. Then from nowhere, he saw the mysterious dreadlocked man's face stuck in between the shifting body parts. His closed eyes popped open and stared directly at Eon.

"Wake Up!" the man said. Eon jumped up from out of his sleep. Violet, about to wake him, jumped back in fear.

"Are you okay?" she asked with true concern. Eon wiped his eyes and focused on who was in front of him.

"Wha…what the fuck are you doing here?"

"I'm sorry. Cassie let me in and told me that I could wake you up," Violet said in hopes that Eon would not throw her out.

"Why would she tell you that? I just went to sleep."

"Well from what she says, you've been asleep for the last four hours," she said.

"Four hours?" Eon asked. He couldn't believe he was snoozing for that long.

"Yeah, well, I sat here for about five minutes and watched you go through something."

"Something like what?" Eon asked.

"Well, you were twisting and turning like you were having a nightmare or something," she said.

"Well, it definitely was a nightmare!" Violet could hear the fear in Eon's voice.

"I'm sorry. I probably should leave." Violet began to walk out of the living room.

"Wait!" Eon said as he held his hand out to Violet. "Listen, I know I haven't been the best during this interview process, especially the last time we saw one another… and I know you didn't deserve any of the energy I gave off on that boat." Violet looked at Eon in shock.

"Is E the MC apologizing to me right now?"

"Yes, but if you tell anyone, I will deny it till the day I die!" Eon joked. They smiled at one another as Eon stood up from the couch and stretched his hands to the ceiling. "Come with me," Eon said as he held his hand out to Violet. She placed her hand inside of Eon's and allowed him to guide her. He took Violet on a tour of the entire brownstone and on each floor told stories from his past.

When they returned to the living room Violet joked,

"Why does this place seem so familiar?" Eon

smiled as he picked up the cracked framed picture of him and his grandmother. "Do you remember that day?" Violet asked.

"Like it was yesterday," Eon said as he ran his finger over his Nana's face as if he were actually caressing her in person. Violet watched his emotions begin to take hold of him. He wiped away a tear and looked up at Violet, who was watching his every move. "You...you tell anyone about this, I'm denying it," he said as he regained his composure.

"I know, till the day you die," she said, finishing Eon's statement.

"Let's go downstairs," Eon said as he led Violet out of the living room.

They stepped into the studio, and Eon sat down in a giant chair.

"Okay, I guess the king has his throne," Violet said sarcastically.

"You damn straight!" he shot back.

"So, you're like the king of..."

"Rock!" Eon pushed a few buttons, and the Run DMC classic chimed in right on cue. She smiled as she sang along with the hip-hop classic.

"You know, there will never be another sound like this...Ever!" Eon said as he bounced his head to the beat. "The fucking sound...the purity of every word...this shit is forever classic." Violet's face turned up with the hard hit of the bass.

"Everybody is fronting now. No one is honest. It's strictly business today," Violet said. Eon looked at her deeply as her words ran through his soul. "It's all about the check! And with the spandex pants they're wearing, they can't even put their hands in their pockets." Eon smiled at Violet's honesty.

"You know, these ignorant mother fuckers can't see how these crackers are just sitting back and cashing in on their stupid ass! I mean, they're getting a half a point for their entire album." Violet nodded her head in total agreement.

One point represented one percent of the proceeds from an album. Many record companies capitalized on the innocence and ignorance of almost all up-and-coming artists. Often times a performer was so excited to get a record deal, they would sign their contract without reviewing it, and even if they did, they never read the fine print. Eon was more than prepared for his time with the record execs. The boardroom gangsters were not able to take advantage of him in any way. Eon's final contract granted him the maximum amount of points available to an artist, in addition to a heavy bonus for every hundred thousand records sold.

This made his deal monumental in the music industry.

"You know, they think they are getting out of the hood, but they end up in more debt than they were in before they signed." Eon looked at Violet as she continued on her tirade of the music industry. "What's even worse is, at the end of everything, when you can't sell another record or can't produce another hit they throw you away like you never existed." Eon just nodded his head in agreement. "So now you are left to return to the same streets you thought you were leaving…and you're more broke than you were before you signed. They create the façade and the look, and then in what feels like seconds, they pull the rug from beneath you. But now you've produced a movement of kids who are walking around looking like penguins 'cause their pants are super tight, hanging six inches off their ass. And that's *with* a fucking belt!" She let out a small laugh at the reality of her comment. "You know it's like we are still slaves in chains." Violet's words stopped Eon in his tracks. He turned his giant chair around and looked directly at her. "They are doing all the work for what…so the master can own the masters!" Eon turned his face up as he allowed her honest lecture to continue. Record companies almost always owned the master copies of any artist's music. This meant that any and all future profit made from any artist's music went directly to the big companies. "I really can not understand how a person can sign their life away just to get a deal."

"Well, I think it's a matter of not knowing any better...just like slavery...we didn't know any better. We had no clue what these pale-faced men were capable of, and because of that, we never completely protected ourselves. They came in peace but left in pure, calculated, manipulative hate," Eon said.

"You ain't never lie...modern-day slavery. What hurts me even more is that *we* should know better. All the information is accessible! I mean, www-dot-whatever, you know?" Violet said passionately.

Eon was surprised that he felt so much comfort with someone in his industry, especially a journalist. He had taken pride in the fact that no one in the business had been able to get into his mind or personal space. Here he was with a female other than Cassie, allowing her access to not just his home, but also his psyche. Eon and Violet discussed the business from two different points of view, the watcher and the watched. Violet talked about her disgust with the lack of content in hip-hop music. Eon spoke about the power of the check writers and how they controlled the artist after a certain amount of time.

"It's like a wild animal that gets captured by the zoo. The animal is trained to do what its handler commands of it. The animal knows that it will not eat if it stays rebellious and doesn't tame itself. Only difference is the trainer cares about the animal." Violet totally understood Eon's analogy.

"So are you tamed, or are you wild?" she asked. Eon glanced over at her.

"I'm my own animal!" Eon pushed a button, and his music began playing. "It's all me!" Eon said with pride.

Violet pulled her chair close to Eon's. He looked at her strangely. He wasn't completely sure of what she was doing, but he knew he wasn't about to deny her an all-access pass. She slowly ran her hand across Eon's shoulder and down his sculpted chest. Eon turned his chair to face Violet. She continued to move her hand south until she arrived below his belt. Eon turned his head to the side, silently asking Violet if she was sure she wanted to carry on with her journey. She grabbed Eon's microphone and softly tugged at it.

"All you, huh?" Violet asked as she checked the goods for herself.

Eon leaned back in his chair as his music played lightly in the background. Violet slowly unbuckled his belt. He looked at her and realized she was not joking. Violet arose from her chair and began kissing Eon. He was shocked at her behavior. Their tongues interlocked and danced around one another as he began unbuttoning her shirt. Violet returned the favor as she took his tank top off, exposing his well-built bare chest. Eon arose from his chair and stood in front of Violet. She looked up at him. He began kissing her face, starting with her forehead and working his way down. Violet unlatched her bra and allowed Eon to venture across her bare chest. She closed her eyes as he softly bit and sucked at her hard, erect nipples. She ran her hands through his hair, directing him from one breast to the other. While Eon continued to pleasure her, she removed her remaining clothes and took Eon's already open pants completely off. He relentlessly kissed Violet's body as he placed her onto his chair. She reclined the chair to an almost horizontal position while he ran his tongue across Violet's belly button, causing her to quiver. As he journeyed down her hairline, he gingerly kissed the top of her vagina. Violet moaned with delight as Eon orally pleasured her. She climaxed and trembled with joy. She pulled at his head as if begging for him to stop; yet he seemed to be on a mission. He continued to taste her until she climaxed a second time. Eon stood up between Violet's legs and looked down on her. She reached up to Eon, seductively requesting his presence in closer proximity.

"Do you have a…"

"Jimmy hat?" Eon interrupted. He reached into a

drawer under the soundboard and pulled out a condom.

A small, sexy smile ran across her face. Violet stopped him before opening the wrapper and sat up in the chair. She softly caressed Eon's stiff manhood as it stood at attention. She slowly placed her mouth around his hard penis and embraced his shaft with her tongue. Eon glanced down at Violet as she moved her mouth up and down at a steady pace. This caused Eon to close his eyes and raise his head to the ceiling in heavenly bliss. Eon stroked Violet's hair as she peeked up at him. He glanced back down at her and noticed his hands moving through a head full of dreadlocks. Eon pulled at Violet's head in an attempt to get her to look up again.

"What, am I doing something wrong?" she said, looking up at Eon, paused in shock.

Eon watched as the familiar, unknown dread looked back up at him; causing him to stop the sexual ride they were both on. He shook his head in confusion, then looked back down and saw Violet looking up at him with desire.

"Is everything okay?" she asked, not wanting to break her oral stride. Eon unsurely bounced his head up and down and grabbed Violet from her seated position. He laid her on one of the couches and put on the condom. She opened her legs and anxiously waited for Eon to enter her.

"Nigger is bugging out." Eon whispered to himself.

"Well, a nigger needs to get it together, 'cause I'm ready!" Violet said sensually.

Eon regained his composure and kissed Violet on her neck and ear. She craved him more with each soft touch of his lips. He cautiously entered her. She cried out in acceptance. He gave more and more of himself with each stroke, and Violet held onto him tightly as he placed all of himself within her moist walls of love. Violet dug her nails into his back, causing him to squint with pleasurable pain. Eon picked her up from her comfortable position and placed himself in her spot, never removing himself from inside of Violet. As Eon sat on the couch, Violet's body interlocked with his in a sexual pretzel. Violet gradually allowed herself to inch down on Eon. Once she felt Eon completely inside of her, she began to move back and forth with precision. He held her breast as he met her half way with every stroke.

"Damn, you got a nigger tripping," he said as she gyrated through another orgasm.

"Your shit is amazing…truly amazing," she said with passion. Eon began to feel a tingling sensation in his feet that he thought meant his climax was close. He closed his eyes in preparation, then opened them in disbelief • • •

He was lost. He observed a line of dark people chained together, at their necks. In front of him was a slab of concrete with wood planks stacked on top of one another. An unchained woman standing at the front of the line was guided to the small stage and commanded to stand still. Multiple white men walked up to the lady and began prodding and touching her. They scrutinized her, lifting her breast, grabbing her buttocks and thighs, as she stood lifeless. A group of people surrounded the woman. A small child stepped up to the woman and poked the side of her leg, almost as if he didn't believe that she was real. The boy's father snatched his hand, pulled out his handkerchief, and wiped the child's fingers. After he brutally cleaned his son's hand, the father threw his handkerchief to the floor and stepped on it. The woman locked eyes with the white man. He walked over to her and stood directly in front of her. Without warning, the man took his hand and began his own vaginal inspection. After sticking his hand inside of her, the man turned to the head salesman and exclaimed, "Wash this one down." The salesman took a bucket of cold water and splashed it across the woman's body. As she shook and shivered with fear and shock from the cold, the group of white men began to bid. Eon watched as the men raised their hands, calling out different offers. Eon suddenly eyed the dread standing in the chain gang line. He turned to Eon, unhooked the chain from around his neck, and walked directly toward him. "Who are you, nigger?" the dread said intently. Eon heard the bang of a gavel. "Sold to Johnson for six hundred and sixty six dollars!"...

"Who are you, nigger? *Shit!*" Violet said as she felt the pleasure of Eon's manhood.

"Get off me!" Eon said as he pushed Violet from atop him. Violet looked at her temporary man as if he were an alien from another planet.

"What the fuck, E?" she questioned.

"I was somewhere else," Eon said as he shook his head in pure mystification. Eon wiped the sweat from his head.

"Yeah, you were somewhere else...like my fallopian tubes," Violet seriously joked.

"Nah, I was at an auction or some shit..." Eon paused and looked at her. She looked back with a weird glare.

"Like a car auction, or I was selling my pussy?" she said in an attempt to understand Eon.

"Get the fuck out of here!" he said.

"No, I'm serious. I want to know," Violet replied. Her voice sounded as if she was a roaming reporter looking for a story and E the MC just so happened to be it.

"No, please listen to me...I am very serious! Get...the...fuck...out...of...here!" The severity of Eon's request was confirmed by the look in his eyes.

"You really want me to leave?" Violet asked as she began picking up her belongings from the floor.

"Listen, Vi, I'm sorry, but I'm going through some real unexplainable shit right now. And before I say, or see, any more crazy shit, I need to really get my mind right!" Violet looked at E and could see that he was not being a heartless prick. He was a confused man who needed some time to get a grip, but that didn't matter to her at the moment.

"Well, good luck with finding yourself," Violet said while she got dressed. As Violet stepped into her panties, Cassie walked into the studio.

"Uh, I guess you're really going all out for this story, huh?" Cassie said with a devilish grin. Eon stood up from the couch naked. Cassie examined Eon from head to toe. She had seen him naked before but never in this capacity.

"Uh, Excuse you!" Violet said quickly, taking Cassie out of her trance.

"Uh, no…excuse you! I live here, *not you*!" Cassie snidely replied.

"Not now, Cassie. Not right fucking now at all!" Eon said, interrupting the brewing catfight.

"Yeah, I know," 'cause the fucking now has stopped, Cassie said as she exited. Eon turned his attention back to Violet.

"Seriously, Vi, it's not you; it's me."

"Yeah, where have I heard that before?" she said with sorrow, closing the last few buttons on her blouse.

"I need to get my mind right." Eon said as he snatched a pre-rolled marijuana joint from a compartment in the soundboard. As Eon lit his special cigarette, Violet rolled her eyes.

"Yeah, I can see you need to get your mind *right*! You know, E, you really need to check yourself," Violet said as she walked out of the studio. Eon took a deep pull from his joint and watched her leave.

"Shit, I damn sure need to check myself...*a.s.a.p.!*" He felt the seriousness of that statement settle into his body.

    The next morning, Eon had Cassie make an appointment with his regular doctor. Eon had been a patient of his for two years now, and the two of them had a connection. It also didn't hurt that his doctor loved music and wasn't interested in selling Eon's medical information for any amount of money. On the drive to the doctor, Cassie sat in silence. She looked out of the window for the entire trip. Eon was so focused on finding out what was troubling him; he didn't notice Cassie ignoring him. As they walked into the office, Cassie went to the front desk and spoke with the receptionist. Eon sat off to the side and tried to blend in with the other patients. Cassie walked over to Eon and mouthed. "Ten minutes." He nodded his head in agreement, happy for the brief wait time. Eon noticed that Cassie chose to sit on the other side of the small room. He pulled his sunglasses down to the tip of his nose and looked at her with wonder. She rolled her eyes and turned her head away from his line of sight. In response to her nonverbal protest, he sucked his teeth and pushed his shades back up into position.

In that moment, a white teenager noticed his face. Eon could see the young boy's emotions getting the best of him. He looked around, wondering if he was the only person who saw the rap god. Eon watched the boy muster up the strength to confront him. He glanced at Cassie, but she was still ignoring him. As he turned his attention away from her, his adoring fan was directly in his face.

"Hey, are you E the MC?" the boy asked as Eon jumped back in surprise.

"Yo, yeah, man, that's me," he said with a smile.

"Oh, shit, you are the fucking man!" the young man shouted.

"Shhh!" Eon placed his finger over his own mouth to emphasize his request for silence. "Where's your mother at, man?" Eon asked as he looked around for the boy's guardian.

"Nah, she's seeing the doctor about her fucked-up tits." Eon's face frowned in full confusion.

"What?" Eon asked.

"Yeah, she has some type of breast cancer or some shit like that. Like Biggie said, my mother got cancer in her breast, don't ask me why, I'm mother fucking stressed. Can I get your autograph, my nigger?" the young boy unconsciously asked as he stuck a piece of paper and pen in Eon's face. Eon grabbed the paper and pen from the boy and stopped before he began writing.

"Hold up, what the fuck you just say?" Eon asked. His smiling face quickly turned to a grimacing frown.

"Uh, can I have your autograph?" the boy repeated without a second thought.

"No, what did you call me?" Eon asked as he squinted his eyes.

"What...my nigger?" The teenager spoke without remorse.

"Yeah, motherfucker!" Eon said.

"What? You ain't a nigger?" Eon thought about the boy's question for a second.

"Yes...No...I ain't *your* nigger!" Eon replied.

"Then whose nigger are you?" Eon grabbed the boy by the collar and dragged him into the hallway so as not to attract any more unwanted attention.

"Wait, before you spazz...I read the inside of your CD cover, and you said that whoever purchased my album, holler at your nigger when you see me."

    Eon thought about the truth of his plea and shook his head in disbelief. His own words seemed to be playing tricks on him. Before he could comment, Cassie came out and told Eon it was time to see the doctor. She appeared numb to the misunderstanding that had just taken place. Eon started toward the office with his eyes on the teenager.

"You gonna sign the paper or what?" Digesting the lesson he had just learned and realizing he still held the paper and pen, Eon stopped to scribble his autograph. He returned it to the youngster and continued walking toward his visit with the doctor.

"Thanks, dude." For fear of a rematch, the boy knew not to use the word again. He glanced down at the autograph that read, *"I am not your nigger anymore!"* The boy and smiled with relief and happiness.

    Eon walked into the doctor's office and sat down. Cassie stood by the entrance. His face was still covered with the shock of the conversation with his fan.

"Can you leave, please?" he asked Cassie without looking at her. Cassie quickly turned the handle and opened the door. She walked directly into the doctor's chest as he was entering. Eon giggled.

"Mr. Montgomery, how are you?" the doctor asked as he shook Eon's hand.

"What's up, Doc?" Eon said with a fake smile.

"So what can I do for you today?" The doctor looked directly into his eyes.

"You look like something is troubling you." The doctor pulled out his pocket light and shined it into Eon's eyes.

"Doc, my mind has been playing tricks on me," he said as the doctor ran his index finger back and forth in front of his patient.

"Really. So which one of the Ghetto Boys are you...Bushwick Bill or Scarface?" the doctor jokingly asked.

"Nah, seriously, Doc. I've been feeling like I'm on a fucking roller-coaster ride through the twilight zone while on crack!"

"Wow...that sounds like a trip and a half. Have you been sampling any crack since the last time I've seen you?" the doctor replied with sincerity and humor.

"Doc, on some real shit, I have seen an entire fucking slave ship and a fucking slave auction!" The doctor's face was now clothed in confusion.

"So, you went to the Blacks in Wax Museum?" he asked, trying to make sense of Eon's statement.

"Hell, no, Doc; I saw the shit as if I was right there."

"Okay…Okay…well, have you been partaking of any drugs?" Eon looked at the doctor with an intense stare. "Other than your usual medicine." The doctor knew that Eon was a marijuana smoker.

"No, Doc, nothing else. But my head hurts like hell because of this shit that's going on…and I've been puffing a lot more lately…and I'm trying to stop!" Eon's comment made the doctor smirk in disbelief. He was well aware of Eon's silent addiction. "I'm fucking serious, Doc!"

"Okay, let's take some blood from you and run a few tests, and we will figure this all out…cool?" Eon nodded his head yes, and the doctor began.

CHAPTER 7

After Eon's day with the doctor, he stayed home, hoping to relax. Cassie and Eon walked silently through the house. They came and went without any contact or conversation. She still felt anger toward Eon for sleeping with Violet, and he felt the coldness of her shoulder. Eon stayed in the house for two days straight without doing much of anything. He avoided his daily regimen of exercise and embraced hibernating in his studio and listening to music.

After forty-eight hours, Eon needed a taste of New York's fresh-and tainted-air. He stepped out of the studio in his bathrobe and slippers and looked up to the morning sun. He walked over to the patio table and pulled up a chair. Eon watched his neighborhood buzz with people. Slumping in his chair, Eon rested his head in his hand. His eyes focused in on two figures that were standing across the street. The two young men cackled with laughter as each new set of people tripped over the man made booby trap. Eon smiled at the boys in one of their happier moments. They all noticed one another at the same time. Eon smiled as the boys trotted across the street.

"So what, you cats is stalking me or something?" he joked.

"My nigger, we watching these crackers bust they ass!" Justin said as he giggled.

"Yo, what's up with the Hugh Hefner look?" Will asked with a smile on his face.

"Man, I've been trying to get my mind right," Eon said in all sincerity.

"Yeah, well, it looks like you're trying to be like Ghost face Killer," Justin said.

"Listen, I feel like someone has turned off the lights in my brain," Eon said as the boys looked on in shock.

"Yeah, well, maybe Lewis Latimer could help you," Will joked. Eon looked at Will as if he was trying to understand the boy's point.

"Uh, duh, He invented the light bulb," Will said with pride. Eon nodded his head in agreement. He stuck his hand into the pocket of his robe and pulled out a medicine stick. Will rubbed his hands together like a hungry boy ready to eat. Eon lit the joint, took two strong pulls, and passed it to Will, who sat to his left. Will slowly took a drag.

"So what, you going crazy or some shit, my nigger?" Justin stared at Will with a glare of anger.

"Hey man, listen, we understand…everyone has a time when shit just doesn't seem right," Justin said in an attempt to help Eon feel normal. Eon looked at Justin like an adoring child staring at his father.

"It's like I'm seeing things...that aren't there," Eon said honestly, staring off into nowhere.

"Damn, my nigger, you sound like you on some crack head shit," Will spoke unconsciously. Justin smacked Will's shoulder to hush him.

"It's cool. I've been saying the same shit myself, fellas."

Cassie walked out of the studio directly into a cloud of smoke. She sucked her teeth and waved her hand in front of her face, swatting away the annoying smoke.

"Listen, the doctor wants to talk to you." Cassie handed her phone to Eon. He stepped away from the table.

"Hello? What's the deal, Doc? Okay, yeah, so what does that mean?" Eon asked, oblivious to the eyes that were watching him. "Huh? A what?" Eon spoke as if he didn't understand his physician. "So what does that mean? You know what? I'm coming to see you right now!" Eon passed the phone back to Cassie as she continued conversing with the doctor.

"So I guess we will see you soon." Cassie walked back into the studio. The boys looked at Eon as his entire mood changed. He was in another world, as a blank look fell upon his face.

"Yo, my nigger, you okay?" Will's question brought Eon out of his trance.

"What?" Eon asked no one in particular.

"Are you alright?" Will asked a second time.

"Yeah...uh, listen, I got to go. I'm going to check you cats a little later." Eon walked toward the entrance of the studio.

"Alright, one...I mean, P.E.A.C.E., my nigger," Justin said only partially correcting himself. Eon turned and gave Justin a half smile as he walked through the door. The boys walked out into the street as they continued sharing the delicious weed.

Eon quickly showered, then dressed for his trip. He entered the car with the doctor's message on his mind. This time, Eon ignored Cassie as the car maneuvered through the city streets. Cassie looked at Eon in hopes he would tell her his situation, but he sat in total silence. The intensity of the moment made it hard for E to sit still. He shifted from side to side. Cassie spoke up.

"What's going on, Eon?"

"Nothing you need to worry about, Cassie." He wanted her to leave him alone.

"Nothing...it sure doesn't look like nothing to me. You haven't stopped moving since we've gotten in the car. Eon Montgomery, what is going on?" Cassie insisted.

"Nothing! Now please leave it the fuck alone!" His loud outburst caused the chauffeur to look back at his passengers.

"Fuck you looking at nigger? Drive!" Eon shouted at his driver, forcing him to stop peeking through the rearview mirror and pay attention to the road and the road only.

"And you say, nothing is wrong, huh?" Cassie turned away from Eon and stayed silent for the remainder of the ride, and everyone else did the same.

Eon walked into the doctor's office and went directly past the receptionist. She screamed for him to wait, but he ignored her request and headed straight to find the doctor. Eon opened door after door, calling out to the doctor.

"Where you at, Doc?" Eon bullied his way through each room.

"Mr. Montgomery!" the doctor said, emerging from his personal office. Eon followed the sound of his voice until he was at the doctor's office. "Sit." Eon plopped down on the chair in front of the doctor's desk. "How are you, Mr. Montgomery?" he asked his not-so-patient patient.

"I'm here looking for you to tell ME that! So what's the issue, Doc? What the fuck is going on with me?"

"Well, like I told you over the phone, we reviewed the test results, and the CT scan showed a spot on your brain." Eon looked on in total doubt. "Because of this, we need to take a biopsy of the tumor." Eon's expression turned from doubt to anger.

"Wait a fucking minute, Doc. You said a spot, not a fucking tumor!" Eon began to feel his pressure rise with frustration and fear.

"Well, E, the biopsy is so we can take a sample of the spot...I mean, tumor," the doctor said in an attempt to calm Eon.

"Doc, which fucking one is it, a *spot* or a mother fucking *tumor*?" Eon's voice rose way beyond the normal level. The doctor saw, and heard, that he wasn't bringing comfort to Eon with his description of their next moves to get him better.

"Yo, E, chill!" The doctor lifted his hands from his desk. Eon immediately calmed down. Even though the doctor's pale face didn't fit the way he spoke, Eon had respect for the practitioner. His straight face and cool demeanor let Eon know that he meant business.

"Look, this is your x-ray." The doctor held the x-ray up to the light. "This right here is a tumor, but it shows as a spot on the x-ray." The doctor used his finger and ran an imaginary circle around the growth. "We need to work quickly and swiftly if we are going to defeat this." The doctor spoke with severity.

"Well, what does it look like?" Eon asked with great anticipation.

"Like a tumor," the doctor said softly.

"And what does that mean?" the innocent rapper asked.

"Well, the truth is, you could have brain cancer." The doctor's words took a few seconds to sink into Eon's body.

"Brain cancer!" Eon repeated the words aloud. "Okay, how sure are you that this is?" Eon did not repeat the two deadly words.

"Well, if you want my professional, honest opinion..." Eon held his eyebrows high in anticipation.

"Yes, I believe it is a tumor. Whenever you have any type of growth on or around the brain, it is best to address it as soon as possible...especially concerning cancer, but we do not know if it is malignant or benign." Eon's eyes immediately dropped to the floor.

"So we need to make sure it's ignorant or benign first before we go any further." Eon's words made the doctor briefly smile.

"Exactly, we are going to take a piece of the tumor and test it to see whether it's malig...cancer inside of it or not," the doctor said.

"Okay, so after we check, then what?" Eon asked as he sat back in his chair.

"That will dictate how urgently we move forward to remove the tumor," the doctor said, hoping that Eon understood.

"Okay, so if it's can...stuff inside of the tu...bump, then we need to remove it a.s.a.p., correct?" The doctor nodded his head yes.

"And if it's nothing in it, then we, what, chill out and go on vacation until we feel like removing it?" Eon asked sarcastically.

"Well, no matter what, we will remove the growth. It's just that if there is anything inside of it, we take the risk of the cancer growing throughout your body," the doctor said with urgency in his voice.

"Okay, Doc, so how early can we get in here?" Eon knocked at his head to emphasize his desire to get the unwelcome visitor out.

"Now we make your appointment for the biopsy first, and then we get you booked for a few treatments of chemotherapy, if and when we need to. Then we schedule for removal of the growth." The doctor pointed at Eon's brain and smiled with a small bit of confidence. The doctor's rundown of Eon's to-do list seemed simple enough, yet it could not have been more complicated and painful. By the end of their impromptu session, the doctor and Eon agreed to work together to get rid of the tumor and work him back into health.

Over the next two days, Eon went to two other doctors for a second and third opinion, and the findings were identical. He had a tumor that needed to be addressed right away, if not sooner. He returned to his doctor and had the biopsy. A week after his sit-down with his physician, Eon was told that his tumor was malignant and he needed to start chemotherapy immediately. Cassie made sure that Eon made every one of his appointments. Once the cat was out of the bag, she became a bulldog in her strive to get Eon back to tip top shape.

Eon was scheduled to attend his chemotherapy sessions three times a week. After his first dosage of chemicals, Eon noticed that the medicine did not agree with him. He would awake in the middle of the night, and his stomach would be in knots. Cassie would listen to Eon as he'd regurgitate his insides into the toilet. Eon struggled through his therapy. He would call his doctor with each new discovery of pain and discomfort. One morning, Eon was screaming at the top of his lungs. Cassie jumped up from her bed and ran into Eon's room. She walked in and saw Eon holding a fistful of his hair. Cassie covered her mouth in shock. She could not believe that Eon was losing his curly locks. He had always called himself Samson, saying that there was never going to be a Delilah that would force him to cut his hair. He looked at Cassie with sadness on his face. The doctor had forewarned E of the possibility of him losing his hair, but Eon did not believe Delilah would come in such a strange form. Over the next two months, Eon made multiple visits to hospitals and other cancer treatment centers. Many of the doctors knew little to nothing about E the MC and were only interested in Eon Montgomery. This took a certain amount of Eon's edge off as his conceit and confidence was replaced with modesty and humility. He listened intently as the physicians explained each level of treatment and what was needed from him for his recovery to go as smoothly as possible.

As the doses became greater, so did Eon's reaction to them. Instead of throwing up once a week, E would puke his guts out numerous times during the day. Although Eon felt like his body was falling apart from the medicine, he was extremely proactive in allowing the medical staff access to his most prized possession, himself. He knew he had to accept the changes that were going on in his body. Eon's doctor was very honest with his explanation of the different side effects that came with chemotherapy. Eon tried to fight the medicine, and its painful consequences with a remedy of weed, weed, and more weed. Where Cassie would usually get frustrated and disturbed by E's marijuana intake, she became understanding and compassionate to his need and desire to feel "normal." Eon would methodically crawl throughout the house. He slowly stepped, like an old senior citizen, smoking while he kept his free hand on his belly. His body's alarm clock would very rarely, if ever, alert him to the auto-reverse button being pushed without warning. Eon threw up whatever was in his stomach at the drop of a hat.

    Three months after the doctor's discovery, Eon was set to have the tumor removed. He nervously packed his clothes. He knew he was going to be in the hospital for at least two weeks. Cassie walked into Eon's room. She could see Eon's uneasiness in the way he threw each article in the bag. Instead of his usual mode of folding every piece of clothing and placing it comfortably into his Louis Vuitton bag, Eon packed with sloppy abandonment. Cassie slowly walked up behind him and grabbed his hand. He shook as her touch startled him.

"It's okay. It's me," she said with concern in her voice as she hugged him.

Eon dropped the underwear he was packing and turned to Cassie. She slowly grabbed Eon around his frail waist. He had been forced to sport a very low haircut because of his battle with the chemotherapy. She ran her hand through his peach-fuzz buzz cut.

"Cass, you have been the only consistent thing in my life for the past five-plus years, and I want to tell you that I appreciate you more than you will ever know." His voice trailed off as he began to feel his emotions getting the best of him.

"Well, I'm your nigger, and it's my job," Cassie said sarcastically.

"No, you're not my nigger...you're my friend!" Eon said as a tear dropped from his eye. Cassie looked at Eon with admiration, as she'd never seen E the MC cry. She knew that the man in front of her was Eon Montgomery. The two hugged for a while as they both cried in one another's arms.

"It's going to be alright," Cassie said as she wiped her face dry. Eon nodded his head in agreement as he grabbed a towel from his bathroom and began clearing the moisture from his face.

"We are going to get through this," he said. He spoke as if he was trying to convince himself of his recovery.

"So, are we done after we get done with this?" Cassie asked with concern.

"I can't even think that far, Cass. If I had to answer that question right now, I would say it's a wrap. I mean, from what the doctors are telling me, it's the game that's stressed me into this *shituation*!" Eon spoke honestly. Cassie could see the frustration in his eyes.

"Well, like you said, let's concentrate on getting better, and then we can revisit this after."

"Hey, what's going on in the matrix?" Eon asked Cassie. Eon would often call show business the matrix. He knew that the entire industry was based around false information and smoke and mirrors.

"Well, they are asking what happened to you, but they aren't kicking our doors down."

"Good!" Eon was more than happy to not have multiple reporters and other tabloid devils at his doorstep, especially with everything he was going through. E the MC was well aware of how his elusiveness had kept many people out of his backyard. He knew the hungry public would love to hear about his current issues. "And Lady Vi?" Eon asked shyly. Cassie rolled her eyes and sucked her teeth.

"I guess you fucked her away." Eon shook his head at Cassie's snide remark as he went into one of his drawers and pulled out a large Ziploc bag stuffed with marijuana.

"Damn, I'm gonna miss my baby," he said like a little boy who had his favorite toy taken away from him.

"The green or the bitch?" Cassie asked. Eon could only continue to shake his head. He knew that he wasn't able to bring his "medicine" inside the hospital with him. Eon rammed his face into the bag and took a deep sniff of its contents. The doorbell rang. Cassie went to the door and opened it. The two boys outside stood still.

"Hey, Miss…I mean, Cassie." Justin examined Cassie's face. "Is everything okay?" Justin asked sincerely.

"Yes, but guys, now isn't really a good time. E is…"

"What up, my young brothers?" Eon slowly walked up behind Cassie and interrupted her.

"Shit, that's what we wanted to ask you, my nigger," Will said unconsciously.

"Listen, gentlemen, I have to go away for a bit, but come on in and we can rap a bit until the car comes to get me." Eon pulled the door open for the boys to walk in. Cassie looked at him in shock as the boys walked past her and into the living room. They both looked around at the many pictures and old trinkets that were all around the room. Justin and Will glanced at each other with a strange stare as they took in the room and its decorations. "So what's up with you cats?" Eon asked as he walked into the room holding the large package of weed.

"Oh, shit, that's a whole lot of green!" Justin said without a second thought. Eon smirked. He watched his two pupils follow the large plastic bag as he switched it from one hand to another. They seemed to ignore Eon's fragile stature and concentrated only on the marijuana.

"Yo, what's going on with that?" Will pointed at the Ziploc bag.

"Well, like I said, I'm going away for a while, sooo…" Eon stretched the end of his statement.

"So what, my nigger? Please don't play with a nigger's emotions," Will said, wanting the goods in Eon's hand.

"Well, I can't bring it with me," Eon said sadly as he looked at Cassie, who was standing to his side.

"I may quit!" E said smartly. The teenagers both looked at Eon, then at one another, and burst out in laughter.

"My nigger, you want us to believe that you're going to stop smoking…and you standing in front of niggers with a pound of goodness in your hand? Get the fuck outta here!" Will smacked five with Justin.

"Well, what are you cats willing to do for this?" he asked as he held the baggie out towards the two boys.

"Listen, I know more about niggers…I mean black people…than school has ever taught me," Will said.

"Word!" Justin agreed.

"I couldn't get much info out of my mom as far as my heritage and family tree goes because she's very serious about my faggot pops being a deadbeat piece of shit, but I will keep asking until she gives me another answer," Will said with sincerity.

"Nah, I need you dudes to keep grabbing all the information you can about yourself and your people. We are a strong race and we are the original man, but we cannot go forward if we don't know our past. We need to gain control over our former masters 'cause they are continuing to keep us down, and we must fight to get better!" Eon felt himself getting caught up in the rapture of his emotions. The boy's faces began to change as they watched their hip-hop super hero begin to cry.

Eon tossed the bag to Justin and looked at both of his students. They finally looked directly at E the MC and noticed the drastic change in his all-around physique. Both of their faces crunched in confusion. They couldn't figure what was eating the rap lord from the inside out. He watched the young men as their eyes tried to answer the question of what was wrong with him. E began to feel more frustrated with every second of their stares. "Promise me that you will research your race!" Eon screamed through tears. Both youngsters jumped at his sudden change in volume as Eon walked away. Cassie gave Justin a bag to carry the marijuana and led the boys out the front door in silence. She could see that both of the young men were trying to understand Eon's emotional outburst as they walked out. She watched them slowly stagger down the street. They glanced back at Cassie every few feet until she closed the door. Five minutes later, a car came to pick up Eon and Cassie to take them to the hospital.

"Okay, so, Mr. Montgomery, how are you feeling?" the specialist asked as Eon lay uncomfortably in his hospital bed. He had spent the last two nights in the hospital being prepped for his operation. Since the discovery of the tumor, Eon's doctor walked with him through every step leading up to this moment.

"Well, I wish I was in St. Thomas sipping on an Amaretto sour with a blunt, but I'm sitting here with a Kojak cut with my ass cheeks clenched together, scared to death...but other than that, I'm great!" Eon joked about his fear of the moment.

"Well, maybe once we get this done, those dreams will be reality," the doctor said as a small smile escaped Eon. "Listen, we are going to take really good care of you, and I will be here as soon as you get out, okay?" Eon grabbed the doctor's hand and shook it intensely.

"Thanks for everything, Doc." Eon started welling up with emotion. Cassie walked over to him as the doctor stepped away.

"I will be right here waiting for you, okay?" she said softly as she wiped her favorite rapper's face. The attendants wheeled Eon away from the doctor and Cassie, who stood at the end of the hallway like anxious parents watching their child go off to battle.

CHAPTER 8

"*Wake up nigger!*" The dread's voice sounded as if he were directly in front of Eon. Slowly awaking from his sleep, Eon scanned the room while trying to gain control of his eyes. The first thing that came into focus was Cassie lying in a chair with a blanket over her. Eon quickly realized he was in the hospital. He felt groggy and weak. He inched his hand up to the top of his head and felt the bandages.

"You have to leave that alone for a while, Mr. Montgomery." The doctor walked into Eon's room, accompanied by the surgeons who had performed the operation.

"Hey there, docs," Eon said softly.

"Mr. Montgomery, how are you feeling? The surgeon asked.

"I'm out of it, but I'm feeling pretty decent...wondering if you can tell me how I'm really feeling." Eon's voice woke Cassie up from her sleep. She looked over at Eon and grinned at him.

"You okay?" she asked as she wiped the cold out of her eyes.

"Yes, I'm okay. I was just about to find out how okay I really am." Eon pointed at the doctors in front of him. Cassie looked up at the men in lab coats and tried her best to straighten herself.

"Cass, they're here to see me, not you," he joked. Cassie waved her hand at Eon and sat up in her seat while listening intently.

"Well, Mr. Montgomery, we have successfully removed the growth from your brain, and the cancer seems to be gone from your body." Eon glanced at the doctors, then at Cassie, who was sitting with tears streaming down her face.

"Okay, what do you mean, *seems*?" Eon inquired. He'd heard everything the medical professionals told him, but he was stuck on the word "seems."

"Mr. Montgomery, I cannot and will not tell you that the cancer is gone for good." Eon looked at the doctors through squinted eyes. "The truth is that cancer can return at any time, so 'seems' is the only word I can use, especially this soon after the operation."

"So what happens if it *seems* to come back? Then what?" Eon asked strongly.

"Depending on how it comes back, we may have to go back to square one and do this all over again. But we don't need to even think that far down the road.

Right now, we need to get you back to health." Eon nodded his head in approval as Cassie walked over to his side and grabbed his hand.

"Okay, so what's next?" she asked.

"We need to make sure he's in a quiet, calm, and peaceful environment," the doctor said directly to Cassie.

"Okay, so we are going back on tour, and then we're attending all the award shows, right?" Eon joked. Cassie smirked and softly tapped Eon's hand.

"Well, Mr. Montgomery, we have all had a very busy few days. We are going to go and allow you to get some more rest," the head physician said with a smile on his face.

"Cool and the gang, Doc, cool and the gang! And again, thank you so much!" Eon said as he readjusted his body in the bed in an attempt to find a more comfortable spot. Cassie turned her attention to E as the doctors walked out of the room.

"Hey, Cass, so what ever happened to the other few shows we were supposed to do? You know, I've been so focused on this shit here that I haven't even thought about E the MC." He closed his eyes for a few seconds.

"Well, I've straightened everything out with all the promoters we were dealing with, and it's all good."

She looked Eon directly in his eyes. "You have nothing to worry about except getting better!"

  For the next few days, Eon watched and listened to the different doctors who would come and check on him. Sometimes they'd take Eon away to run more tests and make sure that everything was going well in Eon's head. One thing that changed on his schedule was Cassie's presence. Cassie had not been around as often as she was, prior to the surgery. Eon noticed, but chose not to make a giant fuss over her absence, especially while he was in the process of getting better. Eon assumed that Cassie had a good reason for not being around. He figured she was getting things done for E the MC and reveled in knowing it would benefit Eon Montgomery. He dismissed his uneasiness and kept a positive outlook on the situation. Eon's body was slowly returning to its regular form. As the days passed, Eon began to feel more and more of his energy.

  After a week of tests and check ups, Eon Montgomery sat in his wheelchair and awaited his release papers. His head was healing well, so much so that he now sported only a bandage on the spot where the incision was made. Cassie stood behind Eon with a giant smile on her face. They both were extremely happy to have made it through such an ordeal. Eon bounced his head to a beat that only he heard.

"You alright, good buddy?" She didn't know whether pain or pleasure was causing her client to move in such a way.

"Oh, now you're checking up on me, huh?" Eon shot back in a sarcastic tone. Cassie sucked her teeth. She knew that at some point she was going to hear about her abandonment, but she wasn't expecting it so soon.

"Listen, mister. I wanted to make sure you weren't having a fucking seizure or anything. I would hate to get you home and find out we gotta bring your ass back again!" She pushed on the wheelchair, causing Eon to slightly jolt forward. Cassie's tone was much more aggressive than usual. Eon quickly turned his head towards his chauffeur.

"Who the fuck you talking to, woman?" Eon asked with a serious look on his face.

"I'm talking to you! Shit! I'm the one caring for you and making sure you're okay, so before we step foot...or should I say roll foot...out this mother fucker, I need to know you are all good." Eon turned around in his chair. Cassie's words struck a nerve. She was the only person he trusted, and she wanted the best for him.

"Cass, let's just get home. I just want to go home," Eon said with sincerity. He knew he was fighting a battle that he couldn't win, so he calmed himself and relaxed in his seat.

"Amen!" Cassie took a deep breath in an attempt to empty her soul of her frustration.

Eon signed the last of his paperwork and shook all of his dream team doctors' hands. Cassie slowly pushed Eon out to the waiting limousine. As he arrived at the door, his usual chauffeur walked over and opened the door for Eon. He looked up at the young man and smiled. The last time they'd seen each other, Eon wasn't the best of passengers. The chauffeur returned a smile and extended his hand to help Eon up from his chair. Eon shook his head and tried to stand up on his own. Eon thought he had already regained his strength. He very slowly stood up, and suddenly his legs gave out, forcing him back into the chair. Cassie stood behind him, bracing the chair for his inevitable fall. As Eon sank his 6-foot-3-inch frame into the car, Cassie turned to roll the wheelchair back to the hospital. Just as she did a 180-degree turn, the chair came close to hitting one of the hospital staff that was waiting to take it from her. He was an attractive man.

"Oh, I'm sorry…I almost took you out," she said, slightly embarrassed.

"Well, you can if you would like to. I wouldn't mind that," the man said as he grabbed a hold of the chair's handle. His hand softly laid on top of Cassie's as they looked into one another's eyes. Before they could say anything else, Eon spoke through his open window.

"Uh, can we stop eye screwing and get going, please?" He watched the two indecisively step away from each other.

"I guess your dad is a little impatient, huh?" the young man said. Cassie smiled from ear to ear as the guy's mistaken identity humored her beyond words. She also loved the fact that he clearly didn't know who E the MC was.

"Do me a favor?" Cassie asked.

"Anything!" His voice was drenched in nervousness as he glanced at Cassie's "dad," who was staring at him. Cassie grabbed a pen from out of the man's green scrub shirt. She softly snatched his hand and began scribbling her number into his palm.

"Call me!" Cassie said like an anxious teenager.

"Let's go!" Eon said aggressively as he rolled the window up without waiting for Cassie's response. The young man walked away from Cassie, peeking at his hand. She climbed into the car with an attitude.

"You know something? That was really rude."

"Oh, I'm sorry. I just finished having my brain opened and a cancerous tumor removed. I'm so sorry I wanted to go home."

"You have to realize that I have a life, too, you know," said Cassie as she sucked her teeth.

"Yeah, yeah...and I support that life and have supported that life for a good stretch of time now," Eon shot back.

"Eon, I would have thought that this ordeal has taught you that money isn't everything." Cassie turned away from Eon and looked out the window.

"You're right, Cassie. It isn't." Cassie turned back to Eon with a look of doubt. She knew that Eon never conceded a point with such simplicity.

"Money isn't the reason these specialists kept me alive...nor is it the reason they helped remove that tumor. They did it because they care," Eon said in a baby voice. Cassie rolled her eyes as she felt the sting of Eon's sarcasm. "No, seriously, I apologize for breaking up you and Dr. Love's make-out session, but I really want to get home so I can get better," Eon said with sincerity.

"I get you, E, and I have made plans to get help for you." Eon quickly turned to Cassie.

"What do you mean, you got help for me?" He understood her comment but didn't know what she meant by it. Cassie could see the doubt and frustration in Eon's stare.

"Well, I hired a home attendant to come by the house," Cassie said.

"When?" he asked. His voice was at a level of screaming.

"Everyday!" Cassie said.

"Come on now, Cass, I don't need no one to help me...I only need you!" She looked at Eon. His honesty showed in his face.

"E, I'm sorry, but I cannot always be there for you." Cassie watched Eon. Her words seemed to deflate Eon as his shoulders slumped. "E, you are going to be fine, and you will get better. These people are professionals, and they know how to make you feel good." She hoped her words were making him feel better.

"But Cass, they don't know me...*you do!*" Eon felt himself getting stressed with the scenario he was facing.

"Listen, E, we...you are going to be just fine!" Cassie was trying to sell him a boost in his morale, and he wasn't buying her product.

"Yeah, whatever." They pulled up to his home. Eon slowly walked up each step. The closer he came to his front door, the more energy he felt. Cassie handed Eon his keys. He unlocked the entrance to his kingdom and stepped through the door with a giant smile on his face. Cassie followed the happy man inside. She dropped his bags and went into her room.

"You know, E, I've really been thinking about what you said about leaving the game, and I think you're absolutely right." Cassie slowly walked towards Eon's room. "You know I have…I mean, we have enough money to…" Cassie stopped as she walked into Eon's bedroom and found him asleep.

For the next week, Eon and Cassie went about their business as if the other weren't there. Eon impatiently waited for his hired help as he regained his energy. Cassie tended to her personal things. One day, Eon was downstairs in the studio when the doorbell rang. He was zoned out in his music. He didn't recognize the sound of the front door until the third ring. Eon listened to hear if Cassie had opened the door. After the fifth ring, the uninvited guest began knocking at the door. Eon felt more and more frustrated with each loud bang. Eon walked out of the studio and called to the person while standing at the top of the stairs.

"What?" Eon shouted. Justin and Will peeked over the top stairs at Eon.

"Yo, what up, my brother?" Justin said with a smile. Eon's temper quickly simmered down when he realized he was looking up at his two students.

"Hey, what's up, fellas? Come on down here." He swung his hand to emphasize his desire for them to step down to the studio. Both of the boys jumped down the stairs and embraced E the MC. The three buddies walked into the studio. Will and Justin looked around as if they'd walked into a museum. "Take a seat and make yourself at home," Eon said with love. He was extremely happy to see the boys. With the way things were going in the house and the distance that seemed to be growing between him and Cassie, Eon was beginning to feel a bit lonely. Will sat in Eon's seat in front of the soundboard. He ran both his hands over the faders and different buttons.

"Wow, so this is what it looks like, huh?" he said. Eon looked at Will with a stare of wonder. "A real studio!"

"We've been in a few homemade ghetto spots, but we have never seen a fully stocked, up-and-running studio," Justin said from his seat. Will jumped up and walked toward the booth. Eon looked at the boys as they both wandered around as if they were in an amusement park.

"This shit is trump tight my nigg...my brother," Will said as he stepped into the booth. Justin moved over to the board and looked at Will. The two played as if they were recording a classic hit. Justin pointed at Will through the clear glass. Will pointed back at Justin as he began shouting multiple verses from his favorite MC through the microphone. Eon looked on at his young apprentices and smiled. He watched Will and Justin in their make-believe session. He pushed a button that made Will's voice audible throughout the entire studio and not just inside the booth. He listened with pride, as Will's flow was identical to E the MC's.

"Yeah, you got it, brother!" Eon pushed a button so that Will could hear him from inside the enclosed cubicle. Will walked back into the room and took a seat.

"So, what's going on, fellas?" E asked.

"Man, we want to ask you that exact same question," Justin said. E looked at Justin and Will, whose faces were cloaked in concern.

"Yeah, man, what's up with you? You don't look like yourself, my dude," Will said.

"You just seem different," Justin added to Will's way-too-honest comment.

"Yeah, I know…well, honestly guys, I've been through a lot in the last few months." Both of the boys looked at E the MC. He took in a deep breath.

"I was diagnosed with a brain tumor." Will and Justin's face turned with confusion. "And the tumor was cancerous, so I needed to have it removed. Before the surgery, I went through chemotherapy, and that's what took my health and my hair," Eon said.

"Shit, my G, that's fucked up," Will said. "You sure that shit wasn't the government?" Will asked. Eon's face turned up with confusion. "What...I mean they have done much more to a lot of other people." Eon started to see the connection. "Nine-eleven, King, the Kennedys, Malcolm X...shit Katrina. Please don't think for a second that they couldn't do some shit to you, E," Will prophesied. Eon shook his head in denial of Will's explanation. "What's even worse is they would put someone black up to do it, too!"

"Niggers don't want to see no one shine, not even themselves," Justin interjected. "It's like the way niggers look at us, especially since we came through in that G4 on wheels that day." Eon smirked at the boys.

"Man, listen. The hood talks like a mother fucker E...you know that," Will said. "And then when we came through with that good green you gave us...shit, it was over!" Eon sat in silence and allowed Will to continue.

"That Willie Lynch really fucked the game up, and that shit is passed down from generation to generation." Eon's eyes grew big as the realization of Will's new found knowledge could be heard in his words.

"E, it's true." He turned his attention to Justin. "Dudes have a lot of hate and envy. It's like if you are successful or want to make it out the hood, then you're a sellout." Eon bounced his head in agreement. "And cats don't see that. They don't even know who the fuck Willie Lynch is, let alone what he's responsible for." Eon could not hide his personal arrogance. He allowed a small grin to run across his lips. He could hear that his students had even gone a step further in gaining information on their people.

"It's crazy. I read his letter to the slave masters, and I couldn't stop thinking about how mother fuckers live right now…today!" Will continued, picking up where Justin left off. "Man, the light-skin mother fuckers think they are God's gift to the universe, and then the deeper the darkness, the more insecure the person." Eon could not believe his ears. He knew that the boys were not just reading, but they were learning. He felt the transformation in how they viewed the world and, even more importantly, themselves. Eon knew that he had impregnated their minds with the desire for knowledge. He listened with appreciation to the birth of the new young men who came from their craving of information. "Now I'm not saying that all light-skin people are the same, but the bullshit shows in a lot of them…and the same for the dark niggers…I mean, brothers and sisters," Will said.

"Shit, I think about back when we used to go to school," Justin began.

"Man, we would call the darker people all type of names…*black*, *crispy*, *burnt*…while a dude would chase the light-skin girl all over school. Man, listen, aren't we all descendants of slaves?" Justin looked at Eon with a very serious face.

"Well, pretty much," Eon said. He reveled in the fact that he was watching little boys show that they were grown-ass men.

"Well, that being the case, the house niggers had, and have, their heads up their ass while the field niggers worked, and continue to work, on the field and live with self-doubt and anger. And now it's even worse 'cause we have been freed from the slave masters and are still living under the same conditions as a people." Eon shook his head and banged his hand on the soundboard.

"What the fuck happened to you cats?" Eon asked with pride.

"You!" both young men said simultaneously. "E, when we last saw you, you weren't looking too good."

"We didn't know if we were going to ever see you again," Justin said. A lump began to grow in his throat.

"And when you said for us to find out more about ourselves, that shit ran through us FOR REAL!" Will said. "We felt like this could have been your final request to us, and we wanted to make good on our promise to you," Will continued. "You were really emotional, and that caught us off guard." Will began to sniffle as he held back his tears. "E, you have to understand that we were never expecting to meet you when we was puffing under your stairs. I mean, we were bugging the fuck out when we left you that first day," Will said.

"And the fact that you were crazy cool with us was really unbelievable. I mean, you are E the fucking MC! Then you started asking us to learn more about ourselves and our people." Justin stated.

"At first we thought it was a little weird, real talk! But as we started learning more and more, we began wanting more and more." Eon looked at his young protégés. He felt the authenticity of their words. Will continued. "We were just trying to make sure the pigs didn't get to us when we were invading the space under your stairs 'cause they are on some bullshit now a days Will said.

"Man, they been on some shit for a lot of days…past, present, and future," Justin said as he smacked five with his partner. "Then you come at us on some knowledge-of-self shit," Justin said. "Man, you fucked us up with that, E. I mean here is the head nigger in the game telling us to stop saying the word 'nigger'...come on now." Justin held his hands out wide as if he was looking for a hug. "Then you didn't just accept us. You made Ms. Cassie accept us, too. Shit was unreal, my dude," Justin said.

"Hey, where is Ms....I mean, Cassie, anyway?" Will asked. He looked around the studio as if he thought Cassie would pop up out of nowhere.

"Honestly, fellas, I don't know what's up with her. She hasn't been around for the past couple of days...and when she does come through, it's as if she'd rather not be here." Both of the boys looked at E with confusion.

"Shit, maybe she's down with the government?" Justin said. The three friends burst out laughing at Justin's comment.

"I really appreciate you cats coming by to see me. Even more, I appreciate you dudes for keeping your mouths shut and not letting the world know that I'm here." Eon spoke in a tone of humility and trust.

"Hey, partner, you have been way too good to us for us to turn around and do you dirty," Will said.

"Yeah, you have opened your heart and helped open our minds in ways we could have never gotten from them bullshit-ass teachers in school." He spoke as if he was upset with his teachers and the entire school system.

"Man, it's like I never want to go back to school. They're not trying to teach us the *real* history. They just want us to believe the hype and whatever they push in front of us and that's just wack!" Will said.

"Well, I can honestly say I know how you feel, J. Them teachers tried to pull the wool over my eyes, and I stopped them cock suckers right in their tracks," Eon continued. "My Big Mama had hipped me to the real. So when they came in with the Christopher-Columbus-discovered-America shit, I was there to shoot that shit down."

"*Word*?" Justin asked.

"And what did they do?" Will inquired.

"They labeled me a troublemaker and tried to kick me out," he said with intensity as his face cringed with thoughts of the past.

"And then what?" Justin asked.

"Well, by the time I reached your age, my third eye was open to all the 'tricknology' traps they were trying to set. I knew that the same people who were setting up our leaders to take a fall were writing and controlling our textbooks and how much info they gave out. I saw past their phony past and the way they were spoon-feeding us." Both boys sat silent like good students. "In between my grandmother, her mother, and the library, I was the wrong nigger to fuck with," Eon said proudly. Justin and Will both beamed with pride and admiration for their teacher.

"Uh, did you just say you were the wrong 'nigger'? Justin asked.

"Well, in the South, that's exactly what you were considered and called!" Eon shot back. "That's why I'm on you cats about the word."

"Yeah, I can dig that, but have you heard any one of your records?" Justin looked directly at Eon with an intense stare. Eon smiled.

"Yes, I have...and I realized that in order to beat the system, you must become part *of* the system." Eon waited to see if his message came across.

"Yeah, right, nigger. You saw a way to get paid and you went after it, didn't you?" Will said.

"Hell, yes!" Eon concurred as the three burst out laughing "No, but seriously, you cats need to understand the game. You think Jay and them named the company Rockefeller for nothing?" Eon asked like an anxious child. He could see that the boys did not know about the Rockefeller Empire. "Now that's going to be your next mission. Look up the Rockefeller dynasty."

"Okay, that's a bet. You mean like the *Dynasty* album? That shit was fire!" Will said. Eon shook his head at Will's ignorance. Will's only knowledge of Rockefeller was through Jay-Z.

"So, Rockefeller and the Masonic movement those are your two assignments," he commanded.

"Oh, you talking about the dude that was down with P-Diddy and went and became a minister and then came back and got down with G-Unit, right?" Will asked. Justin sat in his seat and took mental notes of the names of the two conglomerates.

"So, do we get the same thing we got the last time we saw you?" Will asked. His greed showed in his eyes. Eon looked at Will and then turned to Justin, hoping that he wasn't fueled by the same hunger for excess.

"Nah, it's cool. We are going to check those two companies out, and we will see you soon, E," Justin said. His words helped assure Eon of his commitment to learn more about his people and the world in general.

"Nah, fuck that, my nigger. We needs…" Justin quickly interrupted Will's tirade.

"We need to be going now!" Justin stood up from his chair and towered over Will, who fell silent. Not wanting to be upstaged, Will pushed his chair back and rose up in front of Justin. The two stood face to face like they were getting instructions from a referee before a boxing match. Neither boy budged. Eon knew that he did not have the strength to separate the two young lions if they chose to begin to brawl. As if on time, the doorbell rang.

"Listen, fellas. We just discussed the seriousness of Willie Lynch, and now we are going to fight each other? C'mon!" The doorbell rang a second time. Eon stood to the side of the two warriors as they stared at one another intensely. "Life is way too short!"

"Yeah, and this chump don't want his life to last too long at all!" Will said as he twisted his face up. Justin felt that it was unnecessary to continue down the path that Will was testing him to travel, so he slowly allowed a smile to run across his face.

"Man, listen, I'm not even tripping." He was clearly taking the high road and trying to move past the possibility of an altercation. Will noticed that Justin was not in the same frame of mind as he was when they first squared up against one another. Eon was silently impressed with Justin's choice to be the bigger man. Will stepped back away from Justin and matched his smile with a smirk of his own.

"I'm good!" Will said with clarity. The two friends looked at each other. The doorbell rang for a third time.

"Hey, I'm not good!" Eon said.

Eon pointed to the front door up above them. He slowly walked out of the studio and yelled to the person at his front door.

"Who is it?" Eon screamed. The lady called down to Eon, who was at the bottom of the stairs.

"It is me!" Eon glanced up at the lady's soft white leather nurse shoes. He ran his eyes up from her feet to her face and realized that this was his hired help.

"Are you here for me?" Eon asked.

"Uh, well, are you Mr. Montgomery?" the happy nurse asked.

"That would be me. Please let me get my house guests out, and then I will be right with you." The lady began making her way down the stairs toward Eon.

"No…wait right there. I will be with you in a minute," he commanded. Eon went back into the studio and saw Justin and Will sitting together as if nothing had happened. He laughed at the two friends. *"Let's get ready to rumble!"* Eon's voice shocked the two boys as they looked at him.

"Nah, we cool!" Justin said.

"Word!" Will concurred.

"We outta here, E," Justin said. The two boys stood up from their seats and made their way to the exit. Eon embraced both of his pupils. "So you cats have your assignments, right?" Eon asked.

"You mean Puff Daddy and Jay-Z, right?" Justin joked.

"Yeah, the Rockefeller and Masonic empires," E the MC said. The boys walked out from the basement studio.

"Good luck, lady. You're gonna need it," Will said as they walked past the stairs leading to the front door. She turned and watched the young men walk down the block as Eon opened the door to let her in.

CHAPTER 9

After a month with his nurse, Eon adjusted to her being there on a regular basis. Ms. Francine was very helpful. She cooked and cleaned everyday and never gave Eon any issues. At first, he thought she was going to be a problem. Ms. Francine was a West Indian woman with an accent. She was nothing like Eon was expecting when he first met her. What was even better, she was great company while Cassie was missing in action. He couldn't understand what was keeping Cassie away for such a long period of time. He knew she was upset with him from the time they'd left the hospital, but he had no idea she would hold her grudge for so long.

From the time Eon's career was launched, Cassie had been a consistent and steady staple in Eon's life. She had not left his side for the past five years, and now it seemed as if she was never going to return. He felt the effects of Cassie's absence in both his personal and professional lives. He'd grown so comfortable with Cassie being in his life, he left all the behind-the-scenes aspects to her and her alone. Eon's main focus was to work himself back into shape.

He showed great signs of improvement, yet there were moments when his mind would wander off to Cassie. Eon was left clueless about his career. He didn't have any of the numbers or contacts that

Cassie used. It didn't take long for Ms. Francine to track Eon and his mood shifts. She took the time to talk to Eon whenever he fell into the trance of feeling alone. Francine reminded him of his Nana and his Big Mama. She was wise in her years and wasn't afraid to speak honestly and with love.

"What go on? You look like ya soul trouble you. You want to give thanks for your life, Mr. Montgomery." It didn't take long before Ms. Francine became a permanent fixture in Eon's home.

On certain occasions, she would even stay overnight. They both held one another in high regard; Ms. Francine kept Eon on a scheduled regimen and never allowed his moments of despair to keep a hold of him for too long. Being a cancer survivor herself, Ms. Francine connected to Eon's feelings in a way that not many people had ever done before. Sometimes the two of them would talk until the wee hours of the night. As weeks turned into months, Ms. Francine helped keep Eon focused on returning to his regular healthy state and away from the negative thoughts of Cassie and her abandonment. Cassie had been gone for some time and didn't show her face until one afternoon.

Francine rushed to the door as she heard keys opening the locks. She knew that Mr. Montgomery and she herself were the only people who had keys to the house. Francine had just arrived at the door when Cassie came in, pulling a roller suitcase. Their eyes met. Cassie held the handle to her luggage out to the hired help. Ms. Francine rolled her eyes, sucked her teeth, and walked away from Cassie.

"You know I hired you!" Cassie said sternly. She stood in the foyer for a second and took a deep breath. Cassie walked to her room and unlocked her door. Eon stuck his head out of his room. He couldn't believe that his old partner was actually home. Eon tiptoed toward Cassie's room. Once he arrived at the entrance, she slammed the door in his face. He softly giggled to himself. He could sense that she was upset; yet he didn't know to what extent. He knocked on the door. Cassie opened it just enough for a small slit of light to come through.

"Yes!" she commanded from the other side of the door.

"Cass, listen. I think we really need to talk." Eon touched the door. He spoke like he was unsure of whether he believed his own words. Cassie peeked out from behind the door.

"You acting like I'm a Jehovah's Witness or something," Eon joked with hurt in his voice.

"What do you want, E? I don't have the time!" Her cold tone was one with which Eon was familiar. The biggest difference was that Cassie resorted to this tone when she was talking to people in the business that she knew could not be trusted, and now Eon felt like a total outsider. He looked at Cassie with love and admiration. He could not understand why she was being so callous and mean.

"Cassie, can we talk without this in between us?" Eon asked as he knocked at the wooden barrier Cassie held half-closed to him.

"E, I'm not dressed, plus I have things to do. So what do you want to talk about?" Cassie talked to Eon as if she were a strict mother talking to her disobedient child. Ms. Francine stood to the side and watched Eon. He ignored Ms. Francine and concentrated on getting his message through to Cassie.

"I wanted to discuss you coming home for a little while," he said. Ms. Francine shook her head. She could see that Eon had given Cassie total control over him. Cassie laughed at Eon's suggestion.

"E, you know when you were sick, I was the only one there…the only one." Eon nodded his head in agreement and then looked down at the floor. "And I've always been the only one here, and I'm tired, and I need some time to myself," Cassie said.

"I…I understand, Cass. It's just that…"

"It's just that what, E?" Cassie interrupted Eon's

comment.

"It's just that...I miss you a lot, and I want things to go back to the way they were." Eon's heartfelt confession had absolutely no effect on Cassie.

"Well, it's nice to hear that, but Eon Montgomery, things will never be the same!" She looked at him as if she didn't know who he was and slammed the door closed. Francine watched as Eon held back tears.

He gathered himself and walked back to his room. Minutes later, Ms. Francine came to Eon's room. She stood in the doorway with a look of concern. He could feel her presence.

"What? I'm good." Francine looked at Eon. It was clear that Eon was not telling the truth. "Listen, Ms. Francine. When I was sick, she was the only sure thing I had, and without her, I would have died." He spoke as if he was trying to convince himself. Ms. Francine sighed.

"Mr. Montgomery, you must know that he never leaves you...Jah, the Creator was with you every step of the way. You cannot and should not give the girl credit for healing you." Ms. Francine looked Eon directly in his eyes and patted his hand. He turned his mouth up, as he didn't want to hear Ms. Francine at all. "The Creator and your will to live is what kept you here! She did not, Mr. Montgomery!"

"She didn't leave my side, Ms. Francine. She never left my side," he said with certainty. "And she never will. She will be here long after you have left me." As if it had been timed, Eon heard the front door close shut. He knew that it was Cassie leaving again, except this time he was not sure of her return. Ms. Francine walked out of the room, leaving Eon alone to sit with the reality of Cassie's decisions.

The next morning, Ms. Francine's knocking at his door awakened Eon.

"Mr. Montgomery, good morning," Ms. Francine said.

"Okay…okay, I'm up," Eon groggily replied. He sat up from his horizontal position and rubbed away the night's cold from his eyes.

He immediately dropped to the floor and began doing his push-ups. Ms. Francine smiled from inside the kitchen as she heard Eon's hands hit the floor to begin his workout. She slowly prepared breakfast. After finishing 100 push-ups, Eon did an identical number of sit-ups. He completed his daily calisthenics. Ms. Francine knocked on the door and entered. She was carrying two giant cups of liquid. One cup was filled with Kangen water, and the other was a concoction that Eon had taken every day since he had started on his road to recovery.

"Good morning, Ms. Francine." Eon grabbed the

towel from Ms. Francine's arm and wiped away some of the sweat. She handed Eon the first cup. He guzzled it without interruption.

Ms. Francine took a handful of pills out of her personal pouch, located around her waist and gave them to Mr. Montgomery. He tossed the vitamins in his mouth and swallowed them with the contents of the second glass. Ms. Francine walked into the bathroom and prepared Eon's toothbrush. She laid out Eon's washrag and walked back to the room as he handed her the empty glass.

"Thank you, Ms. Francine." She walked out of the bedroom and into the kitchen while Eon began to brush his teeth. Ms. Francine created a regimented schedule that became a daily routine with the two partners.

Eon walked into the kitchen and sat down at the table. Ms. Francine placed a plate of wheat toast, an egg-white cheese omelet, and turkey bacon in front of him. She pushed a bowl of fruit to the side of his plate. He smiled as he inhaled the aroma of goodness. He grabbed the remote control and turned on the dummy tube. He watched as his face flashed across the screen. Eon immediately turned the volume up.

"And rumor has it that E the MC is BROKE!"

Eon spit out his piece of bacon in laughter,

making Ms. Francine jump in surprise.

"What you do?" Ms. Francine yelled at Eon while ignoring the television. He pointed up to the screen. They both paid close attention to the news reporter.

"A very reliable source says that E the MC's financial situation has kept him out of the limelight." Eon shook his head.

"You assholes! I never wanted to be in the limelight!" Eon screamed at the television as if the reporter could hear his voice.

"That same source says that E the MC, whose real name is Eon Montgomery, has been keeping his money woes a secret along with some other personal health issues."

"Fuck you!" Eon said. "Broke? Man, I should break my foot off in your ass!" Ms. Francine looked at Eon in shock. She had never really heard him talk in such a manner.

"A few months ago, Eon Montgomery, aka E the MC, performed a show on a boat and gave the audience much more than they bargained for."

The screen showed Eon throwing up on stage. Eon quickly calmed down as he relived the embarrassing moment in his mind. The reporter moved on to the next story. Eon stood up from the breakfast table. His blood boiled with anger.

"These mother fuckers don't know ME! They don't know who I…" Eon replayed the reporter's words back in his mind. Ms. Francine watched as Eon's face changed.

"Are you okay, Mr. Montgomery?" Ms. Francine's voice snapped Eon out of his trance.

"How the hell did they know me?" Eon questioned.

He remembered the reporter had said his government name. Eon knew that he'd kept his true identity unknown to the public. He stared at Ms. Francine. Suddenly a light bulb went off in Eon's head. He rushed to Cassie's room and began brutally banging at her door.

"Cassie, you bitch! Why would you give them my government? Why would you spread those lies? Why would you…" Before he could finish his tirade, the reality of the moment hit him like a ton of bricks. He began kicking the door. "You bitch!" Eon shouted with each kick.

Ms. Francine stood and watched like a child at a wrestling match. He continued to thrust his foot into the wooden door, and soon the frame began to give way. After the fourth kick, the door swung open. Eon stood at the doorway in disbelief. The room was empty, with only the bedroom set intact. Eon walked inside and ran his eyes around the entire area. He sat on the bed with his mouth ajar and glanced up at the mirror in front of him. Eon saw his reflection and closed his mouth. He noticed an envelope sitting on the base of the mirror with his name on it. Eon walked over, snatched the envelope, and pulled out the hand written letter inside. He read the words aloud:

My Dearest Eon Montgomery,

If you're reading this letter, then it's evident that I'm long gone. I'm sure you're upset, but if I know you the way I think I do (and I do), you'll quickly bounce back just as you always have. Please understand that this has been the hardest, but easiest, choice I've ever had to make in my life. I've battled with myself for years to stay in this room, to live under this roof, knowing I was capable of doing my job without being underneath you. I knew you needed me, so I held you down and made it so you would want for nothing. I seasoned my skin in rapture of the divine meal, and no, it wasn't business, money, or power, but the essence of love. Yes, LOVE...Eon, I loved you with all I had, yet whenever I tried to tell you, you were either high, about to get high, wasting time with them little niggers from down the street, or dick deep in one of your skank-ass bitches. Then when you got sick, I was there every step of the way. Eon, please know that we were both in the process of treatment and being cured. I never left your side, and yet you still treated me like I was an employee and not your friend, like a slave and not your equal, like an associate and not your real true love. My understanding of our relationship was never clearer than when you first came out of the hospital. You screamed on me as if I was totally expendable! Both you and I know...I WAS NEVER EXPENDABLE! It is because of ME that you are E the MC! You did nothing but take from me. I gave my time, my talent, my mind, and my heart, and you never even attempted to get to know me. So, it was only right *to shed my skin of you. You'd become a SNAKE that had punctured my soul and infected my life with your emotional venom! Please know that I am gone for good, never to return. My number has changed, and I have moved out of the country. If you haven't noticed by now, I QUIT THIS SHITTY JOB! I have accepted my package deal in return for my resignation and left the rest for you. Eon, please know that I will always love you, and don't worry; you will get back on your feet soon!*

Love Always and Forever,

Cassie, aka YOUR NIGGER

Eon looked at the letter as if it were going to magically disappear. He glanced up from the paper and saw Ms. Francine standing in the mangled doorway.

"Her loss!" she said with pride. Eon smirked at Ms. Francine's comment. He glanced back at the letter and reread the last two lines. He snatched the house phone in Cassie's room and began punching numbers. Just as someone answered, the doorbell rang.

"I will get it," Ms. Francine said as she went to answer the door. Eon's face changed from mad to worried. "Mr. Montgomery, there's…" Eon lifted his index finger to Ms. Francine, stopping her words.

"How much?" His voice cracked with uncertainty and concern. "Are you fucking kidding me? You must be fucking kidding me!" Eon screamed at the top of his lungs. "Listen to me. I am going to come down there to that fucking bank and rip your heart out of your fucking chest! Then I'm going to cut your fucking head off, 'cause you're not using it anyway!" Francine watched Eon's frustration level grow with each passing second. "Who the fuck gave her the authorization to do some shit like this?" He quickly changed to a look of seriousness as the person's answer cut through him. "*I did?*" Eon knew the answer was true but did not want to face it at all. He took a giant breath and spoke into the phone. "Okay, I'm coming down there right now, so please don't allow anyone access to my shit, please. Okay?" Eon spoke as if he were talking to a second-grader.

Eon hung up the phone and sat with a blank look. Ms. Francine stood speechless. Eon looked as if he wanted to talk, but words were simply not coming out of his mouth.

"Mr. Montgomery..." Eon interrupted Ms. Francine a second time.

"They just told me that they released eight million dollars of my money to this bitch." He sat motionless. "Eight million." He repeated the number softly. Eon stood up and walked past Ms. Francine as if she weren't there. As he passed the living room, Eon caught a glimpse of two figures sitting on the couch. He slowly doubled back to the living room entrance and readjusted his eyes. His head was shaking, but again words were escaping him.

"Wa...wa...what the fuck are you doing here?" Eon asked the woman. "And why the fuck are you with *him*?" he asked as he pointed at the young man sitting next to her. "Who the fuck let you in here?" Eon asked.

"Well, I was trying to tell you, Mr. Montgomery, that I let them in," Ms. Francine said from behind Eon. "I seen the young man, and I remember his face. The boy says he really needs to talk with you, and I could see it in his eyes. He says this is his mother, so I let them in," Ms. Francine said sternly. She knew Eon was upset, but she was not about to allow him to speak to her in any type of way.

"What the fuck do you want? You thieving bitch!"

Eon said with callousness.

"Yo, my nigger, you can't be talking to my Moms like that!" Will stood up from his seat.

"Well, if your Moms wasn't a thieving bitch, that camped out at photo shoots and snuck around after-shows and shit, I wouldn't have to talk to her like that!" The woman grabbed Will as she stood up from her seat.

"It's okay, William. It's quite all right. I wouldn't expect absolutely anything less from this…deadbeat!"

"Deadbeat?" Both Eon and Will spoke in unison as they tried to make sense of the lady's comment.

"Yes, deadbeat! Listen, William, I never told you about your father because I didn't want to hurt you." The lady then turned to Eon. "And I didn't tell you about William because I knew you wouldn't have wanted him, plus I didn't want you to feel like I was trying to trap you. We were both very young." Eon and Will squinted in confusion. The lady looked and saw how much they actually resembled one another. "Eon, Will is your son."

"How?" Eon asked. "I mean…we didn't meet until…"

Eon stopped speaking as he looked into the lady's face. He started to remember how familiar she looked at the photo shoot. The lady bounced her head as she could read Eon's eyes. He had met her many years ago, just after he had moved to New York. They shared a weekend of love together and then went their separate ways.

"Why didn't you say something at the photo shoot?" Eon asked.

"Yeah, right. I'm going to tell you I'm your long lost girlfriend from high school, and, oh yeah, we have a son! C'mon, you would have had security throw me out on my butt. And then when you brought me home with you, I thought you might've remembered me...especially when you cooked breakfast and all that...but then you threw me out on my butt anyway," she said. Although it sounded like a joke, the lady was extremely serious. "I tried to take the picture 'cause I wanted William to know who his family was. We would talk for hours about your life in the South and how much you loved your Big Mama and your Nana ...remember?" she asked.

"Yeah," Eon said softly.

"So I came to the concert because I was going to tell you then, but you had that bitch Cassie throw me out! Oh, Lord, please forgive my mouth, for its only speaking my heart!" The lady placed her hand over her heart. Eon stared at the woman in disbelief. "Listen, Eon, I am a woman of God now. Yes, I was young and running in those streets, but I know now that the only answer is my Lord and savior, Jesus Christ!"

"Oh, so you're one of *those*," Eon stated.

"Yes, I'm one of those…God's soldiers…and if you had any sense, you would've told your manager to make sure she got some God in her life, too!" The realization of Cassie's underhanded actions quickly returned to Eon's mind. He cringed on the inside as he continued to listen to the lady. "So William is walking around the house researching his history, black history and other worldly things, like he's Alex Haley or something. So I ask him what's going on, and he tells me that he's been chilling with E the MC, his favorite rapper. I thought that God was trying to tell me something." Eon interrupted the young lady before she could continue.

"So you're Shug Avery or something?" he asked sarcastically. The lady rolled her eyes.

"Anyway, once I found out it was you, I immediately told William I needed to meet you. William has been a lot happier since you've come into his life." She looked Eon directly in his eyes as she spoke.

"Well, you must mean since I've unknowingly come *back* into his life, right?" Eon asked.

"Well…I guess you'd be correct in saying that. I didn't want to believe that you were the same person I knew so long ago." Eon snarled at the woman. "What? You were an extremely intelligent man when I first met you, but I know that the business can dummy anyone down. I mean…it dummied you down!" Eon watched the woman carefully. The honesty of her words was a bit rattling to his soul.

"I'm still intelligent. Shit, I made your boy want more out of life than just being in the fucking streets!" Eon's voice rose as his disgust with the woman and the all-around state of his life showed in his face.

"Well, my boy is your boy!" she quickly shot back at Eon. Eon shook his head. He could not believe what was going on with his life.

"This shit is un-be-fucking-liev-able!" Eon said aloud. He'd had enough of the crazy roller-coaster ride of a day and wanted to get off immediately.

He closed his eyes and placed his hands over his face. He removed his hands and looked at the three people staring back at him. The three sets of eyes didn't budge. They wondered what the rapper/patient/father was going to do next.

"Okay, wait…first and foremost…nah…Will, you know me!" Will nodded his head in agreement. "I honestly cannot believe that you are my child. I was your age when we met. Me, and your mother only spent a weekend together! I mean...what the fuck is your name again?" Eon asked the lady.

"My name is *Mary*!" She spoke with an attitude.

"Mary, huh? How fitting. You must be the fucking Virgin Mary 'cause this dude here is the Immaculate Conception." Eon's words shot out like daggers. He thought of no one's feelings but his own. Mary looked at him with rage in her eyes. "So what you're telling me is that the one time we did fuck. I helped to make this mother fucker here!" Eon pointed at Will as if he were a pet.

"Exactly! That's exactly what I am telling you!" Mary's voice matched Eon's aggressive tone as she pointed directly at Eon.

"Get the fuck out of here!" Eon rolled his eyes in disgust. "That boy ain't my..."

"The boy belongs to you!" Ms. Francine's voice exploded from the other side of the room.

Eon whipped his head to the left and watched Ms. Francine as if she had stolen something from his home. He knew he couldn't win the stare-down contest; so he slowly turned his head, and his attention, back to Will and Mary.

"Listen, I'm sorry, but I really can not take this shit

right now. I just received some bullshit, and this shit right here just takes that shit to another level."

Both Mary and Will looked at one another and then at Eon. The heaviness of the moment began to grab a hold of Eon. He held his head, as it felt like it could explode at any minute.

"Okay, you both can leave now, and when I get back, we can discuss this further," Eon said in a serious tone. Mary sucked her teeth and rolled her eyes.

"Yeah, right, go ahead and leave. That's what you're really good at...leaving!" Mary said sarcastically.

"Look, Mary! On some serious shit, you can not blame me for leaving a situation that I knew nothing about." Eon stood directly in front of Will and Mary. His stance was that of a principal who was disciplining two bad students. "Now, had I known of William, I can not say that I would have stuck around anyway...but you never gave me any idea of his existence, so please don't be so shallow and selfish."

Eon slowly walked toward, his room as he continued to speak.

"Ms. Francine, please take a contact number from Mary and Will...excuse me...William, the same name as his alleged grandfather!" Will smiled to himself as he heard Eon's voice in a whole new light. He was hurt by both Eon and his mother Mary's words and actions, but somehow he felt different. A small piece of him felt like he could rule the world.

Just before they left, Will snapped his fingers as if he had just thought of a plan to end world hunger. He walked to Eon's room and stuck his head through the crack in the half-opened door.

"Oh, yeah, Jay-Z and them is one of the first oil babies. And P-Diddy's dude have their hand in the running of the world!" Will shouted. Eon turned and looked at Will, whose head looked as if it were wedged in the door.

"Who?" he asked, already knowing the answer to his question.

"The Rockefellers and the Masons…they run a lot of everything, and they built their shit on the backs of slaves of all colors!" Will said with pride as he remembered his last assignment. With all that he'd gone through in such a short amount of time, Eon could only muster a small smirk as he answered the anxious child.

"They sure as hell did, Will! And still do!" Eon continued to get dressed as he heard Ms. Francine escort Will and Mary out the front door.

CHAPTER 10

The gypsy cab turned down the street where Eon lived. He saw a group of reporters standing in front of his place.

"Keep driving!" Eon ordered the cab driver.

"Papa, I no drive too far without extra pesos," the Spanish man said.

"Listen, just drive around the corner to the bodega." Eon sunk down in his seat as they passed his residence. The driver drove to the store around the corner and stopped.

Eon walked out of the cab and stepped cautiously into the small mini-mart. There was a man behind the counter. He caught a glimpse of Eon and smiled.

"*¿Mi hermano como esta?*" the man asked Eon.

"*Bien mi hermano...bien,*" Eon replied. The two extended their hands to one another. The clerk motioned for Eon to come to the back. He followed the man's silent command. They both arrived at the rear of the store together.

Eon slowly walked into a giant freezer. He looked back at the man, who, again, spoke only with head movement. Eon opened the door and stepped into the cold storage unit.

Once inside, Eon walked to the back of the compartment.

"Adios!" The man bid Eon farewell as he closed the big door behind him.

Eon ran his hand against the cold wall until he felt a switch. Eon smiled to himself as he flipped the switch up. He then pushed the wall as hard as he could. The giant piece of steel began to move backwards slowly. Eon slid himself through the small crack left in between the wall and a totally different area. He stepped into the other side and pushed the wall back to its original place. Eon was standing inside of his recording studio booth.

He stepped out of the booth and made his way upstairs to the main level, where he tiptoed into the kitchen. Ms. Francine stood with her back to Eon as she washed the dishes.

"Hey!" Eon made Ms. Francine jump.

"What you do, boy?" Ms. Francine hit Eon with her wet hand.

"Shit is crazy, Ms. Francine. You see the circus show starting outside?"

"Yes, I noticed them. They showed up about an hour after you left," Ms. Francine said about the reporters who were camped outside of Eon's front steps.

"You know, that bitch really took this shit too far!" Ms. Francine could see Eon's frustration pulling at him. "The assholes at the bank say I have four hundred thousand dollars left," Eon said softly.

"Hmmm…that's better than forty thousand, huh?" Francine said jokingly. Eon smiled at Ms. Francine as her words made him feel a very small amount of happiness.

"Where did you come from?" she asked.

"Wouldn't you like to know?" Eon joked. He knew that she wanted an answer to her question.

"Well, Big Mama had a place in the basement where the wall was really weak. When she passed away and left the place to me, I had some people check the other side of the wall." Ms. Francine watched Eon in anticipation of what he was going to say next. "We found that it was connected to a small warehouse on the other side of the building. That warehouse was turned into a bodega, and we cut out a piece of the wall on both sides and controlled it with a release switch. It opens from a freezer in the store and the back wall of the studio." Francine looked on in amazement. "So whenever I want to be incognito, I take the Batcave!" Eon joked. "When I rolled past the house, I saw all these cock suckers outside my door, and I went around the corner to…"

"The Batcave!" Ms. Francine finished Eon's statement. The two grinned at each other.

"Damn, I must really trust you, 'cause I've never told anyone about that passageway, not even Ca...." Eon stopped short of saying Cassie's name.

"So wait, this out here is because of you? For what?" Francine inquired, as she glanced at the reporters outside.

"Cause the fucking vultures got false information from that bitch Cassie, and they think I'm broke, but..."

"You are?" Ms. Francine interrupted Eon's explanation for the second time. Eon stared at Ms. Francine with an angry frown. He took a deep breath and regained his composure. "Listen, you're broke and my broke are two different 'brokes' altogether!" Ms. Francine said. Eon allowed a small welcoming smile.

"So they tell me that I own this place here and the house down in Mississippi," Eon said. "I owe a heap of taxes on the house down south. That plus what I owe for this place will take a nice piece of what I have left." Eon could only shake his head in disbelief.

"Mr. Montgomery, you must keep yourself in the light. You must keep a positive attitude and know that the Creator brings you to it to bring you through it!" Ms. Francine would always talk in different tones depending on the severity of the situation. She allowed her accent to come and go as she saw fit. Eon completely loved the way Ms. Francine spoke her mind. He knew that she was one of the only people who talked from her soul and didn't allow the craziness of the world to interfere with her thoughts.

"So now what?" Ms. Francine pointed toward the small mob sprinkled around Eon's front steps.

"Well, I don't think they are going anywhere anytime soon." Eon was angered by their presence.

"But maybe I need to," he said unconsciously. Ms. Francine looked at Eon. She was trying to make sense of what Eon just said.

"You need to what? Are you going back to the Batcave?" she skeptically inquired.

"No, I may need to get out of New York soon," Eon said with a certain tone of comfort. It seemed like his mind was already made up as to his traveling plans. She could see that Eon was extremely serious about his decision.

"And what about Will?" Ms. Francine asked. Eon peeked out the side of the window at the roaming reporters.

"Well, I don't know what him and his mother are planning on doing, but I may just give them this!"

Ms. Francine stopped in her tracks as the complexity of his declaration settled into her mind.

"Are you serious?" She felt like Eon had returned with a totally new attitude. "So where this new boy come from, hey?" She wanted to know how Mr. Montgomery had shifted from the tremendously, terrible, angry guy to this mild-mannered man willing to leave his home to his "son" and his mother.

"Well, I left here and sat down with the bank people. They told me that I had given Cassie the green light to take as much as she wanted…and she did." Eon cringed with hurt. Ms. Francine nodded her head, showing that she understood him thus far.

"So all the time that I was sick, she was taking my entire savings, piece by piece…fucking bitch!" Eon screamed. Ms. Francine gave Eon a look of concern. "I'm okay!" he said as he took in a deep breath. "Anyway, after they explained to me how much I had left, I caught myself before I went straight postal on the suit and ties. I stopped and kept my composure. I heard your voice telling me to *simmer down*." Ms. Francine smiled at Eon's honesty.

"That's really good, Mr. Montgomery, I'm really

proud of you! So where's your driver at?" she asked as she looked around.

"I told him that I wasn't in need of his services anymore, and he left…which was good 'cause when I pulled up in the gypsy cab, they didn't even notice me. Then I sat down with my attorneys, and we spoke about what I can do with the rest of my money." Eon smirked as he finished his statement.

"Wow, I thought I was going to hear about you on the news when you left here, Mr. Montgomery," Ms. Francine said.

"No, ma'am I had to think about it and realize that the only person who's to blame is myself. I can not be mad at anyone else but me!" Eon said.

"Well, I can say that your Big Mama and Nana would be proud of you right now." Ms. Francine tried to make Eon feel good about a bad situation.

"Well, I think they would first smack the shit out of me for putting so much trust in Cassie's scandalous ass. But with everything that I've gone through in the last year, they would want me to leave the game altogether…which is funny because before all of this, I was telling Cassie that I wanted to retire and leave the game," Eon said as he shook his head at the realization of his current situation.

"Oh, so you're also a basketball player?" Ms.

Francine asked. Eon laughed at her innocent ignorance.

In an instant, Eon realized that Ms. Francine was unaware of his star status. She had given him her love and affection unconditionally. He appreciated her even more in that moment. He was so accustomed to people dealing with him because he was E the MC that he truly couldn't grasp Ms. Francine's genuine concern and kindness. She had never been anyone other than herself since the day she walked into his home. Eon looked at Ms. Francine with admiration and respect.

"So, after we finished discussing things, I came back home in a gypsy cab, which was good 'cause when I pulled up to the house, they didn't even notice me." Ms. Francine could see and feel that Mr. Montgomery was learning a tough life lesson. She knew that the lesson was extremely harsh and severe, but she felt good knowing that Eon could see things more clearly than he did before. "My lawyers tell me that I need to make sure that Will is my son before I allow him or his mother to step another foot inside of here!" He spoke as if he were a lawyer himself. "So if they come back here, then you need to tell them to return at some other time," Eon said.

"Well, how will you be able to tell them that this is all theirs?" Ms. Francine moved her hand outward as if she were displaying the kitchen to Eon. "Do you want me to call them?" Ms. Francine picked up the phone. It was as if she knew that Eon wanted to contact Will and Mary.

"What you gonna do?" Eon said in a Jamaican dialect. Ms. Francine smiled as she held the phone toward Eon.

Deep inside, he wanted to speak with Will and inform him of his past, his life, and the decisions he had made before and after they'd met. Eon felt connected with Will way before he learned how connected they actually were.

"What makes you think that I want to talk to him?" Eon asked.

"Well, one reason is 'cause you loved that boy way before his mother dropped this bomb on you. Plus, no matter what your lawyers say, you are not going to turn your back on that young boy." Eon stuck out his bottom lip out and nodded his head yes.

"Another reason is that you are truly ready to leave all this craziness behind you and just live your life. That's just what I think! But what do I know? I'm just an old lady." Ms. Francine's truthful words made Eon think more intensely about the things that were already heavily on his mind. He looked at Ms. Francine with a strong stare. She could see the wheels turning in his mind. Francine held the phone out to Eon.

"Ms. Francine, listen to me!" Francine pulled the phone in away from Eon and pinned it to her chest. She turned her entire body so she was facing Eon, watching him carefully. Francine waited like an anxious priest in a confessional booth. She felt Eon was ready to tell her his deepest feelings about his life's weird and sudden change in direction. He came close to Ms. Francine before he spoke.

"Ms. Francine..."

"Yes, Mr. Montgomery," Francine said softly.

"I really, really, really want to smoke some weed right now, and honestly, I'm going to."

Ms. Francine backed away from Eon with a look of disappointment. She wanted Eon to release his inner pain and hurt, figuring it would help him move on with his life. Instead, Eon chose to slow down his "processing system" with drugs.

"You can give Will and his mother a call. Please tell them to come by in another three or four hours. I will be downstairs in the studio." Eon walked to his room.

"But what about...?" Ms. Francine removed the phone embedded in her chest and pointed it at the reporters who were still waiting outside.

"Hopefully they will be gone by the time they get here. The vultures don't like the dark," he said as he walked out from his room with a giant bag of marijuana. Ms. Francine's eyes grew big when she saw the large Ziploc bag.

"Uh...okay!" She could not believe the amount of ganja Eon was carrying. He walked down to the studio as Francine started dialing the number from the piece of paper on the kitchen counter.

Eon puffed away as he listened to the calming sounds of Bob Marley and the Wailers. Every few verses, Eon would sing along with the great, reggae legend. "Don't worry...about a thing...'cause every little thing...is gonna be alright." Eon sang with love as he took every word to heart. He looked around the studio, letting his mind wander. He turned around in his chair and reminisced on the time he had with Violet. Each place he looked, Eon remembered a moment of their lovemaking. The time played back in his mind like a wonderful movie where he knew every single part. Within a few seconds of his beautiful dream, Eon saw the dread's face in between his legs.

"No!" he shouted. He shook his head in disapproval as he shut the music off. Eon stood up and turned to see Ms. Francine swaying to the rhythm.

"Don't worry..." Ms. Francine continued to sing with her eyes closed. Eon watched her as if he was at a show and she was performing. Her voice was heavenly. She sang every word in the exact same tone of the great reggae star. As Ms. Francine finished her singing, she opened her eyes and saw Eon standing with a lighter in the air. The stream of fire rolled back and forth as Eon's hand swayed. "*Yeah!*" Eon made the noise of a grateful crowd who wanted more from their star singer. Ms. Francine smiled as she blushed with embarrassment.

"Damn, Ms. Francine, you got me thinking you were one of the *I Threes*. I didn't know you could blow like that."

"Well, Mr. Montgomery, there are a few things you don't know about me," she said with a grin.

"Damn, I may have to put you in that booth!" Eon pointed back at the empty recording booth. She didn't believe Eon's statement.

"Anyway, Mr. Montgomery, I spoke with Will and his mother, and they are going to be here later tonight around ten." Eon plopped back down in his seat and relit his ganja stick. He inhaled deeply and closed his eyes, allowing the power of the marijuana to seep into his brain.

"Okay, cool. Come get me at nine-forty-five." Eon blew the smoke out into the air as Ms. Francine turned to walk back upstairs. "Wait!" Eon said. Ms. Francine turned around and faced Eon. He pushed a button on the giant soundboard. "This is what I'm known for."

As his song blasted out from the small speakers, Eon watched Ms. Francine. She slowly moved her head to the beat. Eon looked on like a child waiting for his mother's approval.

"Wow...it's a lot of *niggers* in that sound, huh?" She turned and walked upstairs. He sat in the studio and thought about Ms. Francine's comment as he puffed away at his joint.

Eon looked at his watch and saw the time was ten-thirty. He peeked out of one of his front windows and saw that there were only three reporters outside. "Fucking crack head mother fuckers." He watched as Will and Mary walked up to the first step. The reporters began to swarm around them. Eon observed Will. The young boy pushed one of the reporters away from his mother.

"Get the fuck away from her!" Will shoved the reporter back onto the sidewalk. As he tried to step forward, he tripped on the uneven piece of concrete in front of Eon's place. Eon giggled to himself. The two other story-hungry correspondents took a step back from the mother-and-son team. They fearfully allowed the two to walk all the way to the top step without any harassment. Ms. Francine opened the front door. After Mary walked through the door, Will turned to the people at the bottom of the steps.

"Leave it the fuck alone! Why don't you report on world hunger and corruption with the same intensity, you cock suckers!"

Will walked through the first set of doors and closed them, leaving behind the three media people. Eon watched the three people gather their belongings and leave the front of Eon's house. He appreciated Will's determination to not allow anyone to disrespect him or anyone he loved. He knew he had the same trait within himself.

Will trotted into the house, Eon shook his head and laughed.

"What?" Will asked.

"You couldn't have told them 'no comment' or something like that?" Eon said.

"Man, them mother fuckers act like they trying to snatch your soul out from you." Eon furrowed his eyebrows together.

"You are one hundred percent correct, William, one hundred percent!"

"Watch your mouth, William!" Mary looked at Eon as she spoke to Will.

"What?" Eon held his palms up toward the ceiling.

"If you don't say anything, then he's going to think

it's okay to talk like that," Mary said to Eon as if he were a child of hers.

"Well, they are some mother fuckers," Eon said innocently. Mary hit him on his arm. They all went into the living room and sat down. Eon took in a deep breath and began to explain his plan to everyone.

"Okay, a little over a year ago, I found out that I had a cancerous tumor on my brain." Mary held her hand over her mouth in shock. "That tumor was removed, and now I am cancer free!" Eon said with a smile.

"To God be the glory! Hallelujah!" she exclaimed as she felt the spirit moving within her soul

"Uh, God bless you!" Eon joked. Mary looked at Eon through squinted eyes.

"So after they removed the tumor, I began my journey to recovery. As I was returning back into shape, I received word that my manager of six years had taken a large sum of money from me. This pushed me very close to being broke." Mary and Will looked at Eon. "After getting that bit of information, I then find out that I am allegedly the father of a child who I conceived 16 years ago. Who, I might add, has been chilling with me for the past few months! So now I'm wondering, what next?" Eon asked rhetorically. "I'll tell you what's next. Clearly I am in need of a change of pace, so I am going to leave New York and move back to Mississippi to the house I was born in." Will looked at Eon with sadness. "Before I leave, I want us to go take a paternity test to make sure, without any question or doubt, that William is my son," Eon said in his calmest voice.

"Which he is!" Mary said under her breath.

"*If* I am William's father, then I will let you guys live in this house rent free." Mary's eyes popped open wide.

"You don't have to do that," she said.

"I know I don't, but I am going to," Eon replied.

"No, we can't," Mary said.

"Yes, you can, and you will. Last I checked you guys live in the projects, correct?" Eon asked, already knowing the answer.

"Yes, we do!" Will said as his mother nodded her head yes.

"If Will is my son, then I should have the right to give him shelter…and that is what I'm going to do!" Eon spoke with a strong tone, letting everyone know that he was extremely serious. "We can not live with this black guilt." Mary and Will looked at him strangely. "We are so used to not getting things that when we have something handed to us, we reject it, thinking that we aren't worthy." Mary dropped her head. She knew that Eon was speaking the truth. She thought of the numerous times when she was given blessings and turned them away for no reason at all. Will looked at his mother. He could see that Eon's words had struck a chord within her.

"That Willie Lynch dude really set us behind our own eight ball!" Will said with confidence.

"He sure as hell did, William. So, again, if the test proves that Will is a Montgomery, then I will leave you two here while I take some time to myself." He could see that Will was worried.

"My nigger...I mean, my dude, I really don't want you to go," Will said sincerely. He looked up at Eon with puppy-dog eyes. Eon could feel his insides twinge as he stared into Will's eyes.

"William, you have seen me at my best of times and at my worst. You know I need to get outta here, man," Eon said in a low tone. Although Will agreed, he couldn't say anything because he wanted to spend more time with E. Eon could see what Will was thinking. "I will be back, Will, and maybe once your mother gets comfy here, you can come down south and stay for awhile," Eon said as he looked at Mary.

"Sure he can. I think that would be great!" Mary

grabbed William's hand and squeezed it tight. Ms. Francine stood to the side and watched everything with a giant smile on her face.

CHAPTER 11

A week after the test was taken, Eon sat in his office with a manila envelope in his hand. Will and Mary sat on the other side of his desk.

"This is some Maury shit for real!" he said in a halfway-joking tone.

"Not really, 'cause there isn't any other possibility!" Mary said as she sat back in her seat. Will, on the other hand, sat on the very edge of his chair.

"We ready?" Eon asked.

"Hell yeah!" Will shot back before he could finish his question. Eon ripped off the top of the envelope and took out its contents. His eyes scanned across the page, reading every word.

"Ninety-nine point nine percent positive that specimen A and B are father and son," Eon said as Will's eyes lit up. "Damn, we specimens? Sounds like we're lab rats or something," Eon joked.

He looked across the table at Mary and Will. He was a father and had a lot of time to make up for. Mary fought to hold back tears while Eon stared at her.

"I told you so!" she said as a drop fell from her eye. Eon could only nod his head in agreement.

"Okay, so in another week, I'm going to be leaving..." Eon stopped as his emotions began to grab at him.

"Let me first say sorry for all you had to go through," Mary said as Eon stretched his hand out to Mary. She grabbed his hand and held it tight. Will placed his hand on top of the two, and they all held on to one another.

"Ms. Francine!" Eon called out to his friend/assistant/helper. She popped her head into the office.

"Yes, Mr. Montgomery."

"Okay, so the test has come back, and I am William's father."

"I told you so!" Ms. Francine said with a smile.

"Okay, I don't need to hear it from you, too!" Eon said as he shook his head. "Anyway, so since I'm halfway packed already, I guess we can start letting William and Mary start bringing their stuff. Y'all can sort it out little by little since they will be living with you...just like we spoke about." Mary turned around and looked at Ms. Francine with concern.

In a short amount of time Ms. Francine had proven that she was more than just a home attendant, she had become a friend to Eon and he appreciated her beyond words. Mary didn't have the same feelings for Eon's new confidant.

"No offense to you, Ms. Francine, but I don't need any help. I've been doing this on my own for the past sixteen years," she said, looking at her son with pride.

"Well, I totally understand that, but this is not for you as much as it is for me!" Eon said in his clearest voice. He wanted to make sure Mary truly understood his reasoning. "Mary, I lost eight million dollars because I chose to put my total trust in someone else. That's never going to happen to me again." Mary sat speechless as the large sum of money continued to rattle through her head. Will sat with his mouth totally ajar in shock and disbelief.

"My...my...my dude, are you kidding me?" Will asked slowly.

"Nope!" Eon said.

"That's some real bullshit!" Will screamed as he began to feel his father's frustration. Mary tapped Will's hand in hopes that he would stop cursing. "She was on some shit even back when I first met her," Will said as his mother smacked his hand again. "What? She was!" he said, unconscious of his swearing.

"Stop cursing, William!" Mary commanded.

"What, Ma? I didn't call her a bitch or nothing, and

she was a total bitch!" Will said as he tried to make his point valid.

"William, stop the cursing now!" Eon said from behind his desk. Will stared at Eon with a look of doubt.

"Oh, so *now* Daddy is in full effect, huh?" His words were drenched in sarcasm.

"Listen, William. We were close before we found this shit...I mean stuff...out, so please don't act like I was on some bullshit...I mean, some stuff...before all this!" Will had to respect the truth.

"You're right, Pops. You are absolutely right! She was still a bitch, though!" Will said in a sneaky tone. Mary sucked her teeth and turned to William, who held his hands up to his side. "What did I say?" he asked with a mischievous look. Eon and Will smiled at one another as Mary shook her head.

In the next week, Eon had Cassie's room emptied out and her twisted doorway repaired. He also had his room cleared out. Eon had professional cleaners come by the house to strip, wax, and buff the floors. Lastly, he had the entire house painted, both inside and out. Eon sat down with Mary and Ms. Francine and allowed the ladies their choice of whatever colors they desired. Eon had his Nana's couch taken from the living room and shipped to the house in Mississippi. He also bought new furniture for his new tenants. "Out with the old and in with the new!" Eon could be overheard saying every time an old piece of furniture was removed or a new piece came in. The only thing that was kept in the old living room was the cracked picture that Mary had tried to borrow unannounced. Both Mary and Eon agreed that it was an excellent reminder, to both of them, of how far they had come.

  During the week, William and Eon spent a lot of time downstairs in the studio. Eon would teach him which knobs did what, and in exchange; Will would disclose his knowledge of music that Eon had no idea about. William was also a lover of pure music. He introduced Eon to today's groups who based their sound on the essence of the instrument. Eon would sit like an anxious child whenever William would pop in another group's cd. They would listen and analyze the entire song, identifying each distinct sound and rhythm. What they enjoyed even more was the fact that they were able to take each track and listen to it individually. The giant soundboard allowed them to dissect one piece of the song at a time. They'd make notes to one another about where each break came and what key the band played in. After a week's time, Eon's home looked like an entirely different place, and his one-week plan was pushed to two weeks because of all the time he was spending with William.

  A few days before Eon was scheduled to

leave, the two-new/old friends sat in the studio. There was a knock at the door downstairs. Eon walked to the door and checked the peephole.

"Hey Youngblood!" Eon said as he unlocked and opened the door to an all-too-familiar face. Justin smiled as he stepped into the studio. Eon embraced him.

"C'mon in, brother." His welcoming tone made Justin look twice. He could feel that Eon was in an entirely different space from the last time he'd seen him.

"So what's up, Big Poppa?" Justin joked as he smacked Will five.

"Everything is great." Justin plopped himself down in Eon's big chair.

"C'mon now, player, you know the king has to stay on his throne," Eon said as he tapped the back of his chair.

"I can dig it, Daddy-o," Justin replied as he jumped out of the chair.

"Okay, I guess you've heard about me and William's news, huh?" Eon said.

"Hell yeah!" Justin blurted out.

"Man, that shit is just crazy." Eon laughed at

Justin's enthusiastic reaction to the revelation of the unknown family tie. "I mean, for us to be chilling together for all that time, and we didn't know you were his pops...shit is really crazy!" Justin said, trying to keep his composure.

"Tell me about it, kid. Imagine how I felt. Learning that this block head was my seed was the best worst thing to ever happen to me," Eon said as he scratched his knuckles across Will's head.

"Yeah, and now you're leaving me...again!" Will said. He still wasn't comfortable with his father moving, especially since their bond was growing stronger by the day.

"We will be fine, William. We will be just fine," Eon said, hoping William found comfort in his words.

"William? Is that what you go by now?" Justin asked in a playful manner. "Hey, if you see my man Will, please let him know that Justin said 'what's up?' and to come back to the block. We miss him," he joked.

"Man, I'm not going anywhere!" Will said with pride. Eon looked at the two friends as they bantered back and forth.

"Let me show you two cats something special," Eon interrupted. Will and Justin looked at one another and then at Eon. "I need your word that you will not show or speak about this to anyone…ever!" he said with a very serious look in his eyes. Justin and Will nodded their heads in silent approval. They could see that this was not a laughing matter.

"Let's go in the booth," he directed. The three friends filed into the small space, and Eon stared at the two young men. "No one…ever!" Eon stated with emphasis.

"We got it my nigger! I mean, Pops," Will said as he cracked a smile. Eon turned to Justin.

"Man, my word is bond. This thing here is top secret. Like the Holy Grail…the Kennedy Files…B.I.G. and Pac's real killers."

"Okay, okay, okay, I got you!" Eon said, interrupting Justin's list of monumental secrets.

A miniature smile ran across Eon's face as he flipped the switch and the wall began to move.

"A yo…what the fuck?" Justin said in shock.

"Yo, this is some James Bond shit right here," Will said as he stepped away from the shifting brick panel. Eon pushed on the wall and forced a small slit between the two spaces. The two young teenagers glanced into the freezer.

"Get the fuck out of here!" Will said as he stepped

through the small crack and into the chilled room. Justin followed his friend inside. The two boys stood in awe of their new location. The cold didn't seem to affect them in the least bit as they both looked around with smiles on their faces. Suddenly the wall began to shut. Will and Justin tried to pull at the wall before it closed. As the wall moved back to its original place, the boys ran their hands across the flat surface in an attempt to find the switch that would bring the space back.

"Yo, E...what's up, bro?" Justin's voice shivered with a twinge of fear.

"C'mon now, stop this shit. Let us out! Let us in!" Will said. Both Will and Justin placed their hands on the flat, smooth surface. They slowly ran their hands across the entire door as if they were reading braille. Within minutes that felt like hours, William felt the small switch.

"Ahhhh!" Will exuded as he flipped it in the opposite direction. As the wall began to move, Will and Justin smacked one another five. They both pushed on the door together, making it move a few inches. Both boys stepped through the man-made hole and back into the booth. As they both stepped back inside, they saw Eon back behind the soundboard. He smiled as he gave them both the thumbs-up sign. Will and Justin moved the wall back to its original position and walked to the control room where Eon was sitting.

"Good job, fellas," Eon said with a smile.

"Man, that's some real slick shit you got right there, E," Justin said.

"That's real talk!" William agreed.

"I have both of your word that you won't…"

"Tell anyone!" both the boys said at the same time.

"Okay, cool," Eon said.

"Well, guys, I wanted to show you that part of the studio because I was thinking that while I'm gone, maybe you two can run it together." Will and Justin looked as if they didn't understand what Eon was talking about. "You cats know enough rappers you could rent the studio out to, correct?" Eon asked, already knowing the answer.

"Hell, yeah," Will said with assurance.

"So you figure you charge them anywhere from fifty to one hundred dollars an hour, and you guys make a nice little profit." Eon smiled at his business proposition. The two friends looked at each other and then at Eon. "For the first few months, you both would learn from my engineer. Now, you would have to pay him about fifty dollars per session, but before long you won't need him, and it will just be the two of you cats." Eon examined both of the boys' reactions to see if they were as enthused as he was. "So are you down?" Both boys smiled.

"Hell, yes, we're down." Will spoke for both himself and Justin. Eon glanced at Justin, who was smiling from ear to ear.

"Now, listen. There are a few rules."

"Ah, shit! What rules?" Will asked.

"Well, for one, you guys can not allow a gang of dudes and broads in here. The artist and two other people…no entourage!" Eon spoke with intensity so that both boys understood him clearly. "Once people think they can bring any-and everyone, they usually do just that…bring any-and everyone!"

"True!" Justin agreed on behalf of himself and Will.

"Number two is no puffin' inside the studio! They must take it outside!" Eon said sternly.

"Hold up, but you puffs in this joint on a regular." Will tried to make a point.

"Well, William, this is my joint!" Eon quickly shot back. "The reason I say no puffin' inside is because dudes get too comfy when they can burn inside of a studio, and I don't want nobody thinking this is their home, ya dig?"

"We can dig it," Justin said softly.

"And the third rule is that no one, I repeat, no one

says or does anything outta line to Ms. Francine! I will shut the studio down immediately if any of the rules are not adhered to and respected, especially the last one!" Eon gave Will and Justin a look to make sure they knew he was serious.

"Okay, we got you!" Will said. He could see the earnestness in his father's face.

"So, you dudes are going to get some paperwork to sign that says you run the studio but under the supervision of Ms. Francine and me," Eon said.

"Paperwork? You doing it like that?" Justin questioned. "Damn, you don't trust..."

"Don't give anyone complete trust!" Eon interrupted Justin's comment.

"The past month has shown me that people don't live up to the titles you give them." Will and Justin looked at E the MC strangely. "Mother, Father, Manager...people don't live up to the title. They have their own agenda, and they go forward with that agenda whether you like it or not. It's the same way that your mother didn't inform me, or you, about each other for whatever her personal reason." Will nodded his head as the message began to sink into his mind. "So just because you give her the title of Mother doesn't mean she's not going to do what she wants." The boys looked at E. "I thought Cassie was never going to leave my side. She was the only person I trusted." Will shook his head. "Not only did she leave my side, she tried to leave my side broke! But you can not break me because I am too strong!" Eon spoke as if he was trying to convince himself more than the boys. "So I say to you, again, do not put your trust in people but more so in *yourself*, because no one is going to do for you more than you will do for yourself." The boys sat silently as Eon's breakdown of human nature seeped deep into their souls. They both thought about the different people in their lives who were supposed to be friends or family and had done them wrong.

"Niggers is just wack!" William said. His blanket statement seemed to have more meaning than he even knew.

"Yes they are, my son. Yes they are!" Eon agreed as Justin smiled at the father-and-son tandem. "So we understand the rules and regulations of the studio, yes?" Eon asked his soon-to-be business partners.

"Yes! No entourage! Ms. Francine is in charge! No puffing unless done in the yard!" Will said.

"Let me find out you got your Daddy's genes, and you're an MC on the low," Eon said to his smiling son.

"Well, that wasn't my pure and uncut dope. That was just a simple sample." William crossed his hands in his official b-boy stance.

"I mean I can give you the raw if you want it." Will's voice raised another level.

"You want the booth or right here, right now?" Eon asked his young boy.

"I don't need no booth 'cuz I speaks only the truth, spit fire like I swallowed lava and had no front tooth." William looked at his father, who smiled, and continued. "I am the future, the youth, your whole career is an excuse, I would take you out but I would be arrested for child abuse." Eon looked on as if he wanted to hear more. "I am the best, please don't test…I'm not a Mason, but I know life's game is chess…I got your girl playing chess in her bare chest…you know the rest!" Will finished and smacked five with Justin.

"Wow! My boy is nice!" Justin said. E nodded his head and smacked five with William.

"That was kind of hot!" E said to his son.

"Just a little something," William said as he glowed with pride.

"Do you play the game of chess?" E asked the boy.

"Actually I don't, but when I researched the Masons, I saw that they align their plan with the game of chess. They put the chess board in a lot of their photos and stuff like that." Eon nodded his head. "So I learned more about the game because I saw how major it was, and still is, to them," William said with honesty.

"It's a great game, and you can learn an awful lot from playing." Eon's face showed how serious he felt about what he was saying. "Learn that game! That's your new assignment!" Eon said as he glanced at both the boys. William and Justin looked at Eon and then at one another.

"Yes, sir!" Justin stood up and saluted Eon. "We will learn the game of life...I mean, chess!" he said with a serious face. Justin stood with his chest out like a true soldier.

"You said it right the first time, private. The game of chess is directly in line with the game of life," Eon said, in his commando voice. "Okay, gentlemen, I have to continue packing and make sure I'm not leaving anything you dudes would want." Eon smirked at his humorous comment. The boys stood and embraced Eon. Will and Justin walked out together, leaving Eon standing in the studio alone.

Over the next few days, Eon packed the last of his belongings with Ms. Francine's assistance. She would fold all of his clothes with care and love. Eon saw so much of his elders within Ms. Francine. At times he would catch himself before he'd call her Nana or Big Mama. He wanted more than anything to bring Ms. Francine with him to Mississippi, but he knew he needed her to stay and watch over things in New York. It wasn't that he thought Mary would do something irresponsible to destroy his place; Eon just wasn't in the right frame of mind to really trust anyone. Cassie had left an extremely sour taste in his soul, and he was nowhere near the point of looking past her despicable act of dishonesty.

The day before Eon was to leave, he sat down with Mary, William, Justin, Ms. Francine, and Joel Rothstein, his lawyer. Eon had Joel type up contracts for each individual and the venture they were attached to. He also made sure that Joel went over every word of each line with everyone, answering whatever questions they had. Eon made sure each arrangement was straightforward and fair to everyone involved, including himself. The contract with the boys gave them total control of the studio with a clause that stated that if they ever did anything disrespectful to Ms. Francine, they'd forfeit their power and lose the studio altogether. The agreement with Mary stated that Eon still owned the house, but she and William were given the right to stay for at least a year. After that year, they would revisit the situation and see where they would go from there. If, for any reason, something happened to Eon, the contracts would still hold up for the duration of a year. Once that year had passed, the power of attorney was given to Ms. Francine, who had her own separate legal documents that she was to adhere to. As they finished the last of the signings, Eon looked around at each person.

"Does anyone have any more questions for J.R.?" Eon asked everyone in attendance. While all eyes were set on him, Mary raised her hand.

"I just wanted to take this time and really thank you for everything!" Mary's voice cracked as her emotions began to get the best of her. She pulled a pack of tissues out of her purse. Eon smiled. He walked over to Mary and rubbed her back. William looked up at his father as he consoled his mother.

"You're welcome," Eon said as he watched William watching him. Father and son gave each other a silent nod of approval. "Okay, everybody, I'm going to see you all tomorrow before I leave."

The group began walking to the front door. Before they could get there, the doorbell rang. Ms. Francine turned to Eon. He looked as shocked as she was to hear someone at his front door. "It better not be them fucking vultures!" Eon said strongly. Ms. Francine looked at him with concern.

"Well, if it is, we'll definitely give them something to report on!" Will said as he readied himself. Eon peeked out of the side window to see who it was.

"Oh, no, it's something even worse." His comment came too late as Ms. Francine had already opened the door. "Hey, you piece of shit. Everybody, this is the piece of shit that wants to offer me a piece of shit for my house, soon to be your house. Piece of shit, this is everybody."

"Mr. Montgomery, let me first say good day to you," Theodore said as he tipped his hat.

"Whatever," Eon said in reply.

"Sir, I am sorry about the small, disrespectful offer we confronted you with last time." Theodore Black was hoping he could get Eon interested enough to ask what his new offer was. "The last thing we ever wanted to do was be disrespectful."

"Yeah, okay, whatever you say, Theo. So now what's your offer? *Seven hundred and fifty one thousand dollars?*"

"Uh, no, sir, not at all. This time the offer is two and a half million dollars." Once again, Eon didn't flinch at Theodore's offer. Everyone else stood by and waited to hear his response.

"Listen here, *Theo*. I'm not some bitch that you can wave a little money in front of so I can just take all my shit and move! You got the wrong one!" Eon said.

"But, sir two and a half million is not a…"

"But, sir my ass...two and a half million dollars ain't shit," he interrupted. "And to be honest, you ain't shit, either, Theo! So for the second time, please take your offer back to your people and tell them they can suck my big black dick!" Eon said with pride.

"Oh, my Jesus!" Mary interjected.

"Two times!" William added.

"William!" she scolded as Eon finished his tirade.

"And watch your step on the way out, you bitch-ass English homo," Eon said. Theodore looked at Eon in shock. He seemed as if he was going to say something, but just then Eon, Will, and Justin stepped forward causing Theo to think better about his next decision. He quickly turned around and trotted down the stairs, taking them two at a time. "The Three Stooges, huh?" Mary said to Ms. Francine, who could only shake her head.

"No, more like the Three Wise Men!" Eon said as he opened his arms to the boys and placed them under his wing.

"Oh, boy, let me get out of here before I get sick," Mary said as she walked past the three friends and out the front door. J.R. followed Mary. As he got to the doorway, he turned to Eon.

"You know, Mr. Montgomery, two and a half

million dollars is a great deal of money. I really think you should at least consider…"

"Consider what? The fact that it's time for you to leave?" Eon said as he looked at J.R. with a serious stare. Joel knew he was fighting a battle that he could never win, so he did what he felt was the only logical thing. He turned and left. Eon tightened his grip on both William and Justin. "I will see you cats tomorrow," he said.

"That's a lot of paper you just turned down," Will said with honesty.

"You think so?" Eon asked rhetorically.

"Hell, yeah!" Will exclaimed.

"Well, I don't think so. I don't think it's worth a penny in comparison to this right here. I just found out about my family, and now I'm going to give it all up 'cause Theo came here with a two and a half million- dollar check?" Eon asked.

"Uh…yeah!" Will said. He spoke as if Eon was supposed to know the answer to his own question.

"No, not worth it at all!" Eon said as Ms. Francine looked on with joy and pride. She could see that Eon had grown from the time she first met him.

"You know, you really don't have to leave," Justin said as he looked up at Eon with puppy-dog eyes.

"You know what, Justin? I really do...I really do!" Eon said with a small smile.

The next day, Eon walked through his entire place. He touched the newly painted walls as if it were his first time there. He went inside each room and looked around at the untouched furniture. A small part of Eon wanted to stay. He felt as if he had created a completely different home from the one he grew up in. The last room Eon entered was the living room. He looked around at the new pieces of furniture. He sat down on the couch and closed his eyes. He pictured the old plastic-covered couch as he ran his hands over the new sofa, caressing the suede. As he opened his eyes, Eon stared right at the picture of him and his Nana. He smiled to himself and spoke aloud.

"I miss you too!"

Ms. Francine stood at the entrance of the living room in silence. She wanted to give Eon his time and space to say farewell to the only home he'd known for the past ten-plus years. Eon took a deep breath and stood up to walk out. He noticed Ms. Francine.

"You make sure you take good care of her!" Eon said as he looked around the room. Ms. Francine nodded her head. She knew that Eon was speaking not only to her, but also to the house itself.

"The car is here," Ms. Francine said. She quickly felt herself overflowing with emotions.

Ms. Francine saw Eon as her son and no parent wants to ever say goodbye to his or her child. Eon grabbed a small bag that he had packed with the last of his belongings and walked to the front door. He turned around and faced Ms. Francine, who was only half a step behind him. Before he could say anything, Ms. Francine grabbed Eon in a tight, warm hug. She squeezed him with all her might and held on as if their lives depended on it. Eon hugged Ms. Francine with the same intensity and love. They both released from one another's grasp and looked into each other's eyes.

"I thank you, and I love you, Ms. Francine!" Eon said as he allowed a tear to drop from his eye. Ms. Francine took her index finger and dabbed at his single tear.

"I love you, too, Mr. Montgomery!" she said.

"Now, you be careful down there, and don't go making no babies, 'cause I don't know if I can wait another sixteen years to meet your next child." Eon smiled at Ms. Francine's moment of comedy. Ms. Francine opened the door for Eon.

He stepped out into the morning sunlight. He took two steps down and looked to his left. He saw William and Justin walking toward him.

"Hey, there are my boys!" Eon said with pride. The boys reached the front of the building just as Eon stepped onto the sidewalk. "Well, I'm out of here. You kids be careful, and make sure you do what you're supposed to, 'cause I'm watching you," Eon said as he pointed at Ms. Francine, who was standing at the top step looking down at her three favorite men.

"Ain't no kids here! Only grown-ass men!" Will said as he stuck out his chest.

"You know what? You're absolutely correct, William. Nothing but grown-ass men here!" Eon concurred. He hugged Justin.

"Thank you for everything! I'm going to miss you, big homie!" Justin whispered in Eon's ear. As the two separated, Eon looked at his son.

"Well, Pops, I will see you soon. We have that chess game to play!" Will said. Eon smiled as he pulled his boy into his chest and hugged him. The two stepped back from their loving embrace. Eon looked at Justin and William and then at Ms. Francine. Will opened the car door for Eon. "P.E.A.C.E., Dad!" Will said as Eon sat down in his seat.

"P.E.A.C.E., son!" Eon's voice faded, as William closed the door behind him. As the driver slowly pulled off, Eon faced forward. It took everything in his power not to turn around, as he knew he couldn't stand to look back, no matter how much he wanted to.

CHAPTER 12

As soon as Eon stepped off the plane, he felt the energy of his hometown. He walked out to the awaiting cabs and different people picking up their loved ones. He looked around in search of an available car. Suddenly a car pulled up in front of Eon. The driver honked his horn as Eon walked toward him. Although Eon knew his days of having car services take him to and from different places were done, he felt as if this car were here for him and him alone. He gave the driver his destination and sat back in an attempt to relax.

While the car drove through the small slender roads, Eon looked around as if this were his first time in Mississippi. After driving through the town, the car soon rode on nothing but red dirt clay. Eon bounced back and forth as each rock sounded like it was trying to come up through the bottom of the car. As the driver went past numerous homes, he would raise his hand to just about everyone he saw. Some would say hello, and some would just mimic his movement. They came upon Montgomery Road. Eon looked at the sign in disbelief. As a youth, he never took time to notice the sign. The driver slowly turned down the long stretch of road. Eon could only get small glances of the house as he tried to look in between the tall, untamed weeds. The car pulled directly in front of the massive house. Eon sat in the car for a few extra seconds. It was almost as if he was scared even to step toward the giant living quarters.

"Uh, here you are, Mr. Eon Montgomery. That will be twenty-one dollars," the old driver said. Eon went to pass the man the money and stopped.

"Wait a minute. How'd you know my name?" Eon asked.

"Well, sir, it's been a long time since I've seen your face, but I knows a Montgomery when I see one," the driver said in his Southern accent.

"You know me?" Eon asked.

"I know your Grandma and your Great-Grandma. I remember you. You look the same, just a little bit older, that's all." The man's words made Eon smile. "Looks like you got your hands full with this here," the man said as he looked up at the large porch. Eon turned to his left and noticed the couch sitting on the porch along with his other belongings that he had sent from New York.

"Fuck me, why didn't they bring the stuff inside?" Eon asked out loud to no one.

"Well, ain't no one got keys but you!" the old man said. Eon turned and looked at the man.

"You're right!" Eon thought about the simplicity and raw honesty of the man's statement.

"Here you are, sir," Eon said as he held out twenty-five dollars. The man took the money and went into his pocket to get Eon his change.

"Keep that!" Eon said.

"Thank you, sir," the man said and smiled. Eon stepped out of the cab. He turned back to the man.

"Hey, what's your name?" he asked.

"I'm Jesse…Jesse Johnson," the man said as he extended his hand to Eon.

"Pleasure to meet you, Mr. Jesse," Eon said as he shook the man's hand.

"You can call me Jesse or JJ," Jesse said as he kept a firm hold on Eon.

"Okay, Jesse. Well, thank you for your help."

"No problem, sir," Jesse said softly and with appreciation.

"Hold on now, wait. If you want me to call you JJ, then you can call me E or Eon," he said as he released his hand from Jesse's grip.

"Okay, then. Thank you, Eon," Jesse said.

"You're welcome, Jesse!" Eon smiled as he turned back toward the house.

"Well, I guess I will be seeing you around. Well then, again, I might not be seeing you for awhile," Jesse said as he peeked around at the back of the house. Jesse waved as he pulled off and drove back down the dirt road.

Eon walked up the rickety stairs. He looked at the old couch, which had changed color from the sun's powerful rays and the dark humidity of the South. The plastic covers had split in multiple areas. There were also boxes that Eon had sent sprawled all over the dry, stained wood porch floor. Eon shook his head in disgust. He walked through the maze-like set-up, pulled out his keys, and stepped to the front door. He took in a deep breath, and he unlocked the door. The odor of old rust and mildew immediately smacked Eon in his nose, causing him to step back. He suddenly remembered being inside of the large dwelling as a youth. He slowly walked through the place, looking everywhere. Eon walked up the large winding stairs and glanced around all the rooms. He returned to the main floor and went into an oversized kitchen. As soon as Eon stepped into the kitchen, he froze in his tracks. His eyes slowly focused in on different parts of the room. Although the space didn't seem to have had any activity in years, Eon saw a fully functional, working kitchen. He watched his Big Mama as she cut greens, split peas, and placed cornbread in the oven. He looked at the old, raggedy table in the middle of the kitchen. He pictured himself at the exact same table as a boy, listening closely to his great-grandmother, remembering the stories she told about everything from life on the plantation to the unwanted voyage the Africans took to get here. Eon smiled to himself as he suddenly felt the rush of anticipation he used to have when he was younger. He always loved sitting with his Big Mama. Her wisdom and love made her seem larger than life.

Eon's mind continued to take him back in time as the run-down house he was standing in provided him comfort he hadn't felt in ages. He no longer smelled the stench that permeated the house. Each section seemed to have a story, or stories, that Eon knew and felt all too well. By the time he came back to the reality of his true location, Eon was in the back of the house, looking out at the large field of untamed farmland. There was a barn off to the right of the acres of tall weeds. Eon remembered stories of Master Montgomery coming into the barn late at night and raping the female slaves. He shook his head in disgust. He walked down a row of steps. As he trotted toward the barn, he turned around and noticed the kitchen window looking out over the fields. Eon pictured his great-grandmother standing there keeping a keen eye on everyone, making sure they were all doing as they were expected. Eon's trip down memory lane was interrupted by the sudden, faint sound of a car hustling down the long road en route to the house. Instead of continuing his voyage to the barn, Eon made a beeline toward the front of the house. As he turned the corner, he banged his knee directly into a mahogany desk, causing him to double over in pain.

"Ouch!" Eon shouted as he bent over in agony.

He returned to his upright stance and looked around in amazement. Eon's entire bedroom set was sitting out on the lawn, along with his dining room set and a few other items from his old home. Eon looked around at the multiple pieces of furniture and shook his head.

"What the fuck?" Eon said to himself. He watched the different bugs and other creatures roaming all over his belongings. He opened one of the dresser drawers and watched as an assembly line of ants trotted from one side to the other. Eon cringed as he closed the drawer. His skin tingled as if the ants were on him and not the furniture. Eon quickly stepped away from his stuff and began patting his arms in hopes that the sensation would go away. He sucked his teeth as he turned and looked back at his stuff. It looked as if he were having a garage sale.

Eon arrived at the front of the house just as a pick up truck came to a stop.

"Hey, cousin!" the unknown man said from behind the steering wheel. Eon looked at the man strangely. For some reason, Eon felt like he'd seen this man's face before.

"Oh, wait, so you been gone that long that you don't remember your family no more?" the man asked.

"Uh, I'm sorry, sir, but I don't think I know you," Eon said with doubt.

"Damn, man, you don't remember me, do you?" the man asked as he stepped out from the truck. Eon stared at the man, hoping that his identity would pop into his head, but it didn't.

"Man, that there is fucked up. You know, Pops told me you didn't remember him, either." Eon paused before he made another comment. "That just ain't right, cousin. We go too far back for you to have just forgotten your family like that!" the strange man said as he stepped directly in front of Eon. "C'mon, man. You telling me you don't remember me, man?" the man said, not believing that Eon couldn't remember him.

"No, I really don't remember you, brother. I'm really sorry," Eon said with honesty.

"You are sorry, man! You are too sorry." A small, innocent smile escaped Eon's face. "Man, it's me, Jesse…Cousin Jesse!" Eon's smirk quickly turned into a wide, broad smile.

"Cousin Jesse!" Eon exclaimed as the name completely fit the face. "What's going on, man?" Eon stopped and thought to himself. "So, wait. That was your Pops?" Eon asked.

"Yep, that was him," Cousin Jesse said with pride.

"Wow, that's crazy! I knew I'd seen him before, but I just couldn't place his face," Eon said.

"Yeah, well, without some damn cotton in his face, I'm sure you wouldn't be able to recognize him," Jesse joked.

"What the hell is up, man?" Eon said, giving Cousin Jesse a giant bear hug.

Cousin Jesse was only a year older than Eon. His father was the child of one of the slaves on Master Montgomery's plantation. Jesse's grandmother and grandfather both stayed and became workers after Master Montgomery passed and Big Mama took over. Although they weren't actually blood related, the two boys were always together. Their tight bond helped in giving him the name Cousin Jesse. Because of their ages, the boys would roam all over the fields, learning each and every job and what it entailed. The two would use their time to play more than learn. Whenever they went inside to Big Mama, she would quiz them both. Big Mama knew that even though the boys didn't want to learn, they needed to gain knowledge of the plantation and how it was run. Every day, the boys would run into the kitchen, which doubled as Big Mama's office, and discuss the different things that they saw while running throughout the multiple acres of land. Jesse's dad was in charge of running the cotton fields, which became the plantation's major source of revenue once Big Mama took total control. Jesse made sure the boys slowed down long enough to listen to him explain the cotton gin and the way to pick cotton, so much so that the boys tried to avoid his section of the plantation as often as possible. Their scheme didn't work for too long, as Big Mama would watch them from her window. She would wait until they ran inside the house and then command them to go outside and see Jesse. Both of the young boys would trot back out to Jesse and listen to his lecture.

"Man, your father was a cotton-picking fool!" Eon joked. The two long lost friends embraced again as the reality of the moment settled into both of their souls. "Man, it's been a long-ass time," Eon said.

"It sure as hell has been! Far too long!" Jesse concurred. "So what brings you back home?" Jesse asked.

"Shit, man, *life*!" Eon said in a strong tone.

"Yeah, right. E, seemed like your life had been straight!" Jesse said with a serious look. "Except for when you threw up on that boat. Now that shit was hilarious!" Jesse said as he nudged Eon. "Now these mother fuckers is saying you broke!" Jesse said as if he didn't believe the MTV news.

"You know they all got something to say," Eon said. His tone sounded as if he was trying to convince himself that he wasn't hurting mentally, spiritually, or financially.

"Yeah, well, you home now, Cousin!" Jesse said as he wrapped his arm around Eon and squeezed him tightly.

"Damn, Jess, you feel like you been pumping iron or something," Eon said as he slithered out from Jesse's strong hold.

"Well, I been in the joint a few times for some bullshit assault charges, and you know, it ain't much to do when you in there except read and work out. And I ain't never been one for reading." Eon looked at Jesse.

"What?" Jesse asked.

"You remember how we would go to class with our heads full of Big Mama's words of wisdom and be checking them teachers? Well, once you left, I stopped going." Eon looked as if his feelings were hurt.

"Man, E, you was always better at putting them lying mother fuckers in their place, and once you left, I felt like I lost my partner in crime, so I just stopped going to school and went into the business with Pops," Jesse said.

"Oh, so it's my fault you…"

"Hey, now, wait a second, cousin. Ain't nobody blaming nobody for what happened to me! I made the choices I made, period, point blank!" Jesse said. He looked Eon directly in his eyes. Eon could see that Jesse was very serious.

"I hear you, Cousin," Eon said as he smiled and relaxed. Jesse smiled back at Eon.

"Anyway, Cousin, what's with this stuff here?" Jesse asked as he pointed up at the cluttered, crowded porch. "You on some wild life shit or something?" Jesse said jokingly.

"Nope, these mother fuckers delivered my shit and left it here and on the side of the house," Eon said in an annoyed voice.

"Yeah, well, you're the only one with keys," Jesse said, repeating his father's comment.

"I know, I know!" Eon exclaimed.

"Down, boy, down," Jesse said as he could feel Eon's frustration level rising. "Well, the milk is spilled, so we have to deal with what's here now," Jesse said in hopes that he could calm Eon down.

"What's here is a bunch of unusable furniture," Eon said as he extended his arms out as if the items were on display.

"Well, honestly, Cousin, I know a lot of things that we can do with this stuff. We can take this over to the Salvation Army and give these things to a family who needs it. There's a lot of those around here." Jesse said.

"A lot of what?" Eon asked as he half-listened to Jesse's comment.

"A lot of families. man, are you listening to me?" Jesse gave Eon a strange look.

"Oh, okay. I'm sorry, Cousin, but this shit got me going a little crazy," Eon said, snapping back into reality.

"Man, listen, I know exactly where you're at right now, E, for real!" Jesse said honestly and with sincerity. Eon tried to calm down. He looked around at all his things scattered throughout the outside of his home. "Listen, we are gonna load this bitch up with everything we can, and we gonna take this shit to some people who really needs it," Jesse said as he smacked his hand against his pickup truck.

"Okay, so, what? Are you going to call some of your homeboys, and they…"

"Call some who? Cousin, we doing this, me and you!" Cousin Jesse said, interrupting Eon.

"C'mon, Jesse. Can we just pay someone to get this shit out of here?" Eon asked, as if Jesse had control over the situation.

"See, that's your problem right there. You've been paying people to do shit that you can do yourself," Jesse said.

Eon immediately thought about Cassie and how he had paid her to do things that he could have, and more so, should have done for himself.

"You are right, cousin. We can do this. We *will* do this!" Eon said with pride.

The two friends spent the next two days clearing out the porch and the side of the house. They made multiple trips, filling the truck to capacity and taking things to different families. Jesse knew everyone, so he was well informed as to who needed what. Eon felt a new energy as they went from house to house. He had never felt so valued and appreciated in all his time. As they went to each house, the elders would look at Eon with a certain familiarity. Some would ask him if he was one of the Montgomery boys. Eon would answer yes as the younger children of the family would look on in awe. They could not believe that the great rapper was in their town, let alone a product of Mississippi. Eon called his son, William, and gave him a rundown of how his first couple of days back home had gone. Will brought his dad up to speed with things back up north. The two spoke for about ten minutes. They both hung up the phone with smiles on their faces, as they really just wanted to hear each other's voices.

As Eon and Jesse finished the last of the moving, Jesse's father came by and helped them with the final trip. The three men sat on the porch and talked about the last fifteen years of their lives. Cousin Jesse talked about his trips in and out of jail and how he was wrongfully incarcerated. His father talked about having to hold things down with the company that they both ran while the younger Jesse did his short stints behind bars. Eon spoke about his life in New York and how he watched his parents literally party to death. Jesse, Sr. spoke highly of Eon's parents, whom he grew up with. He reminisced on how excited the town was for them when they left.

"Man, you would've thought that the president was leaving or something. Everyone was talking about it!" Jesse, Sr. said with a smile. "Everybody just knew that they were gonna make it big in the big city," he said as he stared off to nowhere.

"Yeah, well, the big city was way too big for them, Mr. JJ. *way too big!*" Eon's voice snapped Jesse, Sr. out of his dream like state. "They both ended up strung out on drugs, and because of their addiction to the fast party life, they died penniless," Eon said honestly. "If not for my Nana, the city would've swallowed me right along with them," Eon said.

"Yeah, Ms. Monty sent her daughter up north to look after the three of y'all. See, your parents were calling asking for money on a frequent basis, and that's what made her send Melissa up to New York," Jesse, Sr. said as he thought back to the time he spoke about. "She was worried sick about them two, but more so about you!" he said as he pointed directly to Eon's chest. "You were her everything, boy! She would sit in that kitchen and just be staring off into nowhere. She was too proud to cry, but she was sure hurt when they took you with them." Eon began to feel his emotions tugging at his heart. "She sent Melissa, and Melissa sent back a message that they were too far gone for anyone to help them. That's when Ms. Monty told her to stay there and tends to you. She knew you was getting a better schooling up there, better than you would've ever gotten down here." Eon listened as JJ continued. "She wanted to get them into a rehab, but they weren't trying to hear any of that." JJ shook his head in disappointment. "You see, Willie would half-listens to his Mama, but when it came down to it, he straight feared Ms. Monty. She was not to be fucked with. Not one bit!" Eon smirked as he thought back to his Big Mama. "But with her down here in the 'Sippi', her arm couldn't stretch that far to keep that fear of God in Willie. She had to keep things straight right here on the farm," JJ said as he pointed down to the ground.

"Damn, she couldn't take a little vacation or

something. I mean, I remember you being her next in command. She couldn't leave you in charge to run shit until she got back?" Eon asked.

"Boy, your Great-Grandma ain't trust nobody with this place but herself," JJ said as he shook his head. "You have to understand that at any moment, she could've lost everything," JJ said.

"Shit, I know the feeling," Eon said under his breath.

"Mister Reverend was trying to get over on her, and then the cotton people was always trying to pull a fast one on her," JJ said.

"Cotton people?" Eon asked.

"That's right. Them big corporations wanted to buy your Big Mama out, and she wasn't budging." Eon looked at Jesse, Sr. strangely. "Oh, wait, you ain't know that your Big Mama was one of the biggest suppliers of raw cotton to the whole East Coast?" JJ asked. Eon stared at JJ with a blank look. "Boy, when you and this knucklehead would be running through them fields, you was running through a gold mine! We were one of the last fully operational plantations in all the South!" Jesse, Sr. said with pride.

"Wow! Well then, why does it look like this now?"

Eon questioned as he gestured toward the untamed land.

"Well, when Ms. Monty died, so did the fields. She was the heart and soul of this place, and when she passed, it all stopped." JJ sighed as he thought back to his good friend. "You know, she was a very, very smart woman, Eon," JJ said. "She made sure her will was air tight and that no one could interfere with her plans on divvying things out to different people once she was gone." Jesse, Sr. took a deep breath. JJ's silence made Eon turn to him. He could see that Jesse, Sr. was starting to get overwhelmed with emotions. Eon patted the old man's back in an attempt to rub away his pain. "You know, she left me a nice amount of money. That's how I started this business. She was just a really good woman who loved those who loved her," JJ said in between sobs.

"I know, JJ, I know," Eon said softly as he continued to caress Jesse, Sr.'s back.

"Damn, E, I ain't know your Big Mama was sitting on stacks like that." Cousin Jesse's voice interrupted the serious moment between the two men.

"Jesse, please shut your damn mouth!" JJ said as he wiped away some of his tears. "You know, Eon down here, all we was around was hate. The white man hated us so much that we begins to hates ourselves." Eon stayed silent and just nodded his head. "And Ms. Monty ain't never choose to live with that hate. Now don't get me wrong. You wasn't gonna just do whatever you felt with her, No sir! But she loved everyone equally, ya know. People just don't do that no more." Eon stopped patting JJ's back and embraced him in a hug of love. Jesse, Sr.'s words made Eon think of his Big Mama and more so of how he used to treat people.

"Oh, man, you two niggers are gay!" Cousin Jesse said as he watched the two men and shook his head.

"Shut the hell up, boy!" JJ screamed from inside of Eon's chest. As the two released each other, Eon wiped his face clean of his own tears. "That ain't nothing but your mother in you that cuts you off from being emotional. I tell you, I wish you and your sister had the same mommy!" JJ said.

"Yeah, then maybe you would love me the way you do her," Jesse, Jr. said with venom in his tone.

"Why, you ungrateful son of a bitch! It ain't my fault that you got yourself into all types of trouble, and when you did, who was there to get your trifling ass out of the joint? Me!" Jesse, Sr. was quickly starting to get annoyed with his oldest child, and Eon could see and feel his energy shifting.

"Whatever, Pop," Cousin Jesse said as if he couldn't care less.

"Listen, boy. You need to realize that the world is way bigger than Mississippi, way bigger!" Eon listened as JJ continued. "And until you take your finger out of your ass and stop blaming everyone else for the shit you do, you ain't gonna get nowhere in life!" Eon could see that JJ was beating a dead horse. Jesse, Jr. furrowed his face as if he had heard his father say this before. "It's like talking to yourself. In one ear and out the other!" Jesse, Sr. said as he looked at his son in frustration.

"You two need to calm down, for real!" Eon commanded as he held his hands out to both the father and son. Eon looked at both Jesses and noticed that they had cooled down. "Now, I need a hand getting this house back in order, and between your knowledge of the ins and outs of this place, JJ, and you helping me with the manual labor, Cousin, we should be able to get things back to the way they once were," Eon said loudly. Both of the men stopped arguing and listened to Eon. "So, now that we have cleared all my shit out from around here, let's put together some type of plan." Eon said.

"Okay, well, the first thing we need to do is walk through the house and see what's needed," JJ said as he started up the stairs. Eon and Cousin Jesse followed behind JJ. JJ walked in through the front door.

"Damn, I remember this place," JJ said as soon as he stepped into his old work place.

"Me too, Pop," Cousin Jesse concurred. The three men walked from room to room together. As they arrived at the kitchen, JJ stopped at the entrance.

"Wow, I feel Ms. Monty all over this kitchen," JJ said in amazement. Cousin Jesse stepped past his father and walked around the large area. He stood over the battered table, and ran his hand along the dilapidated antique.

"She would stand right here and talk to us, remember, E?" Cousin Jesse asked as he pointed to the area Big Mama would frequent.

"Yep! She would tell us the different stories about the slaves that worked here," Eon said. He stared at the spot his Big Mama would stand in.

"That lady was always thinking, always!" JJ said, also walking down memory lane. "You know, when Master Montgomery died, Ms. Monty took over all decision making for the plantation. She was already running the place before he passed, so it wasn't such a drastic change when she legally became the owner." Eon and Cousin Jesse listened intently. JJ thought for a second. "Well, actually, there was a change," he said as if he'd just remembered a point. "She made sure everyone was paid a very decent salary, which was unheard of in that time," Uncle Jesse said.

"Shit, even today don't nobody wanna pay you

what you're worth," Cousin Jesse said matter-of-factly.

"Yeah, well, that's what I'm saying as far as Ms. Monty was concerned. You were given what you deserved, period!" Eon nodded his head as he thought back to how everyone who worked on the plantation seemed so happy.

When he and Jesse would run through the fields, all the workers were cordial and kept smiles on their faces. No one ever complained or told them to get away. Eon never forgot those people and the joy he felt from their energy.

"You know something, JJ? I always remembered you and the other workers being so happy whenever we saw you guys," Eon said as JJ nodded his head in agreement. "It just felt as if you were all family and didn't have a care in the world," Eon said proudly.

"Yeah, well, we all had your Great-Grandma, Ms. Monty, to thank for that!" JJ said with a feeling of joy.

"Damn, Pop, you talk about her like she was God almighty or something," the younger Jesse said as he looked out of Big Mama's window.

"Well, to be honest, son, she was like God to us." Cousin Jesse quickly turned and looked at his father in disbelief. "Seriously, she changed all of our lives when she took over," JJ said. "We all received a job as opposed to being slaves doing slave labor. She made us all employees of the Montgomery plantation. She paid us every week, and with that money came pride in knowing that we were truly getting what we were worth," JJ said loudly with happiness.

"C'mon, Pop. *God*?" Cousin Jesse questioned. The older Jesse looked at his son with an intense glare.

"Boy, you need to realize something. Your Grandpa was traded from the Johnson plantation to Mr. Montgomery in 1915 at the age of five," JJ said.

"But, JJ, I thought slavery was abolished in 1863," Eon said, interrupting JJ.

"Eon, just as we had the Underground Railroad, the slave trade went on, secretly, way into the early 1900s. And if you really want to, how you young boys say, keep it real, they are still trading people in other countries till this day!" JJ said.

"You ain't never lie, Mr. JJ!" Eon said as he turned to face JJ.

"Man, you two niggers don't know what the hell y'all talking about," Cousin Jesse said as he walked out of the kitchen. Eon and JJ looked at each other. They both shook their heads at Cousin Jesse's lack of knowledge of the world he lived in.

CHAPTER 13

 For the next three months, the Montgomery house went through an extreme makeover. With the help of JJ, his son, and their connections, Eon was able to have the house back in livable condition. Eon stayed with the older Jesse, who tended to the fields. His company, J&M Agriculture, specialized in plants of all kinds. Because of his past in the very same fields, JJ took extra pride in making sure every part of the large mass of land was given life again. Because the ground had not been tended to in such a long time, Jesse spent a large amount of time fertilizing the soil. He watched over the multiple patches of land. Although he'd been in the business for more than 20 years, JJ took this job more seriously than any before it. He had many different vegetables growing in one particular area, while the majority of the open terrain grew cotton. A month after planting the seeds, JJ began to see the plants and vegetables sprouting out of the earth. Eon had JJ take him out to the rows of open space and describe each and every green stem and what it represented.

"Sow the seed, E! You reap what you sow!" JJ said to Eon as they stood in between the rows of what were once tall weeds. "Lemme show you something," JJ said to Eon as he walked toward the barn. Eon looked at him strangely as he followed the old man to the giant wooden hangar. JJ waited until Eon stood directly in front of the large door.

"What?" Eon said as he shrugged his shoulders, anticipating the unknown. JJ pushed the door back and watched Eon's face to see his reaction. Eon looked at the hunk of metal and turned to JJ with a frown of doubt. "Wow, is that what I think it is?" Eon asked with curiosity.

"Boy, dat there is a cotton gin!" JJ said with a wide smile. Jesse pushed a button that started the gin. Eon looked on like a young kid whose eyes were caught watching the spin cycle on a washing machine. "I can't believe you don't remember that there thing." JJ pointed to the machine as if Eon should have recognized it immediately. "Do you even remember what we used to call it?" JJ's face scrunched in hopes that Eon wouldn't disappoint him any further.

"Dorothy!" Eon said as the light bulb turned on in his head.

"That's right, son. That there is Dorothy, named after Dorothy Dandridge, the finest black woman to ever be seen on television or movies." Eon smiled as he reminisced back to when JJ would show them how Dorothy worked.

JJ would scream for them both to stay clear of Dorothy. If she were even breathed on, he would know about it. Eon giggled to himself at the thought of how he wasn't allowed to touch the machine, ever. He slowly walked over to Dorothy and lightly ran his finger along her side.

"Hello, Ms. Dorothy," he said while the gin continued to crank.

"Hey now, boy, you keep your hands to yourself now, ya hear!" JJ commanded as he snatched Eon's hand away from touching his lady.

"Damn, she's running like brand new. Where'd you get her?" Eon asked.

"Well, she was sitting up in this here barn just where I'd left her. She was close to dead, but I resurrected her!" JJ said with the pride of Dr. Frankenstein.

"Great job, Mr. J, great job!" Eon exclaimed.

Eon and JJ walked back into the house. They watched the different men working relentlessly. The house was seventy-five percent done, and Eon was extremely happy. He had made a deal with JJ, who was the foreman of the entire job. The deal was if the job were finished within six months' time, then he would pay everyone's team an additional one thousand dollars. Here they were, four months in, and Eon could see that he was going to lose the deal, which he'd actually win in the long run. Eon's finances were quickly dwindling, but he continued on with the completion of the house he loved. JJ noticed Eon's face showed worry.

"Listen, son. If you need to, you don't have to pay my crew that extra money. E, you've been more than generous with paying us our rate," JJ said in hopes that Eon would take the deal he was offering.

"Shit, we looking at an entire month early in this bitch! Cousin, please pay me my money!" Cousin Jesse said from atop a ladder in one the rooms. Cousin Jesse was always eavesdropping, especially when his father was talking. Eon shook his head.

"Don't worry, Cousin. Everyone is going to get what we agreed on. No one will be shorted." Eon gave a half smile.

"That's my nigger!" Cousin Jesse went back to touching up the ceiling with a final coat of paint.

Eon immediately thought of Cassie and wondered what she was doing with all his money. His smile turned into an evil glare. JJ noticed Eon's transformation and swiftly walked him into the kitchen. The kitchen was completely done. There were new appliances throughout the entire room. The only thing that wasn't removed and replaced was the old metal table and chairs. JJ had the table and chairs refurbished. Amazingly, the ancient pieces seemed to blend in well with the new, more modern items. Eon and JJ both looked out from Ms.

Monty's window into the rows of soil.

"Mr. J, I have to tell you something, and I want this to stay between me and you only." Eon turned and looked JJ directly in his eyes.

"Talk to me, son." JJ stared back at Eon then pulled him to the furthest part of the kitchen. JJ wanted to make sure that his son could not listen in on their conversation, as he could see that what Eon had to say was serious.

"Mr. J, in the last two years of my life, I have gone through some crazy shit! I trusted someone who ended up stealing eight million dollars from me, leaving me very close to broke. I then found out that I had a teenage son who I knew nothing about. And before all of that, I was diagnosed with a brain tumor that was cancerous," Eon said honestly.

"Damn, son, that's a lot! God is amazing, though, I tell you that!" Eon looked at him with a weird stare. "Well, you don't think for a second that God didn't want you to learn from all these things, now, do you?" JJ asked. Eon shook his head no. "So be grateful that you are still here, because he spared you so that you could realize your position in this world! I've watched you from afar, and I always knew you would come back home. I never knew it would be in this capacity, but nevertheless I knew you'd come home." Eon stood and listened to his 70-plus-year-old father figure. "You know, your

Great-Grandma would be really proud of you, boy." He patted Eon on his shoulder.

"I don't know about that one, Mr. J. After all the shit I've done and my music being so unproductive, I think she would have me stay in this kitchen with her for a few years." A look of sorrow fell upon his face.

"Boy, that woman taught you about life so that if you ever were in a situation like this, you would be able to control yourself and keeps your mind tight!" JJ said.

"Well, even that's felt like it's fading away," Eon said straight up.

"What you talking about, boy?" Mr. J questioned.

"Nothing, Mr. J, nothing," Eon said. He was hesitant to bring Mr. J into his world of crazy dreams, so Eon held back on telling JJ everything.

"Look, son. We have finished the majority of this house. Now if you don't mind me asking, how far is you from broke?" JJ inquired.

"Well, after I pay everyone, I will probably be looking at about anywhere from fifty to sixty grand, give or take a couple of thousands," Eon said with clarity.

"Okay, well, let me ask ya something else. Are you

going back into that there hippy-hop world?" JJ asked, wondering if Eon had plans to return to his music career.

"No sir, Mr. J. I am done with show biz!" Eon closed his eyes and raised his head to the sky.

"Okay well then, we gonna relive the past." Eon looked at JJ as if he were speaking a foreign language.

"Relive the past?" Eon repeated Mr. J's words more for himself than for anyone else.

"Yes man! We got a field full of cotton out there, and we ain't about to let it go to waste, No sir!" JJ spoke with confidence as he pointed to the growing plants. Eon thought about Mr. J's words as he looked out at the open earth.

"Well, how do we do this, Mr. J? I don't know how to pick no cotton, and I'm not about to let you get down on your hands and knees, 'cause you ain't no spring chicken," Eon joked, although he was very serious.

"Well, you gonna have to learn, son, and I will be right here with you every step of the way. And, son, please know that you are not alone. I battled colon cancer for two and a half years, and I stand in front of you cancer free for the past ten years!" Eon smiled. He felt more connected to Mr. J than ever before. The two men hugged as they both felt the joy of going up against the deadly disease and winning. Cousin Jesse walked past the kitchen and stopped in the entrance.

"You two niggers are gay!" he said as he kept walking. JJ waved his hand at his son as he continued to embrace his other son.

The entire Montgomery plantation was back in tiptop shape after five months of work. Eon had a barbeque at his home and invited all the workers and their families. In the time it took to fix the house, each of the men had built a relationship with Eon. He valued all the workers not just for their workmanship, but also for the fact that each handyman did everything that Eon requested. With the large amount of home and land to cover, the craftsmen took their time in making sure the job was done right. Eon loved the fact that everyone respected his wishes.

At first, he considered hiring unlicensed scabs in an attempt to save money. JJ advised Eon to pay the professionals to do professional work. Eon thought back to when he had fixed up the brownstone in Harlem. He had learned a hard lesson in the remodeling of his home. In trying to cut corners, Eon ended up having to spend much more than he had originally budgeted for the job. Instead of hiring professionals, Eon gave work to every unlicensed Tom, Dick, and Harry who quoted lower than the qualified workers. Halfway through the job, Eon released the scabs and hired experts to give him the results he wanted. He remembered hearing Cassie's voice: *"You get what you pay for!"*

Once the smoke cleared, Eon ended up paying almost twice as much to change the interior of Nana's house. Oddly enough, back then; Eon had the funds to pay the certified workers what they'd asked for. And now here he was on the brink of being flat broke and he knew in his heart that the best way to get the best job was to pay for it.

At the cookout, Eon and JJ sat on the giant porch.

"Uncle J, I want to thank you for all your help and assistance. Your expertise and advice is and always will be priceless." They watched the children running around.

"Son, it is truly my pleasure. Please know that your Great-Grandma is so proud of you, and so am I!" JJ patted Eon on his back.

Even though she was gone, JJ often spoke about Ms. Monty as if she were still here in the flesh, especially since the house was now up and running. Whenever Eon spoke with Uncle J, he felt a certain assurance of love. Their relationship reminded him of his life with Ms. Francine. Both were wise beyond their earthly years, and they always made Eon feel as if they wanted nothing but the best for him. The fact that Eon's names for Jesse, Sr. had gone from JJ to Mr. J to Uncle J was a true sign of how much progress they'd made within a short amount of time. Uncle J knew, before he was even told of the craziness in New York, that Eon's heart and soul were very fragile when he returned home. Uncle J silently became Eon's guardian and mentor as he watched over Eon with the same intense love that Big Mama did many years ago.

"You know, Uncle J, I wish your daughter could have came through. I really wanted to meet her," Eon said.

"Don't worry, son. You will soon enough," Uncle J said with assurance. As the two men stood in front of the house, they watched as a car made its way down the long strip toward the house.

"Now, who could this be?" Eon asked no one in particular.

"Don't know, but we about to find out," Uncle J said in a slick tone.

As the car pulled up to the front of the house, Eon peeked into the vehicle from the porch. He couldn't get a clear view of who was in the car, but he could tell that there was more than one person inside. Eon tilted his head from left to right to get a better glimpse of the people.

"Who in the hell is that?" he impatiently asked. The door swung open, and a tall, slim figure stepped out of the car. The young man immediately looked up at Eon and smiled.

Eon's heart began to beat fast as he recognized the all-too-familiar face. Just as he began to say something, Eon noticed a second lofty gentleman stepping out from the other side of the car. Eon's smile became even bigger as the two giants walked up the stairs toward him.

"What it look like, Pop?" William asked his father.

"Things are really looking good, son. Especially now!" Eon opened his arms wide and embraced his son. The two hugged for what felt like an eternity.

"Damn, so I get no love, E?" Justin said. He stood off to the side of the father-son team.

"Hey, Jus, come over here, man!" Eon demanded as he released his son and grabbed his second son. "How did you guys get out here?" Eon asked as he let Justin out from his clutches.

"I brought them," a stern female voice said from in front of the car. Eon looked down the stairs and saw Mary. She was waiting for someone to take the bags out of the trunk. "You boys better come over here and help me," she commanded.

"Oh, excuse me, Miss, but I will damn sure get those for you!" Cousin Jesse swooped in from out of nowhere like a superhero saving a damsel in distress. Eon smiled and shook his head at Cousin Jesse.

"Why, thank you, sir. At least there are still *some* gentlemen left on this earth!" Mary watched Cousin Jesse remove the last of the bags from the car.

"Yeah, well, if that's your idea of a gentleman, then God help you!" Eon quickly shot back as he smiled at Cousin Jesse, who was sizing Mary up while she looked up at Eon. As she turned back to Cousin Jesse, he stopped his roaming eyes, straightened up, and faced her with a large grin.

"Welcome to the 'Sippi' family," Cousin Jesse said in his most sexual voice.

"Thank you. I think I'm going to like it here!" Mary basked in the attention she was getting from Cousin Jesse.

"Ms. Lady, you better watch out there, now. You lay down with dogs, you gonna wake up with fleas!" Uncle J said from atop the porch.

"And ticks!" Eon added for good measure.

Cousin Jesse ignored Eon and his father and kept his concentration on Mary. Mary walked up the stairs as Cousin Jesse stood by the car and watched her derriere swing from side to side.

"Hey, Dad E!" she joked. Eon shook his head.

"You are too crazy, lady," Eon said as he hugged Mary.

"Damn, cousin, you look like you don't know what to do with that there," Cousin Jesse shouted from the bottom of the stairs.

"Oh, believe me, cousin. I know what to do, and have done it!" Eon spoke with confidence as Mary looked up at him with desire. "Mary, Jus, Will, this is my crazy Cousin Jesse," Eon said as they all looked at Jesse. Cousin Jesse quickly jumped the stairs, grabbed a hold of Mary's hand, and softly kissed it.

"The pleasure is all mine, Ms. Mary!" Cousin Jesse said.

"Please call me Mary," she replied.

"Oh, then Mary it is!" Jesse said as he kept his eyes on hers.

"Anyway!" Eon said as he turned his New York family to the side to face the rest of his down-south family.

"This is his Dad, Uncle J," Eon said.

"Oh, I know Uncle Jesse," Mary said as she walked

over and hugged the old man with all her might. As Uncle J squeezed Mary he looked at Eon, who was staring at him in confusion.

"Uncle Jesse is who arranged for us to come out here," Will said as he waited for his mom to release the elder Jesse so he could get his hug.

"We've been talking with him for the past few months, E," Mary said as she stepped away from Uncle Jesse.

Eon could only watch as his son wrapped Uncle J in his long arms. Once Will released Uncle Jesse, Justin stepped in to show his affection and appreciation.

"You!" Eon said, as more words seemed to escape him. Uncle J looked at Eon with the face of an innocent child.

Eon placed his arms around Will and Justin and turned them toward the front door of the house. The three walked into the large house. Uncle Jesse stuck out his arm as Mary interlocked her limb with his. The two walked behind the three-man team. Cousin Jesse took up the rear with his eyes fixed on Mary's rear.

Eon gave Mary, Will, and Justin a tour of his house. The boys looked up at the high ceilings in awe. Their mouths were ajar as they took in the beautiful walls and large rooms. With everything being new, the boys couldn't believe their eyes.

"Damn, Pop, this shit looks like a museum or some shit," William said.

Eon smiled to himself as he looked at his boys. Mary was also caught off guard by the massiveness of the house. Each room looked as if it were out of a magazine. The floors were stripped and waxed so they sparkled with an incredible shine. The entire house was fully furnished, which gave the place a whole different feel of comfort.

Eon walked behind Uncle J as he gave everyone a brief description of each area. Uncle J spoke about how each room looked back when Ms. Monty owned the plantation. He also spoke about how he and Eon had made slight, and in some cases major, changes to enhance the ambiance. After showing them every part of the inside of the house, Uncle J walked Eon's functional family out to the backyard and the large field of plants and vegetables. As they stepped out of the back door, Uncle J introduced them to everyone at the cookout.

"Hey everybody, this is Eon's son, William: his best friend, Justin: and William's mother, Mary." The group of workers, along with their families, waved at the three new faces. As Will, Mary, and Justin walked amongst the people, mingling and enjoying the summer day, some people simply nodded hello while others stopped and shook the new comers' hands.

"Damn, this feels like a welcome home party," William said, as he embraced the warm Southern hospitality from everyone.

"Well, it is!" Eon said. "I mean, you are home!" he added, smiling at his son, who smiled back at him.

"And we are so, so happy to have you!" Cousin Jesse said from out of nowhere. He slowly crept up behind Mary, making her squirm with discomfort.

Cousin Jesse had broken off from the pack as they toured the house.

"Where in the world did you come from?" Mary asked.

"Well, that dude right there, but don't hold that against me." Cousin Jesse pointed to his father who looked at him with disgust. After they made their way through the crowd of people, Eon guided Will and company over to the barn.

Uncle J slowly opened the door, giving the group access to enter. Mary sighed in disbelief as they all surrounded the cotton gin. Uncle J began to introduce his favorite machine.

"Okay, lady and gentlemen, this here is…"

"Dorothy!" Mary exclaimed, interrupting Uncle J.

The elder Jesse smiled at Mary. He was extremely proud, and shocked, at her knowledge of his beloved cotton gin.

"How about that. You are absolutely correct, Ms. Mary. This here is my Dorothy," Uncle J said. He spoke to Mary but kept his eyes on Eon, who could only smile and shake his head.

"What does she do?" Justin asked as he went to touch Dorothy's side.

"She does whatever I ask of her as long as you don't touch her!" Uncle J smacked Justin's hand away from the machine. "And you better not even think about it, 'cause Uncle J sees and feels everything Dorothy does!" Mary added.

"Damn, Ma, how you know all this stuff about Ms. Dorothy?" Will asked his mother.

"Well, your father would talk about her," Mary said honestly.

"That was a very long time ago, son," Eon said.

"And she remembered!" Uncle J interjected as he looked at Mary and gave her a wink.

"Okay, so Dorothy is what people call a cotton gin. She takes cotton and flattens it, along with extracting any seeds that are left inside," Uncle J said. He looked at his small class of students to make sure they were all receiving his lesson. "Okay, so where's the cotton?" Will asked curiously.

"Great question, young man. Follow me!" Uncle J said as they exited the barn. He walked his group over to the cotton fields, which were in bloom. Uncle J raised his hands out over the field. "Here's the cotton, son!" he exclaimed with excitement. Will, Justin, and Mary all looked over the long rows of plants.

"So this is what it looks like in the raw, huh?" Justin said. He bent down and touched one of the fluffy patches. "Shit!" Justin said as he quickly pulled his hand back.

"You have to be careful, son. Those leaves dry out, and they get razor sharp," Uncle J explained as Justin inspected his pricked finger.

Uncle J pulled a pair of leather gloves out of his back pocket and put them on. He slowly knelt by the same plant that Justin had just stepped away from and picked the boll of cotton from the plant. Uncle J held the small amount in his hand and looked at his three pupils.

"This is how you pick cotton," he said as he moved his fingers, grabbing the white, soft material.

"Don't they have machines that can do all of this?" Justin asked as he sucked his finger like a little baby.

"Yes, they do, Justin, but Ms. Monty never relied on anyone but her own hands, so neither do we," Uncle J said with pride.

"Uh, plus my father probably can't afford any of those machines, either," William said as he looked at his dad.

"You are absolutely correct, William!" Eon said without hesitation.

"So who are we getting to pick all this cotton?" William inquired.

"We got you and Justin," Eon said. William looked at his father strangely. Eon's face showed that he was not joking in the least bit.

"I don't know about that, Pop, for real," Will said as he shook his head.

"So you don't know about making seven hundred a week?" Eon asked his son.

"Where's do I starts Boss?" William said as he shucked and jived in front of Eon.

Everyone smiled at William's change of heart except Uncle J, who walked away from the group in silence.

"Ah, damn, I didn't mean to offend him, Pop," William said as he watched Uncle J slowly trot back toward the house.

"Son, you have to realize that he comes from a time when shit was a lot different around here. He can remember when that same shit either kept you alive or got your ass killed!" Eon said. William nodded his head. He knew his father was speaking the truth.

"You know what's crazy is me and Justin see the remnants of that same buffoonery in the studio." Eon listened as his son continued to explain himself. "Brothers feel like the only way to make it is to 'keep it real,' which is the phoniest shit on Earth," Will said.

"Man, if I hear another nigger talk about they niggers and the niggers they killed and the bitches they fucked and the money niggers better pay them or they gonna kill more niggers," Justin said in total frustration.

"You better watch your mouth, Justin!" Mary said with a stern voice.

"Okay, I'm sorry, Ms. Mary," Justin said.

"What's even worse is we know each and every one of these dudes, and they have never even thought about the thought of picking up a gun! Just about all of them live with their mothers. And they all have never smelled no parts of any puss…"

"Watch your mouth, young man!" Mary interrupted her son before he could speak of the small kitten.

"I know it's the gift and the curse," Eon replied to his son.

"Well, what's the gift? 'Cause they are damn sure the curse," Justin said. Mary gave Justin an angry look. "I'm sorry, Ms. Mary, my fault," Justin said to her silent reprimand.

"Well, the gift is the fact that they can make a ton of money if they are picked up by the right company and promoted the right way," Eon said.

"Yeah, and then after that, they trust some scandalous bitch who takes them for all their money," William said. He looked to his mother, expecting to hear her chastise him for cursing.

"Oh, no, Cassie was a female dog!" Mary said.

"Son, are you trying to upset everyone down here?" Eon asked.

"No, I'm sorry Pop," Will said as he hung his head in shame.

"Now, I think you need to go find your Uncle J and give him one of those, too," Eon said. William nodded his head as he walked back toward the house.

As William came closer to the back of the house, he saw Uncle J in the kitchen window. As their eyes met, Will felt as if Jesse was looking past him. He slowly walked into the house, taking his time with each step. William finally made it to the entrance of the kitchen. Uncle J felt his presence but did not move from his place at the window.

"You know, your Great-Great-Grandma used to own this land. She was a very smart woman, one of the smartest I have ever known, past and present. She ran the entire plantation from right here in this kitchen. She would send your father out to those very same fields you were standing on. He and my son would give messages to all of us, letting us know what we needed to do and how soon she wanted it done. She was a fair woman. If you did the work, then you were paid accordingly. You know, I look at you and your father, and I envy you two." Will looked at Uncle J strangely as he slowly stepped into the kitchen. "You two love the mess out of each other, and it shows in everything you both do. Your Dad has made some mistakes and so have I, but I feel like my boy doesn't see the love I have for him. He just doesn't get it! You know, you need to cherish every moment you have with your father because your relationship is based on love, and that can take you any and everywhere you want to go." Will nodded in silence.

"My father was hanged for my 16th birthday. He was out in town trying to buy me something and was in such a happy daze that he made the mistake of brushing against the wrong white person. Because he was smiling so wide and seemed so happy, the white man made him dance a jig. After he finished dancing, they tied him up to a tree and whipped him to within inches of his life. They then poured alcohol on the open wounds and continued to beat on his body. They locked him up in a jail, where he lay in a pool of his own blood. That night, the Klan came to the jail and took him to our house. By the grace of God, I wasn't there. I had stayed here with Ms. Monty, which was a normal thing for me to do." Will could feel both Jesse's and his emotions beginning to get the better of them both.

"They destroyed my house and everything in it. They then pulled my entire family out and hung them all, leaving my father last so that he could watch his loved ones die. Everyone was dressed in his or her Sunday best. They were all going to come here to sing 'Happy Birthday' to me and give me my gifts. Instead of seeing my father's pickup truck rolling down the long road to the house, I stood on the front porch and watched a police car rumbling up to the house. The officers said they had found my family. They had all been murdered." Will looked at Uncle Jesse. He could see that he was reliving the moment in his mind. Tears slowly began to run down Uncle Jesse's face. William placed his hand on Uncle Jesse's shoulder. He could tell that he didn't want to talk anymore.

"Uncle Jesse, I am really sorry about the way I acted out there. I wasn't trying to be disrespectful in the least bit. Please forgive me? Please!" William pleaded. He began to relate to Jesse's pain.

William thought about how it would feel to lose his father, especially since he'd just become part of William's life. As his mind wandered into the negative space, Will contemplated someone murdering Eon. Uncle Jesse turned to Will and saw that he too was crying.

"It's okay, son. I forgive you...I forgive you!" Uncle Jesse said as he comforted William in a strong embrace. As the two hugged one another, the younger Jesse stood at the entrance of the kitchen, shaking his head.

"You two niggers are really gay," he said as he walked away from his father and William.

"Listen, son. Please ignore my son and his silly comments. He truly doesn't know any better." William smiled as he could see that Uncle J was coming out of his funk.

"It's cool, Uncle J. I'm just a little worried about us

making ends meet out here. Are you sure we can make money just from cotton?" William inquired.

"Son, this entire plantation ran on the money that was made from us picking cotton. There were a lot more workers back then, and the price per pound was much more, also." William looked at Jesse with confusion. "Well, son, we were paid thirty-three and a third for each pound of cotton. That number has changed drastically with the fact that cotton has gone corporate, bringing the all-around value down." William nodded his head. "You know, Will, Dorothy used to be the size of the entire barn." William's eyes bulged as he considered the compact piece of metal taking up the whole barn. "And again, that there corporate world got a hold of things and downsized everything!" Uncle J said with a twinge of anger.

"So then, how are we gonna..."

"We are going to be fine, son" Uncle J said confidently, interrupting Will's concerned question. "You will see...things are going to be fine." William looked directly in Uncle J's eyes. For some strange reason, he believed every word he said.

CHAPTER 14

Because Uncle J had never moved away from either the business of plants and crops or Mississippi, he knew exactly what type of plant and vegetable each piece of land grew. This gave him an advantage on the competition. In most cases, he knew the land better than the owners themselves. Yesterday's sharecropper had become today's businessman. Many of the people who owned land received it through inheritance. In many cases, they were not interested in anything but making a profit. Their land was looked at as more of a low-risk investment. Because of this, most landowners would cut corners when it came to planting and growing. They would leave a handler in charge of running the grounds. Uncle J, and his company were called on for maintenance of many of the properties. Not only did he know when every crop grew, he knew the harvest time better than anyone. After comparing the different amounts that each company paid for cotton, he narrowed it down to one. The elder Jesse had learned how to do business from one of the sharpest minds in the world. He knew that because of his color and age, many people were going to try to take advantage of him. Being that he was already well versed in running his own business, Uncle J took on running the plantation with pride and comfort. He never allowed anyone to get over on him and always ran his company with dignity, being fair to each and every one of his employees.

    Because he was so close to Ms. Monty when she was running the plantation, Jesse knew the exact price that was paid for each pound of cotton. The going rate was now between five and eight dollars per pound, depending on the quality. Uncle J settled on six dollars. He knew that he could've gotten more, but he also knew that the contract would've come with restrictions and deadlines. Because he was dealing with a much smaller team that was inexperienced in the skills of picking cotton, Uncle J didn't want to place too much of a work load on himself or his workers. Eon was the owner of the company with Uncle J as a silent partner. More than anything, Eon wanted to make sure that he continued the tradition that his Big Mama had set forth. He and Jesse both agreed to be fair to all their workers. The majority of the people who were working on the Montgomery plantation were from Jesse's company. They knew a lot about agriculture, yet the actual process of picking cotton was new to them all. Even still, the twenty-man team all signed up for the one-year deal. William and Justin both agreed to work in the fields. They knew that the money they'd make was much greater than what they were getting from running the studio. Plus, they both missed being around Eon. Mary also became part of the team. She stayed in the house, working as the office assistant. She was the liaison between the fabric company and Eon's business. Mary was more than happy to have steady work, and even more, she missed Eon.

The average slave would pick anywhere between two hundred and fifty to three hundred pounds of cotton in a day. Eon and Jesse only expected a minimum of one hundred pounds from each worker. If the person picked a minimum of 100 pounds of cotton, then he or she was given the agreed-upon pay, which ranged from five hundred to seven hundred dollars a week, with Saturday being an optional day of work. The company was closed on Sunday. This was the same schedule that Big Mama ran the plantation on when she was alive. Jesse also did all his planting based on the *Farmer's Almanac*, which was Ms. Monty's way of judging when to plant. The best time for harvest was between August and November, when the heat was breathtaking. Eon and Jesse would allow the workers to start at twelve in the afternoon and work an eight-to-nine-hour shift. This took them into the night, when they didn't have to deal with the strains and effects of the blaring sun. Eon had rows of floodlights placed around the seventy-plus acres of cotton. This made it much easier to see in the late-night hours.

The first few months of business ran pretty smoothly. The company turned a profit almost immediately. With all the workers happy, even Cousin Jesse, B.M.C. (Big Mama's Cotton) quickly became a part of the Southern fabric corporations. Their quality of cotton was worth way more than they were getting for it. Because of this, Eon knew that he could monopolize the entire industry, at least in Madison and the neighboring counties. Uncle J and Eon agreed, when they first started the business that they would not step on anyone's toes. This is why they dealt with a company that had never done any business in the state of Mississippi. They also dealt with only the one contract they had. Eon and Uncle J could have hired more people and made more money, yet they prided themselves on not being greedy, but being fair. Every day someone would call hoping to do business with B.M.C., but Eon had Mary take the information for possible work for the future. Between running the company and actually working in the fields, Eon's body and soul began to feel the effects. Although the physical labor was extremely strenuous, Eon felt good knowing that he was finally working for himself, but the constant wear and tear showed in Eon's face.

One day, he went into the office, which was one of the many rooms in the house that had been transformed. Mary quickly handed him a piece of paper.

"What's this?" he asked Mary.

"Your doctor's information. You, Mr. Montgomery, have an appointment for this Thursday at two o'clock," Mary commanded. She kept her head down, tending to the papers on her desk. Eon stood with his mouth ajar.

"But I don't have a doctor."

"Doctor Jackson will see you this Thursday," Mary said, interrupting Eon.

"You've got to be kidding me," Eon joked. Mary slowly looked up from her desk and stared at Eon.

"What? I mean, I didn't even know I had a doctor in Mississippi, and now you're telling me I'm going to see the moon walking gloved one who's allegedly dead but doubling as a doctor…c'mon!" Eon said with a glare of seriousness.

"Michael Andrew Jackson is the son of Dr. George Jackson." Eon looked suspicious, as the name seemed familiar. "Dr. George Jackson was your physician when you were a teenager!" Mary said. Her voice was coated with honest sarcasm. Eon took a second to respond.

"You know, I remember running around his father's office whenever his dad and Big Mama sat down to discuss my health," Eon said.

"That's funny, 'cause he remembers you, too!" Mary said as she shook her head at Eon. Eon nodded as he stepped out of the office.

"But wait. How in the world did you know that?" Eon asked.

"Uncle J knows more about you than you know! He is the person who contacted us and arranged for us to come out here in the first place. E, that man loves you like a son," Mary said as she went back to her papers on her desk. He walked out of the office with a smile on his face.

Eon walked into the barn. He looked at Uncle J running the cotton gin. He slowly crept up to the machine and touched the base of the gin. "Get them hands off her!" Uncle Jesse said from the other side of Dorothy. Eon could only smile, as the connection between Uncle J and Dorothy seemed unbelievable.

"Hey, Uncle J," Eon said as he walked around to Jesse.

"Hey, son," Jesse replied.

"So Mary just gave me an appointment for Dr. Jackson?" Eon questioned.

"Yeah, and?" Jesse asked.

"Well, I was wondering what made you think I needed to go see a doctor, and how did you get this information?" Eon inquired.

"Well, Eon, I know that running this plantation ain't

easy in the least bit. I also know that you need to make sure your health is in order 'cause you ain't no good to no one, especially yourself, if you're stressed out and sick." Eon nodded his head in agreement. "And I knew Michael Jackson's father for as long as you've been alive," Uncle J said.

"Who, Joe?" Eon joked.

"Son, your Big Mama made sure that I was aware of everything that went on here on these grounds. You were part of what went on here, so you were my business, too! Now, George raised *Andrew* to be a doctor, and now he is one. I wish I could've raised my boy to be something other than an ungrateful leech, but I didn't…hey, that milk is already spilled," Jesse said with a tone of disappointment. "Listen, Eon. We are going to need to either buy a bigger gin, or we may have to take this stuff over to Mister Reverend to get cleaned."

"I thought he only had the farmers' market," Eon said with doubt.

"No, sir, Mister Reverend owns one of the biggest cotton gins this side of the Mason Dixon." Eon stared at Uncle J with a look of surprise.

"What?"

"You thought we were going over there just getting fruits and stuff?" Jesse said, speaking about the trips they used to make back and forth to Mister Reverend's marketplace. "Whenever we went there, we were going to get our receipt of the cotton that we'd dropped off earlier." A small smile escaped from Eon's face as he remembered back to the time Jesse talked about. They would always drive to the back of the farmers' market and park. Every time they went, the boys would both stay in the truck while Uncle J went in through the back entrance. Eon knew, especially back then, that the remnants of slavery were still very present, especially in the backwoods of Madison, Mississippi. Mister Reverend was a tall, slim white man. He wore overalls and smoked a straw pipe. Whether he had tobacco in it or not, Mister Reverend kept his smoking utensil close by, often allowing it to hang from his lips. Sometimes they would have to travel to Mister Reverend's home. Eon and Cousin Jesse would sit and watch as Jesse, Sr. walked up to the rear entrance. He would always aggressively wipe his feet before he entered the domain. Eon was dreaming with his eyes open.

"Boy, that man was always the head white man in all of Madison County. Do you remember his church?" Uncle J asked.

"I sure do!" Eon said as he snapped back to reality. "I remember we would pass his church whenever we were going to ours. Big Mama always said they had a slower line to God," Eon said, quoting his great-grandmother.

"Did you understand what she meant?" Uncle Jesse asked.

"Well, I figured because they were always taking their time in church, she meant they were taking their time to get in touch with the Lord. We were always singing and celebrating and just rejoicing in our love for God, and they were always staying in one place while they went about their service." Uncle J nodded his head as he could tell that Eon understood Ms. Monty. "She also said that just because they were slower and softer in how they praised that they weren't any worse or better than us!"

"Amen to that!" Uncle J said as he raised his hand to the sky above.

"So, wait, he's still alive?" Eon said unconsciously.

"Yes, he is, E. The man is old as dirt itself and still the same," Uncle Jesse said with a look of disgust.

"So do we have to deal with him?" Eon asked, hoping there were other options.

"Well, no, we don't. But for us to keep up with cleaning the cotton, we are going to need to buy a larger gin. That could cost about a hundred thousand dollars, and that's not counting the maintenance," Uncle J said.

"Shit! Well, what else can we do?" Eon asked.

"We could take it to a different gin. The only problem there is that it's in another town. We spend way too much just in traveling expenses." Eon shook his head with disappointment.

"So, really, our only real option is dealing with the Rev, huh?" Eon asked, already knowing the answer to his question. Uncle J stayed silent. He answered with only the nod of his head.

Eon made his doctor appointment. For the first time in a long time, he enjoyed his visit. Instead of the usual poking and prodding, Eon went through a regular checkup. Seeing his old friend made him feel even better. They talked and reminisced on their past, catching up on one another's lives. The doctor made sure he spoke to Eon about getting the proper rest and considering letting someone else pick cotton for him. Eon didn't want to seem as if he was milking his position as owner of the company, but it was in his best interest that he take a break from physically working so hard.

"You know, it's really kind of crazy that you are really picking cotton nowadays. You know, they have machines that can do all that work for you," Dr. Jackson said.

"Yeah, I know, MJ, but that's for people who have

the available funds to purchase those items. Plus, I love watching my son get his hands dirty. It makes me feel good that he is earning his money," Eon said with pride.

"Well, you are E the MC, aren't you? Or are you saying that those crazy rumors about you being broke are true?" the doctor asked in hopes of getting the scoop on the great rapper.

"You know something, Doc? If I didn't know any better, I would think that you were trying to pry a little bit into my business," Eon said as he gave the doctor a strange look.

"Well, is it true?" the doctor reiterated.

"Listen, Doc. Stick to what you know. Leave the snooping and reporting to the scandalous, story-hungry news people and the gay community!" Eon said as he shook Dr. Jackson's hand and left his office. Eon walked out with a clean bill of health and a feeling of joy that he hadn't felt in years.

Eon returned to the house and spoke with Uncle J. He talked about leaving the fields and concentrating on getting the company new business. Eon suggested that Uncle J do the same thing. Jesse was of retirement age. Even though he did move with the bounce of a man much younger, Jesse had given years and years of his life to his passion for plants, and the manual labor had taken a toll on his body. Jesse agreed on leaving Dorothy on one condition, that no one else touch her and that the company deal with Mister Reverend. Eon didn't want to deal with Mister Reverend, but he knew that they didn't have the money to buy another cotton gin. He also knew that buying one meant that Uncle J would have to be on call for whatever maintenance would be needed on the machine. This would go totally against the plan for Uncle J to retire from such intense work.

 Miraculously, Eon and Uncle J stepped into their new roles without a glitch. All of the employees accepted both men's choice to leave the physical work to them. As opposed to the people feeling slighted and wronged, the entire crew embraced both men. Uncle J's men felt that it was overdue. They had watched Jesse, Sr. work as hard as they did on each and every job. He never took a day off and always was the first person to show up to a job and the last one to leave. Because of the relationship Eon had built with everyone, none of the workers said anything. They all gave him credit for working as long as he did. Both of these men were bosses in the literal sense, yet they treated themselves as equals to their employees, never looking down or degrading anyone. This was a new way of working for Eon. The past two years of his life had made him much more humble. Also, the fact that his son was working alongside him gave Eon a feeling of love and light that he hadn't felt in a long time. William and Justin also accepted their comrade's decision. They both knew what Eon had gone through and were happy to see him take a break for once.

Now that they had more time, Eon and Uncle J secured more work for the company. They'd set up another one-year contract that paid them almost double their current agreement. It was another company that was new to the cotton business, keeping B.M.C. clear of stepping on anyone's toes or interfering with any company's established arrangement. The two men felt good witnessing their growth as businessmen and as friends. Over the past year and a half that Eon had been in Mississippi, Uncle J had seen Eon in a new light.

Eon pulled the truck up to the front of Mister Reverend's house.

"What you doing, son?" Uncle J asked from the passenger seat. Eon smirked as he put the truck back in drive and rolled around to the back of the house. As the car came to a halt, Eon looked at the giant, old house and then at Uncle J.

"Do we really have to?" Eon asked with the voice of a small child.

"We're here now, son. I mean, what you wanna do? You want to stay or go?" Uncle J questioned Eon, who looked doubtful.

"Uncle, I don't know about this. I mean, what if he doesn't want our business?" Eon asked.

"Listen, son, Mister Reverend did business with your great-grandmother for more than twenty years. Now, I ain't gonna sit here and say he's some kind of saint or nothing," Uncle J said as if he was trying to convince Eon.

"Uncle J, I hear you, but..."

"But what, son?" Uncle J asked, interrupting Eon.

"But I'm not Big Mama!" Eon said. He stared at Jesse to see if he understood his point.

Uncle J nodded his head as he glanced at Eon.

"You're right, son. You are absolutely right! You are not your Great-Grandma." Uncle J spoke slowly to make sure Eon knew he'd gotten his point across. "You know more about the world than she did," Jesse said. Eon looked at Uncle J with doubt and confusion.

"How can you say that?" Eon asked.

"Well, you must understand that with all the information she gave you, along with the fact that you have pretty much traveled the world, that makes you more informed as to people and their ways. Ms. Monty never left that kitchen. Now that doesn't make her any less wise than she was. It just means she only knows what she knows." Eon looked at Jesse as his words began to sink into Eon's body. "Again, we can go in there right now, or we can leave. We have already scheduled this sit-down, and he knows what we are here for, so it's not like we need to be here too long at all," Uncle J said. He was hoping that Eon would trust him and his decision to do business with Mister Reverend. Eon began to nod his head. He could see that Uncle J was sincere and honest. The thought of leaving slowly crept out of his system.

"Okay, let's go," Eon said as he opened the truck door and stepped out. Uncle J smiled to himself as he left the truck.

The two businessmen walked up to the back door. Uncle J began digging his feet into the old rug that sat at the entrance to the rear of the house.

"What the fuck, J?" Eon asked.

"Listen, just wipe your feet, please!" Uncle J demanded. He spoke in a serious tone.

Eon quickly ran his feet over the mat. Uncle J looked at Eon as if he didn't believe he had really wanted to clean the bottom of his shoes.

"What?" Eon asked as Uncle J knocked on the door. A short black man answered.

"May I help you?" the man asked.

"Yes, we are here to see Mister Reverend," Uncle J said in a stern voice.

"Right this way," the man said as he opened the door wide enough for the two men to walk inside. Eon and Jesse followed the man into the house. They walked into a study with a mantel and a fireplace.

"One second. Mister Reverend will be right with you," he said as he walked away, leaving Eon and Uncle J alone.

"Excuse me, sir, who might I ask is visiting, and what is this in concern of?" The butler's voice shocked Eon, who was concentrating on three mason jars that sat upon the mantle.

"We are the owners of B.M.C. We are here to discuss business with Mister Reverend," Uncle J said.

The man turned around and walked out from the study. Eon turned his attention back to the jars. They all were full, yet he could not make out what exactly was inside. Eon took a step toward the containers. He tilted his head in hopes that a different view would allow him to see the contents more clearly. As Eon took another small step toward the mantel, an old, shaky voice sounded from behind.

"That first one there is my Granddaddy's. That one in the middle is my Daddy's. And that last one there is mine!" Eon turned and faced Mister Reverend, who stood in his overalls.

"Jesse, who this here you brought up in my house?" Mister Reverend asked as he peeked at Eon from head to toe.

"Mister Reverend, this is Ms. Monty's great-grandson," Uncle J said as he held his hand on Eon's shoulder.

"What! Boy, you sure is bigger than last I seen you," Mister Reverend said.

"Yes, sir," Eon said as he stared at Mister Reverend's pipe dangling from his mouth.

Uncle J could feel the tension between Eon and Mister Reverend. He hoped that Eon would keep his composure.

"So these jars are what…pickled pig feet or something?" Eon asked. Mister Reverend chuckled softly.

"No, boy, these here is our trophy case." Uncle J stiffened with discomfort as Eon squinted with confusion. "Boy, these here is niggers' balls that me and my family done cuts off! We keeps them as a reminder of how worthless niggers are!" Eon looked at Uncle J with a stern stare of disgust and anger.

"Speaking of worthless, did you two wipe ya feets before you comes in here?" Eon stared at Uncle J.

He couldn't believe his ears. Eon began walking toward the back exit. Uncle J stepped in front of Eon, stopping him from leaving. He spoke to Mister Reverend as he looked directly at Eon.

"Yes, sir, we did. We wiped them really good." Eon shook his head as his blood boiled.

"Mister Reverend, we want to discuss using the services of your cotton gin. We have a lot of cotton that needs to be cleaned," Uncle J said.

"Yeah, well, you can't clean it over there at the Montgomery plantation? I hears about you two harvesting some good cotton and sellin' it for cheap. That just don't makes no sense. But then again, that place ain't made no sense for a long time now. Mr. Montgomery didn't make sense with how he ran that plantation. Giving niggers a place in the world just don't ever make sense…*ever*!" Eon stared at Jesse. Jesse could feel the intensity of Eon's glare.

"Listen, Mister Reverend. If we are to do business, can you please find a way to not use that type of language?" Eon asked. His voice rose with rage and annoyance.

"What you mean, English?" Mister Reverend said sarcastically. He looked at Eon and smirked. He could tell that Eon was irritated with him, but he truly didn't care.

"Now, you listen to me, boy. Niggers been calling each other niggers for a long time now! Shit, them hippy-hopping niggers call each other nigger every day." Mister Reverend sat down in his chair.

"Yes, but you're not a nigger!" Eon said as he balled his fist at his side.

"You got that shit right!" Mister Reverend spoke with pride. "And I would never want to be mistaken as one of them, either. I would kill a motherfucker for even thinking that I cared about a nigger. I've killed…"

"Mister Reverend!" Eon interrupted Mister Reverend's comment. "How much will you charge us to use your gin?" Eon asked. He could tell that he was fighting a battle that he just could not win.

Mister Reverend was completely stuck in his ways, and there was nothing that anyone could say or do to change his mind.

"You boys are gonna pay me a dollar per pound and a dollar-fifty for every pound after the first thousand," Mister Reverend said as he settled into his chair.

"Okay, thank you, sir. We will have someone contact you when we've made our decision," Eon said as he began to walk out.

"Good day, Jesse," Mister Reverend said nonchalantly, ignoring the exiting Eon.

"Good day, Mister Reverend. We will be in touch," Uncle J said as he walked out. Mister Reverend sat in his chair with his face turned away from Jesse.

Jesse walked out of the house. He looked at Eon, who was sitting in the truck, waiting for him. He could see that Eon was extremely upset.

"Uncle J, there's no way we should even consider doing business with that racist pig!" Eon said.

"E, have you ever heard of sticks and stones?" Uncle J asked as he tried to make light of the situation.

"Yeah, and this mother fucker needs to have a stick shoved up his ass and be stoned!" Eon's voice began to rise along with his rage.

"Son, I told you he wasn't no saint, " Jesse said.

"Yeah but you ain't say he was the Devil himself! Jesse, He has three men's testicles in Mason jars on his mantle!" Eon closed his eyes as he took in a deep breath. Jesse shook his head clear of the thought of his father and the ordeal he had gone through.

"Listen, son. The man is giving us a great price to use his cotton gin. We are still going to make the same amount of money even after we pay him. With our next contract, we are going to make double what we are making now. That means us paying him is pennies when you think about it."

"I know, Uncle J, I know! I was just sitting here doing the math." Eon didn't want to agree with Uncle J, but he couldn't deny the truth.

"Well, I don't want to have anything to do with him. I don't want to drop off nor pick up any cotton. And his checks are *all* in the mail." Uncle J nodded his head. He understood Eon and his reasoning for not wanting to ever see nor contact Mister Reverend again.

"He comes from a time when colored men didn't have a chance to do or say anything. They just went about their life without a thought of success, just plain survival!" Uncle J's voice trailed off as he reminisced on the many men who'd lost their lives simply because of their skin color.

Uncle J slowly began to move the truck out from the spot behind Mister Reverend's house.

"Like I told you about my father..." Eon peeked at Uncle J with a look of doubt. Jesse stopped short as he thought of the moment he had with Eon's son.

"Shit, I told your boy this, not you." Uncle J shook his head as he remembered speaking with William.

"Okay, well, you need to tell me now!" Eon exclaimed. Uncle J acted as if he didn't hear Eon.

"Jesse!" Eon shouted as he grabbed Uncle J's hand, forcing him to stop the truck in the midst of his turn. Eon looked at Uncle J as the truck sat in front of what looked like a guesthouse.

"Talk to me, Uncle J!" Eon commanded. Jesse gripped the wheel of the truck. He looked over at Eon, who impatiently waited to hear what Jesse had to say.

"Eon, my father was murdered because of his color. He was hung along with my mother and the rest of my family." Jesse looked at Eon.

"Shit, and here I am calling myself and those who adore me niggers! What type of monster am I?" Eon asked.

"Son, everyone has demons. And you are not a nigger anymore," Uncle J said. Eon's eyes were focused on someone or something outside of the truck. "Son, are you listening to me?" Uncle J asked Eon. He could see that Eon was in another world. Uncle J looked in front of the truck.

The lights beamed on a white woman who was walking out of the guesthouse. Her head was wrapped in a scarf. She slowly and gingerly moved her fragile body out the doorway. His eyes were fixed on the gauze that stuck out from under her head wrap. Eon immediately thought to his time when he was sick. He remembered the discomfort that came from the bandages. Eon touched his head. He ran his fingers over the small remnants of the scars.

"Eon Montgomery!" Uncle J screamed, snapping Eon out of his trance. Eon turned and faced Uncle J.

"Yes, "Eon said as if he had no idea of his whereabouts.

"Son, are you okay?" Jesse asked as he turned and faced the lady. The woman stumbled directly in front of the truck. Eon jumped out of the truck and helped the lady. Uncle J remained in the driver's seat.

"Are you okay?" Eon asked. His words were drenched in worry and concern. The lady slowly got back to her feet with Eon's assistance.

"Yes, I'm okay. I've been better," she said jokingly.

"Please take me back inside. My granddaughter would kill me if she knew I was out here." The lady cautiously looked around. Eon could see the worry in her face.

"Listen it's okay. Take your time. Okay. Take your time. Everything is okay?" Eon said. The lady placed her chin on her chest and glanced up at Eon.

"Everything isn't okay, young man please know that," she said as she stood as upright as her broken body would allow. The woman snatched her hand out of Eon's grasp.

"Hey!" Eon shouted as he pulled his hand back. Uncle J rushed from around the other side of the truck.

He figured Eon had done something to irritate the old white lady. Uncle J warily grabbed the lady's free hand. She quickly turned and stared at Jesse. Before she could speak, Jesse softly tapped the top of her hand.

"Ma'am, please forgive my partner. He truly didn't mean any disrespect. Ma'am, are you okay?" Jesse asked the lady. She seemed stuck in one place as she watched Uncle J as if he were her favorite television show.

"You wouldn't happen to be Jesse Joe Johnson's

boy, would you?" the old white woman asked Jesse.

"Why, yes, ma'am, I am!" Uncle J said with pride and curiosity.

"My name is..."

"You are Lil Jesse?" the lady said, interrupting Uncle J's introduction.

"Yes, I am!" Uncle J said. The lady looked at him in awe. She rubbed his hand as she walked him into her front door. Eon stood outside with a look of total shock. He slowly followed the two inside her house.

"My name is Ethel, Ethel Jones," the old lady said as she plopped down in her chair.

"Well, you already know who I am," Uncle J said with a smile. His desire to know how she knew his father was eating Jesse from the inside out.

"This is my partner, Eon Montgomery," Jesse said as he pointed his hand to Eon, who had just entered Ethel's domain. The old lady looked at Eon.

"Hmm, so you is Mildred and William's boy, huh?" Ethel said as she took a second to really check Eon out.

"Yes, ma'am, I am. You knew my parents?" Eon asked, clearly knowing the answer.

"Yes, I did. I knew them. I knows your Grandma and your Great-Grandmamma," Ethel twisted her body until she found a comfy place in her chair.

"Jesse, I can't believes it's you. Your daddy loved you soo much. He thought the world of you," Ethel said as she looked at Jesse. Her eyes began to fill with water. She dug into her bra as if she was trying to find something. She grabbed a piece of tissue out of her bosom and wiped her eyes. Ethel pointed at one of many pictures sitting on a table across from where she sat. Uncle J reached out and took one of the framed pictures. His eyes popped open. Jesse pulled the photo in close to his face as if he couldn't believe his eyes.

"This...this...this is my daddy!" Uncle J said. Ethel and Eon could hear the lump form inside of Jesse's throat. "How do you know my father?" Uncle J asked Ethel as if he was still alive.

"I knew your father very well. He was my life...my love...my everything!" Ethel said. She began to feel herself going into a place of pain and sadness.

"Jesse, your father loved your mother very much, but not in the way a husband loves his wife. He loved her for giving him you!" Uncle J nodded his head. "He and I would sneak around to see each other. My father was a partner with Mister Reverend, and whenever they went away on business, I would find a way to see him. As you know, blacks and whites weren't allowed to be seen together, let alone be in a relationship." Uncle J stood with his eyes plastered on the picture of his dad while he and Eon listened to Ethel.

"How long did you know him?" Eon asked.

"I knew him just about from birth. Our fathers were partners. I told you! On his deathbed, my father made Mister Reverend promise to take care of me if I ever needed him. So when I got brain cancer, he brought me in and let me stay in the guesthouse. My granddaughter came down and has been helping me get around," Ethel said.

"Hold on! Wait one minute here! You said your fathers were partners? Are you trying to tell me that Mister Reverend is my Daddy's Daddy?" Jesse screamed at the top of his lungs.

"Jesse, you need to go talk to him," Ethel said with compassion. Jesse closed his eyes.

As the disbelief continued to build in his soul, Jesse ran out of the guesthouse and made a direct line towards Mister Reverend's house, carrying his father's picture with him. Eon stood inside of Ethel's place with a blank look on his face.

CHAPTER 15

    Jesse pounded on the back door. As the butler opened the door, Uncle J pushed his way into the house. Before the butler could regain his composure, Jesse was inside the study. Mister Reverend was still sitting in his favorite chair.

"What the hell has gotten into you there, Jesse?" Mister Reverend asked calmly.

"Mister Reverend, how do you know my father?" Jesse asked. Mister Reverend took his pipe out of his mouth. He looked down into the pipe.

"Well, Jesse, I knew your Daddy really well. You know back when this here plantation was up and running; I would often go in the barn and pick me a nigger woman to have relations with. One day, one of them say that they pregnant. Now, when the baby comes out, he don't look like he's a colored baby at all. Come to find out, that there baby is mines. That there baby is your Daddy, Jesse," Mister Reverend said as he pointed his pipe at Jesse. Jesse stood motionless. "Now, I ain't abouts to be claiming no nigger child, so I trades him to the Johnson plantation for two hogs and four chickens when he was a young'n. From there they treats him like he's a nigger slave, as they should, 'cause that's what he is." Mister Reverend spoke about his son as if he were livestock and not a human being. Jesse closed his eyes as he gripped the framed picture tightly.

"As your Daddy gets older, he begins to take a liken to Ethel, my partner's daughter, who's a white woman. Now, it ain't no way that no nigger is gonna loves no white woman…that's just plain impossible, so I have him traded to the Montgomery plantation. There the boy finds your mother, and they have you. Now I'm thinking that everything is okay with him leaving Ethel alone, but comes to find out, he ain't leaves her be." Mister Reverend spoke as if he were telling the story of someone other than his actual son. "They still sneaking around, and that's just not gonna happen here in Madison, Mississippi. No, Sir, it ain't! And then comes to find out that Ethel is pregnant! Well, that there was the straw that done broke the camel's back," Mister Reverend said as he banged his hand down on the armrest of his chair.

Meanwhile Eon continued to sit with Ethel.

"Ethel, whatever happened to Uncle Jesse's father? He was just about to tell me how he passed away when I saw you stumble and fall." Ethel looked directly at Eon.

"Son, Jesse's dad was murdered!" As she continued, a woman walked out from the back of the house. She had her head down while she punched buttons on her Blackberry. Eon listened intently as Ethel told the story.

"The day that I had Jesse Joe's baby, my daughter,

they went and found him in town. They beat him badly and then left him inside the jail. After that, they brought him to his house." Eon put his head inside of his hands, as it hurt for him to hear the story. While Ethel explained, Eon began to feel the familiar rush in his feet.

Eon felt the heat from the burning crosses that stood in the middle of the front yard of the house. He looked at the front door, which was wide open. Eon watched as the hooded men pulled two small children out of the house. The kids were eight and nine years old. They kicked and screamed as they were unwillingly escorted out of the house. The men placed nooses around the small kids' necks. Eon watched as the two children helplessly twisted and turned until their bodies gave way to the pressure on their necks. Their bodies twitched one or two more times, then went completely limp. He then watched as an old lady was taken out of the house. She tried to release herself from the grip of the Klansman, but it was useless. The men pulled her up by her neck. Because of her weight, she took a shorter time to die. Eon tried to turn away, but he couldn't. As Ethel continued to tell the story, Eon continued to see it like a movie that he could not leave. Next they walked an older man out of the house. Unlike everyone else, the man did not seem to put up any type of struggle. He walked out without a fight. As they placed the noose around his neck, the man seemed to be muttering to himself. They raised his body up the tree, and he coughed through the Lord's Prayer until his body gave up the fight to live. Next there was a middle-aged woman escorted out. She screamed and yelled as the men pulled her from the now-burning house. As they brought her to the tree, she cried at the sight of her kids' and parents' feet dangling above her. She sniffled and cried as they placed the noose around her neck and tightened it. As they pulled her up, she slowly twitched as life left her body little by little.

Eon watched as the men all gathered around one man. As Eon caught a glimpse of the man, he saw that it was the same person who he'd been seeing in all his dreams. The same man from the boat and from the auction, except this time he didn't have dreads. His face seemed lighter. Eon watched as one of the hooded men walked over to the man who seemed very close to dead. Before they placed the noose around his neck, the one man pulled his hood off. Eon watched as Mister Reverend looked at the man dead in his eyes. His cold stare burned into Eon's soul. The hostage spit blood from his mouth onto Mister Reverend's Klan suit. Mister Reverend had his cohorts stand the man up as he took a giant machete and cut the man's genitals off. The blood splattered all over as Mister Reverend had them pull the rope and lift the man's already lifeless body up on the strong branch. Eon looked at the man. His eyes popped open, and he spoke loudly...

"I am not a Nigger! I am not a Nigger!"

Eon screamed as he opened his eyes and lifted his head. Ethel looked at Eon. She could see that he was going through an intense moment.

"Baby, can you please go get this gentleman a glass of water or lemonade?" Ethel asked the lady who was still concentrating on her Blackberry.

"Which one you want, water or lemonade?" she asked without raising her head. "Water or lemonade?" she asked a second time. As Eon sat motionless, the lady took her eyes away from her cellular device and faced him.

"Water or le..." Before she could finish, the two looked at one another with pure shock and fear.

"Eon?" she said, not understanding why he was there.

"Violet?" Eon asked with the same confusion. "What the hell are you doing here?" he asked Violet.

"I'm here with my grandmother. What are *you* doing here?" she asked.

"I'm here with my partner. We're getting work from Mister Reverend. Oh, shit, Mister Reverend!" Eon exclaimed loudly.

"Ethel, are you telling me that Mister Reverend killed his own son because of his hate for black people? Because his son was part black?" Eon asked his question quickly as if he had somewhere to go.

"Yes, that and the fact that he had gotten me pregnant with Violet's mother. Mister Reverend felt as if Jesse Joe was wrong because he wasn't a white man and he was in love with a white woman. So he killed his only son and placed his testicles in a jar." Eon shook his head in pure disgust.

"Oh, shit, Uncle J!" Eon said as he shot out of the house and ran across to Mister Reverend's home.

As he ran through the back door, Eon looked as Uncle J had a pillow covering Mister Reverend's face. The butler stood to the side and did not seem interested enough to stop Jesse as he pushed the pillow down onto Mister Reverend's face. While Eon was getting brought up to speed, so was Uncle J. Mister Reverend had told him the very same story that Eon had heard and lived through across the way at Ethel's. As Eon grabbed Uncle J's hand, he slowly pulled the pillow back from Mister Reverend's face. His eyes were blank, and his lifeless body sat motionless.

"No, Jesse no! Why?" Eon asked. Jesse turned to his partner with a look of calmness.

"My grandfather killed my father, so I killed him. For years I thought his death was random, but it wasn't. It was totally calculated and planned. And he orchestrated it all!" Jesse said, still in his calm state.

Eon looked at the butler who was standing to the side of Mister Reverend's chair.

"At least he died in his sleep," the butler said as he walked over and took Mister Reverend's pulse. After a minute, he shook his head and closed Mister Reverend's open eyes. "You guys need to go back to your visiting Ms. Ethel. I will call the authorities in another thirty minutes. You guys should be gone by then." The butler seemed to be arranging the room back to its normal state. Eon walked Jesse back over to Ethel's home.

"My picture," Uncle J said. Jesse still sounded as if he were tripping on acid or some kind of drug that caused him to be as calm, cool, and composed as possible. Eon went back to Mister Reverend's and picked up the picture. As he looked down, he saw Jesse Joe looking back at him in the photograph.

"Good to finally meet you again!" Eon said as he walked back into Ethel's place. Eon looked up from the picture and saw Violet standing next to her grandmother. His mind began to put the pieces of his craziness together.

"It was you!" Eon said as he pointed directly at Violet.

"Me what?" she asked Eon.

"Whenever I saw your grandfather, you were there.

When I was in the photo shoot, you had come by to do the interview, but you said you left, right?" Violet nodded her head yes. "Then on the boat, you were trying to make your way to me, but it was too crowded. Then when we were having sex, I saw him again!" Eon said as Ethel's eyes widened. "And just now, you were directly in front of me when I saw the whole thing of Jesse Joe's family being massacred," Eon said. "I always saw him!" Eon said as he pointed at the picture of Jesse Joe. "Your grandfather has been talking to me through you!" Eon said as if he had cracked the case of how he'd mysteriously gone crazy. Violet glanced at Eon. "We need to be going. Violet, I will talk with you very soon. Ethel, it was a pleasure, and I look forward to talking with you again in the near future." Eon and Uncle J both exited Ethel's as the night air brushed against their faces. They got into the truck as Eon pulled away from the house.

The two men rode home in complete silence. As they walked into the house, Eon held Uncle J's arm.

"Are you okay?" he asked as he looked into Jesse's eyes.

"Yes, I'm okay. I want to go talk to my son," Uncle J said. He showed no remorse for what had just happened, and Eon couldn't blame him. Because the house had more than enough space, everyone had a room. The two men walked up to Cousin

Jesse's room and slowly opened the door. Eon walked in and stood in horror. He watched Dr. Jackson on his hands and knees as Cousin Jesse plowed into him from behind. Eon turned and exited the room just as Cousin Jesse realized that he had unwanted company.

"Cousin, Cousin!" Jesse screamed as the door slammed in his face. Eon chuckled to himself as he stood outside the room with Uncle J.

"What?" Uncle J asked, oblivious to his son's extracurricular activities.

"Nothing. You know, Uncle J, I don't know if we want to really have this conversation with Cousin Jesse. I mean…you know he may not be mature enough to understand and comprehend where you're coming from. I'm not saying he's a child, but he just may not be ready to handle such a heavy message right here, right now." Eon spoke with tenderness in his tone. He didn't want Uncle J to know the real reason he wasn't allowing him inside of his son's room. Uncle J simply nodded his head, went off to his room, and cried himself to sleep.

The next day, the word spread throughout the town that Mister Reverend had passed away in his sleep. Eon sat at the breakfast table and watched the town news on the television. As the story of Mister Reverend came across the screen, Uncle J walked into the kitchen.

"Good morning, everyone," Uncle J said to his family at the table. Will, Justin, Mary, and Eon all replied with warmth and love as they wished Jesse a good morning.

"Uncle J, you hear the news that Mister Reverend passed away last night?" Eon asked Uncle J.

"No way! We were just sitting discussing business with him, too. That's too crazy!" Uncle J said. His voice sounded as if he truly could not believe that the man was gone. Cousin Jesse then came down into the kitchen in his house slippers, a pair of boxers, a tank top, and a robe. As soon as he sat down, he looked at everyone but Eon.

"Hey, cousin," Eon exclaimed with a giant smile on his face.

"You hear the news?" Eon asked. He could see the worry in Cousin Jesse's face. Cousin Jesse did not know exactly what the news was, but he sure hoped that he wasn't it.

"Mister Reverend passed away in his sleep," Uncle J said.

"Good for him!" Cousin Jesse said confidently.

"Even though he was the meanest, scariest, white bread piece of shit in all of the 'Sippi, he has got to feel a lot better being out of this shit here," Cousin Jesse said as he poured himself a bowl of cereal.

"Well, everyone is in some shit, one way or the other, ain't we, Cousin?" Eon watched Cousin Jesse squirm with discomfort.

"True, true, Cousin," the younger Jesse said under his breath. From that moment on, Eon did not have any problems from Cousin Jesse.

Six months after Mister Reverend's death, his estate was given to his next of kin. Because he didn't have a will when he died, all his land and money was left to Uncle J. Violet's grandmother fought through her battle with brain cancer and won. Eon connected her with his specialists, and they helped her to survive, just as they had helped Eon before. Violet and her grandmother grew together in health and in life. Eon and Uncle J felt an extreme closeness to Ethel. After the spiritual roller-coaster ride that Eon had been on, he felt a bond with Violet that was undeniable. The two first started to speak on the phone, and then slowly but surely, they started to date. Eon no longer had the flashes, but he felt as if the message was clear. Because he owned so many acres of land, Eon was able to harvest a smaller amount of cotton and still make a really good amount of money. He and Uncle J still kept their deal with Mister Reverend and used his cotton gin at the same price they agreed upon. Because Uncle Jesse now owned Mister Reverend's land, they were able to do whatever they wanted with it, and they did.

Eon transformed both his plantation and Mister Reverend's into interactive museums. The Montgomery plantation was turned into Ms. Monty's, while Mister Reverend's land was changed to Jesse Joe's Cotton Gin. They were open only from Thursday to Monday and only on select weekends. It started with kids from New York. Eon had signed a deal with a few different group homes and other agencies that specialized in troubled teens. As the word spread, regular schools were calling to arrange for their classes to come to Mississippi. In every case, the kids were picked up by bus and driven to Ms. Monty's. As soon as they exited the bus, they were treated as if they were slaves. The two guides were Will and Justin, who had extended their stay with Eon. Eon had made an agreement with them both. They were to finish their schooling and get their diplomas. After they'd received the documents, the two boys would each have a nice secondhand car waiting for them. This gave them more incentive and drive to finish school. Justin's family, which consisted of only his single mother who really didn't care much about Justin's well being, had signed over her parental rights to Eon. Once Mary felt that Will was safe and secure with his dad, she returned to the Harlem brownstone and stayed with Ms. Francine. The two ladies ran the studio from the upstairs part of the house. They hired an assistant who dealt with the engineer and whoever the artists were who came to record.

Because of the similarity in age, most of the kids visiting Ms. Monty's would listen to the two young men. They spoke to the young adults with venom and contempt. Some of the troubled teens would try to flex their muscles, but along with the two teenage boys were two grown men who were dressed in guard outfits. Cousin Jesse and Dr. Jackson stood watch with looks that could put fear in the hearts of the kids. In most cases, all it took was to make an example of the loudest ringleader, and the rest of the teens would fall in line. The youth were first taken out to an ark-like boat that sat on the side of the plantation, the former location of the barn. They were chained together with plastic bracelets on their necks, arms, and ankles and told to cram into spaces that were tight and uncomfortable. Each kid lay directly next to the other with little to no room between them. They were kept in the tight quarters for at least an hour. Many of the toughest kids would cry as the silence and all-around energy felt like death. After their time on the boat, they were each walked out to a stage. Each person was unchained and led onto the stage where a group of men would yell out numbers and prices for each. Some were sent to the Johnson plantation while some were sent to the Montgomery plantation. In every case, the kids were yelled at and called nigger. Once they were bought, they then were sent out to their owner's land. At the Montgomery fields, they were forced to pick cotton. They would work an entire shift. The "slaves" had to tend to the cotton and all the other crops and vegetables that were in the fields. Eon had livestock added to Mister Reverend's old land. Those "slaves" who were sent to the Johnson plantation (Jesse Joe's) had to make sure all the cows were milked, pigs were fed, and whatever other upkeep was needed for the animals that lived on the land. The workers then stayed in a barn where they slept on haystacks that doubled as beds. Their food was served on metal trays. They were only given a spoon to eat with. There was a water well that allowed the kids to drink as much as they wanted without a hassle from the two bosses and their enforcers. The next morning, the workers from the Montgomery plantation would bring the cotton over to Jesse Joe's, where the giant gin was used to clean and compress the cotton. There, the slaves would be traded from Montgomery's to Johnson's. This allowed them all to feel the exact same thing that the others felt. After the second day, the "slaves" were ready to leave, but they couldn't. After they finished their work, they were sent to a classroom-type setting. They all sat down and spoke to Violet. She would talk with them and get their feelings about the torture they'd just been put through. Each kid spoke openly about how degraded and disrespected he or she felt. Many cried. They couldn't believe that people went through the same things, and a lot worse. Eon would watch the slaves-turned-students through a one-way mirror. He never showed his face, as he didn't want the kids to lose the feeling of hurt they had all because E the MC showed up. Eon would watch as Uncle J would walk into the classroom and talk with the kids about what happened to his father. Uncle J would talk about his love for his father and how much pain he went through when he found out the truth about his death. He told them the story about how Mister Reverend had killed his own son, his own flesh and blood, because of his hatred for people of color. Violet would then line up the students and give them each two dollars and fifty cents. All of them would look at the money as if it were foreign currency. "This was the going rate for slave work," she would say. The kids would all leave the trip with a newfound respect for themselves and a hatred for the N-word.

One day, after a field trip of students had all packed up and left, Eon and Violet sat inside the classroom. They had been in business for six full months and had made a substantial amount of money. Between the "museum" and the actual cotton that they picked, Big Mama's Cotton was making more than enough money. Eon sat in one of the chairs and looked at his love.

"So what do we do now?" Violet asked.

"Well, you know, you never was able to get your interview," Eon said sarcastically.

"Yeah, but you still got your money, didn't you?"

Violet said in a matter-of-fact tone.

"Well, I didn't, but I'm sure someone is spending that money," Eon said, making fun of his past.

"To be honest with you, Lady Vi, I wouldn't have it any other way. I learned a whole lot about myself and my true family," Eon said with pride.

"You know, it's really a great story!" Violet said. Violet and Eon looked at each other as the light bulbs went off in both their minds.

Violet walked through the giant glass doors of the tall building. She walked with confidence and composure. She looked stunning in her business suit. As she walked up to the security guard, she flashed her credentials. The guard quickly nodded his head and allowed her through the checkpoint. Violet held her bag as she rode the elevator to the top floor. Once she arrived, she stood at a desk and spoke with the secretary.

"Yes, I'm here to do an interview with Shawn Carter," she said with a soft smile. The lady picked up the phone and spoke for a few seconds.

"Mr. Carter will see you now," the lady said as she held her hand out toward the two giant wooden doors.

As Violet walked closer to the doors, they slowly began to open. She walked through and directly up to the large desk that the music mogul sat behind.

"Have a seat," he said as he pulled his chair closer to the desk.

"No, thank you. I just wanted to drop this off to you. Please contact the number on the card." Violet pulled the bonded paper out of her bag and placed it on the table. Mr. Carter looked at the card that was attached to the front of the paper.

"B.M.C.?" he read aloud to himself. He placed the business card to the side and looked at the first page of what seemed to be a book.

"The E.O.N." The Evolution Of a Nigger.

E.O.N.